Boys from the Backfields

Derec Jones

OPENING CHAPTER

First Printing, 2013

ISBN 10: 1-904958-34-6

ISBN 13: 978-1-904958-34-5

published by

*Opening Chapter
Cardiff, Wales*

www.openingchapter.com

To Dad

2013

The door to my past opened easily, it was a surprise. I'd intended to confront Angel directly, but she was out when I arrived. Considering her profession, she should have changed the locks.

I was hiding in the attic when she came back in.

I'd climbed up there to see if I could find any clues among the bits we left behind when we'd gone to LA in the nineties. The questions raised by the anonymous emails needed answers. I found a heavy wooden box crammed with old photos, and two large manila envelopes, stuffed with my scribbles about the events that had come to define my life.

I was sitting in an old deckchair waiting for Angel to go to bed. The answer had to be there, in those damp, limp bundles, some detail I hadn't realised was important when I'd written it down.

My cell phone vibrated as another text arrived. It was my PA, Helene, again. No. I couldn't think about work, or too much about Helene. I had to focus. The past had to be resolved before I could think about the future again.

I wrote the first 'book' in the late seventies, when I felt I was able to give some time to myself, after half-a-dozen years of frantic success. Hell, I even considered retiring then, before my thirtieth birthday.

The paper was thin and stained, but the typewritten text was still crisp and bold.

I started to read.

BOOK ONE
1963 – 1973

CHAPTER 1

Have you watched those wildlife programmes on the television and seen the images of big cats dealing with porcupines? That was me and trouble. I sniffed at it in a circumspect way, and then, when it showed any sign of life, I ran like hell. That was me usually, but that day the taunting just got to me.

The smirking face begged to be squashed into the muddy grass of the field. It was a wet summer and I had recently come into that phase of life that marks your earliest memories, the few vivid incidents from early childhood that you remember when you eventually emerge into the heaviness of adulthood.

The boy's name was David, an innocent sounding name for what was a vile specimen of childhood. Like the serpent in the Garden of Eden, he slithered and oozed his way around my consciousness, an evil, ugly, smelly, little boy. I knew him as Snobby, a name that invoked gross images of dirty dried-up snot and filthy fingernails.

The lesson he taught me was worth a lot I suppose. His existence showed me that there is evil in the world, and dealing with him gave me my first practical lessons in coping with it. He was a year or so older than me and a lot bigger, a real bully.

Some people talk about their earliest memories with pleasure, the feeling of warmth and security, the excitement of a trip to the seaside, even the wonder of their first days at school. The memory of that encounter was pleasurable too, the elation of pride and triumph, the look of astonishment on Snobby's face, as I, the quiet helpless victim, fought back. I squashed his face hard into that mud, singing inside and juddering with fear at what the consequences might be. As it was, he yelped like a hurt puppy and loped off home to his equally hideous mother. I suppose he was only six years old himself.

They told me that at that time travelling showmen presented real Punch and Judy shows on the field. I had a vague memory of dodging through a crowd of adult legs and tree trunks, and feeling a sense of occasion. Soon after, the council felled the remaining trees, and in the years after the incident with Snobby, I played boisterous games there, on the rough grass of the field that passed for our village green.

The Backfields Estate was split into three sections. I don't know if the council intended it that way when they built it, but nature demanded it. The bottom site was the oldest part, and as I remembered it, the toughest. The top site was the newest part, and apart from small gangs of fiercely territorial boys, was then relatively quiet and refined.

I lived in the middle site, a motley collection of colourful families gathered from all over the town. Those were the beginning of great times, the late fifties and then the sixties, when we thought we could change the world, as if we alone in all human existence had the opportunity to participate in major evolutionary and revolutionary changes.

Early in the history of the estate, before bitter memories and endless vendettas developed, we all came together on the field. I remember long summer days when dozens of children tumbled with primal joy on the damp grass and rushed home en masse for dinner, and a scolding for the green and brown stains on their knees and clothes. Small groups would converge from the top, middle, and bottom sites, and join in friendly tests of strength. Piggy-back and shoulder-back fights, and games where everyone collapsed into a laughing, sweating heap were the best.

These exciting tribal games were punctuated by the occasional match of football, cricket, or rugby – pretty tedious stuff. Those games were for the real competitors, who charged about the field, panting with determined looks, sweating to claim the glory of a goal or a try, or contorting in athletic ways catching and smacking hard leather-clad balls.

We made French arrows by slitting the tops of small sticks of bamboo and forcing folded paper flights into the grooves. We hurled them across the field with lengths of waxy twine twisted around our fingers, not aware of or not caring about the consequences.

The bottom site was separated from the middle by the main road, an uncrossable barrier for a young child alone, unless, like many of the parents then, yours didn't care or were too stupid or naïve, or too exhausted by debt or poverty, to keep the reins of caring tight. Even then that road was busy, the busiest in the county they said, the main road from our town to the next, full of trundling noisy motor vehicles.

The barrier between the middle site and the top was more subtle, yet just as effective. I lived on the edge of that barrier, a row of larger private houses that loomed and bragged about their affluence with deep bay windows and bleached lace curtains. The few children who lived there had piano lessons, took week-long holidays, and got driven around by parents with cars. Our small comfortable council house faced the posher people across the road, and the view from my bedroom window bequeathed me bothersome hang-ups about background and social status.

In one of the owner-occupied houses lived a lively, nosy old lady known to our small gang as Betty Fish. Her husband had been a fishmonger who drove around the estates in a small white van selling overpriced fresh fish. Friday was his best day. A couple of years earlier on a Friday night visit to the pub to drink some of his profit he'd collapsed and died. Betty Fish remained, living alone in that big house. The van had been driven away a few months after her husband's death, with her perched on the edge of the pavement waving

3

good-bye to the new owner with a smile and a bundle of fivers in her fist. As a single woman Betty became nosier and happier, spending most of her time bustling to and from the few small shops on the estate and chatting in a patronising manner to the natives from the council houses.

One late summer day in 1963 Betty Fish was murdered. I was thirteen years old and I saw it happen.

Our gang had gone out quite early due to plans we'd made the day before to pick blackberries. The most fruitful place was in a small overgrown field that buffered some of the private houses from the top site. That's where we were.

"You're useless," I said to Pogo, clearing my throat and spitting at the bramble bushes to emphasise my lack of uselessness.

"It's not my fault," replied Pogo, in a small hurt voice, adjusting his large black-framed spectacles with his purple-stained index finger, the top of his curly-haired head a good four inches below mine. "You pinched the best bush."

"Shall we nick some apples from Betty Fish?" It was Trevor Thomas, Trev as we called him, a wise, calm person, tall and sinewy with ruddy complexion and tousled fair hair. Trev was not a know-all but he knew it all. He was immensely respected by us lesser mortals and was the natural leader of our group.

The fourth member of our regular gang was, much to my chagrin, Snobby. Yes, that Snobby. I didn't like him, but Trev kept him under control. More than once Snobby had been given a quiet word and a black eye behind a hedge or in a dark alley. He'd become more subdued than he'd been before I viciously retaliated that day on the field. Maybe he'd learnt his lessons, life isn't easy for anyone, and perhaps he couldn't help his obnoxious personality? So being a level, tolerant person I put away my misgivings and put up with him.

Snobby, trying to impress Trev, was already hanging over the top of the mossy stone wall at the bottom of Betty Fish's garden before we had a chance to react to Trev's suggestion.

We put our blackberry gathering basins behind a bramble

bush near the wall and followed Snobby's example, intending to retrieve the basins later and carry on gathering the fruit. Then we would plague the houses on the estate, our haul of berries tastefully displayed in wicker baskets decorated with fern leaves. We could get a shilling a pint for the soft black fruit (even maggot-ridden). We'd use the money we earned to buy a pack or two of five Woodbine cigarettes from Tight Bert, the newsagents on the main road.

As we approached the wall Snobby dropped down back towards us unexpectedly, and said in an uncharacteristically faltering way: "Let's not bother boys, I've got a much better idea."

Trev laughed: "Your ideas are never better."

He pushed Snobby aside and we scrambled up the wall.

I poked my head up and began a slow recce of the garden. At the foot of the wall inside the garden the bramble bushes from the field had spread their tentacles, creating a wild unkempt area. Beyond that were the mature apple trees laden with ripening fruit. Betty Fish wouldn't miss a few apples, many were already rotting on the ground. Through the gaps in the trees my eyes swept over the lawn, tended every week by Jacko's father, the squint-eyed alcoholic from the top site, for the price of a bottle of sherry.

Behind the trees, if we moved carefully, we would be hidden from the view of anyone but a determined observer from the house, and if we were spotted we could always make a run for it, at least Betty Fish didn't have a dog. I saw no sign of any activity, so I hauled myself over and dropped into the blackberry thorns. I heard the others following me and soon we were creeping around, stuffing the apples into our jumpers, adrenaline pumping, hearts beating hard with the excitement. I nearly dropped my haul when I heard a muffled cry from the direction of the house. I looked up. Through the open curtains at the rear window I saw two darkened figures struggling.

We froze in our positions, like that silly party game, and stared intently at the scene. One of the figures fell away and the other disappeared into the depths of the house. I looked over at Trev, who shrugged, then at the bewildered baby face of Pogo. Snobby had disappeared.

Long slow motion seconds later the back door sprang open, and a person, under cover of the rhododendron bushes that shielded the door, came out. The distance was too great to see clearly but there was something familiar about the shape and the gait. The person jerked its head quickly from right to left, composed itself, and set off down the side of the semi-detached towards the street where I lived at the front.

Pogo whispered first: "Let's go boys, I don't like this at all."

Trev, ever the boldest, moved slowly towards the house. I followed cautiously a few paces behind. We approached the rear window from its side and peeked in nervously. We pressed our faces right up against the glass. Lying sprawled on the red Persian carpet was a distinctly immobile Betty Fish.

"Fucking Hell!" Trev said.

"Fucking Hell!" I echoed.

"Blooming Heck!" came a small weak voice beside us.

I looked at Trev, his sun-bleached eyebrows lifted. We all turned and ran back to the shelter of the trees. Pogo's little legs pumped unbelievably fast and by the time Trev and I reached the small orchard he was over the wall and gone. We crouched, panting, gathering our thoughts.

"Let's go and phone the cops," I said. "We don't have to say who we are."

Trev nodded breathlessly. We jumped over the wall together. At the top of the wall I glanced back and saw the trail of apples, strewn from the rear window of the house, over the lawn, and into the trees. There was nothing I could do about it so I dropped down and followed Trev.

We headed for a phone box that normally worked, on the far side of the top site. It would mean risking our lives by going through other gangs' territories, but we were more afraid to go to our usual box in the middle site in case the police traced the call. My fears about the top site were realised when from a side alley a group of three boys and two vicious-looking dogs appeared and almost bumped into us.

The boys were older and bigger than us, and looked mean, so I increased my pace to get away from them, all the time glancing sideways to make sure the dogs hadn't picked up the smell of my fear. Trev touched my arm.

"Wait a minute. Don't panic. You'll be all right."

One of the boys shouted "Oi!"

Trev stopped and turned to face them, I had no choice but to do the same.

"Trev, isn't it?" the stranger said, smiling paternally.

Trev smiled and nodded.

"You're OK you are, what you doing?"

"Looking for my dog, Smokey. He's like a sheepdog, lots of black and white, you know. Have you seen him?"

"He's a good rabbit catcher isn't he? We'll keep an eye out."

Trev could handle every situation, he knew everyone, and everyone liked him. We carried on walking purposefully, pretending to look around for the dog, whistling and calling for Smokey. The other boys turned down another alley, I sighed with relief.

"You worry too much," Trev said. "There's the phone box."

Luckily, although the coin slot was jammed, the telephone still worked for 999 calls.

Trev did the talking, he was older and more composed.

"Police? I think there's been a murder."

"Yes, it's Betty Fish."

"Betty somebody, I don't know..."

"It's in the Backfields."

"In the private houses."

"Opposite the council houses."

"In Meadow Road."

"No, sorry."

Click.

We carried on walking, talking excitedly.

"How do you know she's dead?" I asked stupidly, because of course Trev knew these things for sure.

"Did you recognise who did it?" he asked.

"No, though there was something about..."

"Yes, I thought there was something."

7

"Do you think Pogo will say anything?" I asked.

Trev laughed, shaking his fair hair in the sunlight. "Got any fags?" he asked.

"Here," I said. "I've got a stump of a Players, I nicked it off the mantelpiece this morning, my old girl won't miss it, there were another five or six there. Have you got a match?"

We reached the outer limits of the Backfields and crossed a busy road where a farm track led into the countryside and a place where we spent much of our time trying to catch rabbits and grass-snakes among the ivy covered ruins of a group of stone buildings. We leant against a hedge just out of sight of the road and Trev lit up. We shared the Players' stump, taking great pride in smoking it down until it burnt our lips and fingers and became impossible to hold.

"Fuck me!" Trev said, spitting the dregs of tobacco from his lips. "We've left the fucking blackberry basins behind."

Preferring to avoid the possibility of another confrontation with the top-siters, we made our way back to the field behind Betty Fish's house by skirting the outer boundary of the estate and walking quietly through a long privet-straddled alley. The basins still sat undisturbed under the brambles and we retrieved them with relief. I couldn't resist a quick look over the wall.

At the back of the house two uniformed policemen plodded slowly examining the ground for clues. I tried to keep very still and quiet, breathing heavily with the effort of hanging on the wall. One of the police turned in our direction and following the trail of apples walked up the lawn towards us. As he came closer I recognised him as Sergeant Conway, a slow determined giant, frightening, but easy to avoid. He didn't worry me. He looked up towards the apple trees and our eyes met through the gaps in the foliage.

"Oi, stop you. Wait!" he commanded in a large voice.

We took our cue, grabbed the basins and ran. We hid in the doorway behind Good Stores for twenty minutes before edging out tentatively.

"Better go home," Trev said.

I nodded. "I'll give you a shout after dinner, we'll see what's going on then."

I turned right up Meadow Road and Trev walked nonchalantly down School Lane towards his house.

A group of neighbours chattered with jabbing fingers on the pavement outside my house. Mrs Lee a small round woman with gypsy black hair talked incomprehensibly fast and pointed unselfconsciously at the police activity across the road. Mr Lee, her dull, thick-set husband puffed on a slipshod example of a rolled up cigarette and smiled with malign satisfaction at the prospect of someone other than himself being in trouble with the law. Snobby's, thin, ferret-eyed father peered short-sightedly and tipsily with a puzzled expression. No doubt he'd walked into the drama on his way back from a lunchtime visit to the Carpenter's Inn.

My mother, a young and always tired thirty-five, commanded her usual position at the centre of the group; and my older brother Ralph sat on the low brick wall behind them, gently patting his hair into shape. I tried to look surprised.

"What the heck's going on, Ralph?"

"Hi, little broth, it's the cops, something's happening in Mrs Johnson's house."

Who the hell is Mrs Johnson? I thought, of course it must be Betty Fish's real name. My mother spotted me.

"Mick, come here, where have you been? Are those blackberries?"

I looked down at my hands, I was carrying two basins, mine and Pogo's, one squashed on top of the other, both almost empty.

"Er, yes, we didn't get much."

"We, who's we?"

"Trev, Trevor..."

I backed away instinctively, she had kind eyes my mother, but those hands, they carried a sting.

"You know I don't like you playing with that boy, where have you . . ?"

"Mick, look." Ralph grabbed my arm, saving me from further interrogation. I was already starting to crack.

An ambulance pulled up outside the house opposite. A policeman looked protectively up and down the street as two uniformed ambulance men dismounted and went up the path carrying a folded stretcher. I took the opportunity of the distraction to slip down my own path and into the open front door. I dumped the basins on the table in the galley kitchen and rushed upstairs to my bedroom where I could watch the developments in comfort and security through the window.

A noise behind me made my heart and my body leap.

"It's only me, Mick."

"Oh, Ralph," I sighed with relief.

Ralph looked good, his oily hairstyle not yet a relic, the black leather jacket a symbol of his maturity and independence. Although he still lived with us he was no longer subject to the same parent-imposed rules as I was. His nineteen years, his job as an apprentice fitter, and the three or four pounds that he contributed to the household expenses each week saw to that. A fatal accident at the site of the new steelworks, where my father was earning big money, working long tiring hours trying to beat construction deadlines, placed the sixteen year old Ralph as the oldest male member of the family three years earlier.

He took the burden uncomplainingly at the time and had since matured, supporting my mother and me with a calm paternal benevolence. I liked Ralph and often confided in him, but I couldn't decide whether or not to tell him what we'd seen, after all we hadn't done anything wrong, had we? Stealing apples was not a capital offence, yet I was reluctant to involve the adult world in the adventure until I'd at least discussed it with Trev.

"What's happening now?" I asked, hoping Ralph hadn't noticed the guilt.

"Old girl's probably had a heart attack or something. I don't know what all the fuss is about. All those police, you'd think they had nothing better to do."

Another police car pulled up and three people got out, a man, a woman, and a girl. She looked like the new girl from the top site to me. I'd seen her around, she was small and pretty, with long golden hair, and seemed to have a bit of a cocky attitude about her. I liked that.

They stopped on the pavement near the ambulance. The man put his arm around the woman's shoulder and took the girl's hand in his.

The two ambulance men came out of the house carrying a laden stretcher, and put it in the back of their vehicle.

The ambulance pulled away sedately and quietly, confirming my supposition that Betty Fish was dead, no rush to the hospital for a corpse. The three people were led into the house by a policeman. Most of the uniformed police dispersed, leaving a man standing by the front door and another walking along the path to the rear. I saw my mother detach herself from the group on the roadside and make her way to our front door.

Ralph looked me up and down. "Been picking blackberries Mick? Where did you go?"

"Just around..."

"MICK, RALPH," my mother shouted up the stairs. "Come and get your dinner. I'm warming it up."

We sat in the living room with bowls of leek and potato soup balanced on our knees. I kept quiet while Ralph and my mother talked.

CHAPTER 2

"There's going to be a storm tonight. My Gran says so. She's always right."

"Bollocks Pogo! Gimme that."

Snobby grabbed the gun and pointed it a street lamp. He pressed the trigger but nothing happened.

Trev tutted. "Give it here, it's not loaded."

Trev took the gun, a long polished air-rifle, the sort that only someone with money in the family could afford, even if they did have to sneak it out under their trouser leg. Trev cracked it open and inserted a pellet that he materialised from nowhere. He casually aimed the rifle at the street lamp and squeezed the trigger. The lead pellet hit dead centre, the light crackled and went out.

"Run," he commanded.

We did, laughing and jostling down the lane behind the off-licence in the darkness we'd caused with our delinquency.

"So, when did the cops go then Mick?" asked Trev, puffing for breath.

It took a few seconds to register, the splash caused by the death of Betty Fish had already ebbed into gentle ripples in my mind.

"Most of them went soon after I got home, there's still one or two there, but they don't seem to care very much, I can see them from my bedroom window, lounging about, having a sly smoke. Ralph says they'll probably come around the houses tomorrow, to see if anyone knows anything. Do you think I should tell them what we saw?"

"Never tell the cops anything you don't have to. My uncle reported a stolen car once, they had him in the cells for nearly two days, they're all bastards."

We stopped before the end of the lane, near the wooden

gates at the rear of the off-license. The gates were open a few inches. I pushed them open wider and peered inside. A light from a back window allowed us to see a little of the contents of the yard. Crates containing the overspill stock of bottles lay against the walls, I walked softly towards them. We didn't need words, an opportunity had presented itself, and there was only one thing to do, take advantage of it, like a pack of hunting dogs, who fall spontaneously silent when they come across a potential victim. We had that kind of rapport, me and Trev, but Pogo lived in his own small world of nervousness and fear.

"I'm going home." Pogo didn't wait for approval, he took the air rifle from Trev's disinterested grasp and faded away.

I stared at the treasure with awe. Trev and Snobby had already grabbed two flagon bottles of cider each. I picked up two more, and we ran quietly out of the yard, back up the dark side of the lane, and through the estate, looking for a safe place to consume our prey.

It was easy to pretend to drink both flagon bottles of the sickly sweet brew because the other two were so engrossed in their own private cider-swigging competition. I suspect that Snobby let more run down the front of his jacket than his throat, but Trev took the drink like the man he was. I'd sneaked a whisky from Aunty Val's bottle once and felt the warmth and disorientation of being slightly drunk, but in the grounds of the school that night, I got truly drunk for the first time. I hated it, even though I suppose it was only the alcohol content of three quarters of one flagon that found its way into my swift adolescent blood.

Within minutes there were six empty bottles lying on the stone steps of the dark school entrance, three of them smashed, the amber glass sparkling in the light from the surviving street lamps. Pogo and his air-rifle a distant memory, I staggered and burped my way home.

Afraid to go in and face the inevitable inquisition and the equally inevitable impact of my mother's loving hands, I crept in through the back gate, slumped on the damp unkempt grass, and stared at the rear window of the living room as it spun round in nauseating concentric circles. Half an hour later my body aching with the violent retching I'd experienced, I opened the back door and fell in. Ralph was alone in the living room. Thank God for Bingo night.

"It's a bit late for you Mick. What the hell?"

"I'm all right Ralph, just been a bit sick."

"You've been drinking, and you stink, better get washed up and off to bed while you've got the chance, it's nearly ten o'clock, the bingo bus will be here soon. I'll say you didn't feel well. I hope the old girl's had a win."

Good old Ralph, he had the answers, always cool and in control.

I lay on my bed, gripping the sides to stop falling off as it spun around the room, for the first time the words 'never again' whistling through my tortured brain. A soft tapping on the door of my bedroom alerted me, time to get control, look ill instead of drunk. It must be my mother home from the bingo.

"Mind if I come in?" Saved again, it was Ralph's voice.

"OK," I said, not at all sure it was.

Ralph sat on the edge of the bed.

"What did you drink Mick, it must have been potent stuff?"

"Just some cider, not much, I think I really am ill. Oh no..."

I sat upright, gagging on the nausea.

"Take it easy there. You all right? Did you find out any more about what happened at Betty Fish's?"

I had to really concentrate to understand what he was talking about. Betty Fish? What was the matter with her? What did he mean?

"Betty? Oh yes, that! Some bloke done her in. I didn't see who it was."

"What do you mean? You saw something?"

I'd put my foot in it, Ralph may have been an easy-going, if paternal, older brother but he was not stupid. I felt close to him, but because of his position as the only man in the house, he represented the grey serious world of adulthood.

"Well, yes, I mean ..."

"Go on, you can tell me, what was it?"

"Nothing really, but Trev says we shouldn't tell the cops, they're bastards."

Miraculously I was sobering up. My head began to throb insistently; I cupped it with my hands and moaned.

"Slow down, it's all right, I won't say anything, if that's what you want."

What the Hell! I thought, and told Ralph everything about our little gang's adventure in Betty Fish's garden. It was easier than trying to resist his damnably enthusiastic and insistent questioning. When I finished I rolled on the bed making agonised groans. Ralph laughed.

"You hang on. I'll get some aspirins. Keep quiet, Mam's home. I told her you've been sick. She said it serves you right for stuffing yourself down the chippy again. Anyway she's too busy counting her winnings, she got the last house, two pounds and ten bob."

Great, I thought, somewhere beneath the agony, we'd have fresh fruit with our dinner the next day. I went sick again, in the bath, in the hand-basin, in the toilet bowl, and all over the yellow linoleum covered floor. I swallowed the aspirins offered by a chuckling Ralph.

"No one's going to care about a few sour apples," he said. "You should tell the police what you told me."

"But Trev..."

"Never mind Trev," Ralph snapped. "He doesn't know everything. Now try and get to sleep, we'll talk in the morning. Night, night."

We were scared, it was like a scene from a cowboy film at the Saturday Morning Cinema Club. The top-siters had us pinned down behind the hedge. We could hear their delighted laughter, the same sound Jacko made when he tore the hind-legs off living frogs before roasting them in the heat leaking from the brickwork furnaces, and feeding them to his equally imbecilic sidekick Jonno. God I was frightened. I heard the crack of the gun and the snapping whoosh as the lead pellet whizzed close by me through the hedge, and the thump it made on the soft earth beside me. That could have been my leg, or my eye.

"Keep still, keep quiet, they'll get fed up soon," Trev said.

Snobby looked even more terrified than I was, and little stout Pogo lay flat, face down in the brambles and the rabbit-shit.

"Let's make a run for it," I suggested, not really wanting to, hoping Trev would disagree and deny me the risk of exposing my back to the guns.

Our attackers had climbed to the top of the ruins, to a height that I'd never known anyone to attempt before.

I willed them to fall off to the stones thirty feet below.

"Now," Trev said. "Come on."

We tried to run in a line from the ruins, keeping the hedge between us and the pellets. Trev's dog ran alongside us, barking excitedly, betraying our position to the cruel older boys from the top-site.

There was a thud. Smokey yelped in surprise and tumbled down on the damp mud of the stony path. He lay there whimpering and looking pointedly at his left back leg. We all stopped and stared. Trev ran to the dog and knelt down to examine its injury.

"Dirty Fuckers!" he exclaimed, and set off towards the ruins waving his fists in the air.

The shooting had stopped. The back end of a lead pellet protruded out of Smokey's thigh muscle; he wasn't seriously hurt, but Trev loved that dog like a younger brother and I'd never heard that tone in his voice before. What would he do? Surely the other boys were much older and tougher than he was.

"Come on boys," I said "Trev will get a hammering. "Hey Pogo! Where are you going?"

Pogo didn't answer. He increased his pace and disappeared around a bend in the path.

"I'm coming Mick," Snobby said, with a pained expression. "It's my ankle, I think I've twisted it. You carry on. I'll catch up."

I looked at that cowardly face and the old hatreds flared up. I felt an urge to squash his ugly face into the dirt of the path, just as I'd squashed it into that muddy field all those years before, but he wasn't worth it. I had to go and help Trev.

By the time I got to the foot of the ruined building Trev had caught the boys on their way down and had one of them by the throat, up against the wall. The boy looked scared stiff, and the other wasn't laughing as he implored with Trev to stop.

"Sorry, it was only a bit of fun, you know we'd never hurt you or your dog. We didn't even know it was..."

I interrupted. "Come on Trev, calm down. What about Smokey? He's over there on the path."

That seemed to bring him to his senses. He let go of the boy's throat, spat at him, and ran back towards the dog.

"Your mate's got a hell of a bloody temper," said the boy who hadn't been choked. The other one was too white and shaken to say anything. I recognised them then, they were two brothers, Paul and Peter Kent. Peter, the older, choked one, must have been nearly sixteen, so why was he behaving like a stupid child? He was old enough to sneak in the back door of the Carpenter's and drink almost legally.

"So what would you do if your dog had been shot?" I asked.

"It wasn't deliberate."

Trev was coming back, followed closely by a limping Smokey, and further behind, a more heavily limping Snobby.

We waited.

"Stupid bastards."

"Sorry again, Trev, if we'd known it was you."

"Fucking forget it. You've only got peashooters anyway. Come on Mick, let's go."

"Wait a minute," Paul Kent said. "You live in the same street as that old biddy who got bashed to death, don't you?"

"So?" I said.

"They've arrested some bloke, lives nearby. My old man reckons anyway, he works with the murderer in the steelworks, a shifty little git, bloke called Robinson. They call him Snobbo or something?"

While we were talking Snobby finally arrived, and was hovering outside the main group looking for sympathy. When he heard the name he gasped loudly. He looked at each of us in turn, his face a picture of horror, then turned and ran towards the path that led back to the estate, not a sign of a limp.

CHAPTER 3

Trev was bathing Smokey's back leg with salt water.
"Do you reckon it was Snobby's old man then?" I asked.
"What?"
"The murder."
"How should I know?"
"So, do you think it's time to tell them what we saw?"
"Do what you want, Mick."
"I'm off," I said.
Trev didn't respond.
When I got home my mother was out the back putting weeds and bits of rubbish into a bucket.
"Where have you been?" she asked
"Just out."
"I worry about you, Mick, with people like that Robinson out there. I hope you're being careful, looking after yourself."
"I heard they'd arrested him."
"Yes something about a bracelet his wife had."
"I ... we, saw who murdered Betty Fish. We were in the ..."
"What do you mean? You saw Mr Robinson doing it?"
"Not really, we couldn't see him clearly, we just saw them struggling through the window. I thought I recognised him, but he didn't remind me of Snobby's father at the time."
"Well that's who they've arrested, she was showing the bracelet off in the Carpenter's Arms last night apparently, silly cow! Now tell me what you saw and then you'll have to tell the police. I never did like the look of that man, him and his horrible little boy, the one who calls for you sometimes."
"Remember I told you we were picking blackberries, well we were, but we decided to nick some apples as ..."
"What have I told you about that, you'll only end up with a bad stomach, probably poison yourself."

She gave me a clip to remind me who was in control.
"Ouch!"

While I was waiting for my mother to get ready to accompany
me to the police station I wandered out the front to sit on the
wall and watch the world go by. I looked up and down the
street and saw Ralph coming towards me talking to Snobby.
Snobby grinned as he walked past but didn't stop.

"Hiya Mick," Ralph said. "I've just had a chat with your
mate there. You want to be careful with that one, he's a right
little snake in the grass."

"He's no mate, I only put up with him because he behaves
himself. What's he been saying?"

"Nothing much, I told him I knew about you lot in Betty
Fish's garden, and I asked him about his father. He doesn't
seem too worried, reckons they'll have to let him go soon,
they've got no evidence."

"What about the bracelet?"

"His mother lied. Her husband didn't give it to her. She
found it on the pavement near their house. And it seems he's
got an alibi for the time of the murder, he was out drinking
with his brother. They've got no proof the bracelet belonged
to Betty Fish either. It's what they call a red herring."

"What?"

"It's bullshit Mick, it's all bullshit."

I was very disappointed, I wanted the murderer to be
someone like Snobby's father, if I hadn't been with him, I'd
like to have believed it was Snobby himself.

"Did you tell her?" he asked.

I nodded.

My mother came out of the house and walked purposefully
down the concrete path. Where did she think we were going?
She'd obviously scoured her meagre wardrobe and spent
some time in front of the dressing-table mirror with her
cheap powders, paints, and perfumes. The overall effect
didn't cheapen her, but it embarrassed me. Mothers weren't
supposed to look like that, they should be grey and
nondescript, like Mrs Rees-Jones from across the road, whose

daughter Lydia played the cello and had a habit of asking me for help with her maths homework.

The police questioned all of us during the course of the afternoon. Afterwards, my mother insisted that I stayed in and did some homework. I did try, but couldn't focus. There were far more interesting things going on in my life.

I got on the bus to school the next morning, but when I saw Trev striding jauntily along the pavement on the main road, Smokey trotting happily ahead of him, I got off at the next stop and ran back to catch him up.

"Hiya Mick," he said, when he saw me approaching. "What's the matter, did you miss the bus? Again!"

I laughed. "Sort of," I said.

"Fuck school anyway," he said.

Trev worried me sometimes, I really admired him, he was so strong and so certain, but he had a tendency to be reckless.

Another unofficial day off school and what would we do? We got fed up of wandering around the estate, crouching behind privet hedges whenever it looked like we'd be spotted. So we escaped the boundaries of the Backfields and traced the courses of the polluted streams that flowed through the industrially-scarred mixture of old factories and half-used farms.

After a couple of hours, we were bored with that too, so we went back to Trev's house to get something to eat. I waited in the garden with Smokey while he went in to see if he could find anything. After a few minutes he came back out, in a foul mood.

"There's fuck all there," he said. "Just my stupid git of a father, and he's already pissed. Come on, let's go and see if we can nick something from Good Stores."

Smokey followed as we went through the back gate into the alley behind Trev's house.

"Stay!" he commanded his dog.

Smokey whimpered and slinked back into the garden.

"We don't want him holding us up," Trev said. "He'll be all

right. At least he's got a few bones buried."

"There was nothing doing in the shop. The old woman with the wart on her nose was there, and she followed us around the shop, giving us the evil eye.

"I've got an idea," Trev said. "Follow me."

I followed him to a quiet corner of the estate that was normally out of bounds to us, seeing as it housed a group of families that were a little better off than the rest of us. Talk was that the councillors made sure their own friends and family were allocated the bigger plots in that enclave.

"What are we doing here?" I asked.

"You'll see," he said, grinning.

I wasn't comfortable in that alien space. "Maybe I should have gone to school after all," I said.

"No time, Mick, there's no time – why bother with all that rubbish – school, and work, and doing things the right way. Come on. I'm going in."

I followed Trev down the drive of a tidy semi-detached to the back door.

"No one will be in," he said. "It's Lionel's house."

Lionel was a posh git; both his parents worked, and he went to school conscientiously, every day. His house, still a council house of course, though with added features, like a clean tarmacked drive bordered with neat shrubs, would almost certainly be empty.

Trev casually put his elbow through the glass panel in the back door, reached inside and turned the key.

"Easy pops," he said grinning. "Come on, before anyone sees us."

We crept around the house at first, my heart beating rapidly. In a wardrobe upstairs we found a coat which had a few pounds in the pocket. Great.

"Let's get out now, someone might come," I suggested hopefully.

"Don't be soft Mick, you go and make a cuppa, and find something to eat. I want a shit."

I obeyed. At least it was just me and him, no Snobby and no Pogo to hold us up.

I found some expensive instant coffee and a packet of chocolate covered biscuits in the kitchen.

I relaxed over the coffee and biscuits, a rare treat for me. We turned the shiny new transistor radio on and closed our eyes, pretending for a moment that this was our own home – fitted carpets and comfortable armchairs, a clean cosy place, somewhere to feel safe in. Trev found the drinks' cupboard and extracted a small bottle of whisky.

"Strong stuff this," I said, completely relaxed, warm, and a little drunk.

"Did the cops give you a hard time?" Trev asked, swallowing the last of the fiery booze.

"Nah, it was a doddle. That bloody detective, Inspector Tudor, s'all he was interested in was my mother's legs. It really pissed me off in a way."

"You're mother's a bit of all right," Trev said grinning. "You can't blame the man. But that other bastard copper, he wasn't so nice to me."

"Conway, you mean?" I asked in a slur.

"Almost tried to pin the murder on me ... fuck, what's that?"

We both jumped up quickly from the couch, knocking over the coffee table, along with the glasses, bottles, plates, and cups. Someone was coming in through the front door. Trev, quick thinking as ever, grabbed two crocheted doilies from the back of the sofa.

"Sling this over your face, quick."

I draped the doily over my head, thank God for house-proud housewives, and we charged towards the door. In the hall a startled woman saw two crotchet covered boys running towards her, and with a look of horror flattened herself against the wall. As we ran past I looked into her eyes through the holes in the crotchet, and felt a deep sense of shame and fear. What had I done? I felt dirty and scared. We burst out of the still-open front door and ran down the street, diving into the first alley we saw.

Five minutes later we reached the block of garages where I'd hidden my satchel, climbed onto the roof of a rather rickety tin-sheet affair, and laughed maniacally until the tension had gone. Then the headaches and nausea began. I wasn't used to the drink and the shock of being the bad guy.

"Jennifer fancies you, did you know that?" Trev said, still a little drunk.

"How do you mean?" I asked.

I was shocked. Jennifer Jones, the sexiest girl on the estate, a year older than me and lumps in all the right places. I'd heard she was a bit of a tart, but me?

Later, I still felt a bit rough after the drink, but the train of thoughts started by Trev's mention of Jennifer gave me enough sexual energy to hit the streets again. I went on the prowl hoping to bump into sexy Jenny. Unfortunately the first person I bumped into was the cowardly Snobby. I didn't want to face the little bastard but he persisted in his obnoxious way to trail along with me. We sat on a wall near Jenny's house, I didn't explain to him why I chose to sit there, and I waited, pumped up with adolescent hormones for the chance of something that I had no experience of but wanted with a desperate urgency.

We squirmed on the brick wall, my arse getting sorer, spitting at the pavement and talking crap for over half an hour.

A girl walked too slowly and hesitantly towards us and with a nervous glance passed quickly. She was small and pretty with golden wind-blown hair. It was the same girl I'd seen going into Betty Fish's house that day.

I could see she felt threatened by the two boys shuffling on the wall and gobbing at the pavement. She could have crossed the street to avoid us, yet she toughed it out, despite her fear. I was captivated by her appearance and her attitude, my eyes followed her. I stopped shuffling, talking, and spitting. Snobby ignored her.

"Who was that?" I asked. "She's new, isn't she?"

"Who? Dunno. Oh yeah, she's just moved into a house in Rosehill Crescent, bit of a snob if you ask me."

"Do you know her name?" I asked.

Then Jenny and her cousin Mags, a squat ugly girl with pale red hair and redder spot-covered complexion, just right for Snobby I thought, came out. Jenny stopped at her gate and looked coy and sexy while Mags came over to talk to us.

"Will you go out with my cousin?" she asked me, no preamble. She stood, hands on hips, waiting for my answer, chewing noisily.

My mind raced as fast as my hormones. "Only if you go with Snobby," I said, as if trying to set up a friend. I glanced quickly at Snobby who had developed a look of panic, too startled to say anything.

"All right then, come on, Jenny's parents are out tonight, down the bingo, we've got the house to ourselves."

We followed in silence, me surprised at my good luck, Snobby still too shocked to do anything else, both of us swept along by a force over which we had no control.

Inside, Snobby and Mags disappeared upstairs and I sat in the front room with Jenny. It was getting dark. Jenny was a beautiful girl, she had shiny dark shoulder-length hair and deep brown eyes, she was small and slim with pointed breasts and full lips. She was wearing a short white blouse, through which I could see a black bra, and skin tight white leggings covered in big black spots.

Jenny spoke for the first time, I hadn't realised just how stupid or coarse she sounded. I tried not to think of her voice.

"I wouldn't do this with anyone you know. I think you're the best of your gang, and I only do this with the best."

She leant towards me and kissed me wetly on the lips, it was the first time I'd been kissed like that. With horror I felt her tongue push its way into my mouth and tried not to pull away, she took my hand and placed it between her legs, I rubbed dutifully and clumsily.

"Ooh," she said, thrusting into my hand, and putting hers on my groin. I responded involuntarily and my penis grew larger and stiffer at her touch.

Her trousers peeled off easily and stayed tangled around her ankles with her bikini style knickers. I crawled inside the oval made by her wide-open legs as she pulled my trousers and pants down. She was very sweet and moist and wrapped her legs around me while I pushed into her. It didn't last long but it was thrilling. Afterwards we both lay exhausted and spent on the fake sheepskin rug in front of the sofa.

I heard a disturbance outside the front window and looked up. I could just make out the silhouette of a couple of younger girls flashing a torch through the net curtains. Jenny jumped up quickly pulling her knickers and leggings up to their proper position. I did the same with my pants and trousers.

"You little cow, Sandra, piss off," she screamed.

I hadn't realised but Jenny's job for the evening was to baby-sit for her little sister Sandra.

"I'd better go," I said meekly.

"You better bloody have," Jenny said sharply. "Solong."

I left the house quickly without bothering to look for Snobby and ran most of the way home. What a day!

CHAPTER 4

They didn't find the murderer, not then anyway. I continued to trudge through the sludge of my adolescence and slowly the police activity diminished. A couple of months after Betty Fish's demise, I bumped into Trev outside Good Stores. It was the fifth of November, bonfire night. The shop's lights blinked out as Trev closed the door behind him. He unwrapped a pack of five Woodbines and offered one to me.

"Thanks Trev." I took the neat white cylinder with gratitude, something to blow away the boredom with.

"Getting dark," Trev observed, looking intelligently upwards at the early evening November sky.

"Yep," I replied, as coolly as I could. "Got any bangers?"

"Course I got bangers, and a couple of air-bombs. Fancy a walk around the sites, see who's lighting fires and that?"

We ambled slowly through the damp concrete streets, smiling like a pair of benevolent uncles at the younger kids running excitedly to and fro, carrying bundles of dryish wood and armfuls of paper. On almost every small piece of spare land, unlit bonfires grew towards the moon, people gathered, chattering in anticipation.

We came to a quiet part of the estate, where a cluster of the older residents lived. Trev walked up a short path to a front door. He pulled a small banger from his pocket and attacked hard with the knocker. Then he lit the firework, waited for it to start fizzing and dropped it into the empty milk bottle on the doorstep.

The glass panel in the door lit up as the occupier responded to the knock. We crossed the road quickly and sat in the shadows on a low brick wall opposite. The door opened and the firework exploded simultaneously. The door slammed shut and we ran away laughing. The fun of bonfire night had begun.

A couple of streets from where I lived was the house of an odd family. The whole family was kind of bent, a little off skew, not all there. They looked slightly strange; their voices came out as if something had corrupted them on the way from their brains to their mouths. Mother, father, and the two children, were all different from each other, but they had this common oddness so that they were all different from all of us. It's as if they were some kind of alien experiment, trying to look and behave in a natural human way, but somehow not quite making it. Another thing – they were all natural victims.

Some people just seem to be like that, you can't help it, some primitive urge swells up inside and you get the overwhelming desire to punch them, to brutalise. You feel that if you leave them alone they'll develop into something really evil and grow up to be the next Hitler or something. They need to be kept down, to be spat at, to be picked on, to be abused and bullied. It could be that it's nature's way of ensuring the survival of your own kind, these natural victims are different in some subtle way. You just can't let them get the better of you. Or maybe it's because they remind you of a part of your inner-self you'd rather not know about, the dark, negative side of your own nature.

"This way," urged Trev. "I think the Dingles are having a bonfire tonight. I saw Beakface with a couple of branches just now."

We ducked into an alleyway between two neatly-kept end of terrace houses and emerged at the back of the Dingles' garden. Sure enough a small bonfire was burning in the middle of the muddy lawn. The odd family were huddled around the fire holding sparklers, and grunting to each other in their unique way. We kept in the shadows.

Trev whispered: "Here take one of these." He handed me a large banger. "These are powerful fuckers," he said.

I took the banger and followed Trev's lead. He lit another Woodbine, sucked hard until the end glowed bright orange and touched the paper fuses of the bangers with the burning tobacco.

"Come on, quick."

We ran down the last ten yards of the alley. As we reached the broken chicken-wire that marked the boundary of the Dingles' garden, we lobbed the fizzing bangers towards the family. They looked towards us, their pointed white faces expressing complete bewilderment. Before their slow minds could react, the bangers exploded in mid-air, almost at eye level. The mother, a tiny, skinny, grey-haired woman, screamed hysterically; the others jumped around in panic. Transfixed for a few seconds, we just stared. The older son saw us, and shaking his fist in the air, lurched towards us, on the attack. We turned and fled back up the alley, laughing with fear and delight.

I paused as we got to the street and looked back. The man was half-heartedly limping after us. He stopped too and looked at me with the most awful look of terror I'd ever seen. He jerked forward, fighting the fear.

Trev called out: "Come on Mick, there's a big bonfire on the bottom site."

I unlocked my eyes from the Dingle and trotted along the street to catch up with Trev.

"Wait for me," I shouted after him, shaking my head to dislodge the image of those tortured eyes.

Another hour of mad adolescence passed in chaotic burning bursts of chemical energy. The remains of the hundred bonfires on the estate still sent ribbons and puffs of grey smoke into the atmosphere. Me and Trev, and Pogo, who we had picked up as a reluctant companion from outside his front gate, sheltered in a bus-shelter from the drizzle that had just started.

Pogo was beginning to show signs of what he wanted to become in later life. He had decided to cope with the awful fucking enormity of life by allowing himself to slip into conformity. He didn't really want to hang around with scruffs like us anymore because it endangered the fragile hold he had on his reality. I sensed this, and being a kind of compliant character would have quite happily left him alone, but Trev seemed to want to drag him along like a reluctant cat on a lead, someone to play with, someone to boss around.

F U C K   O F F, Trev scrawled the thick black letters on the thin grey-painted metal of the bus shelter.

IF YOU WUNT A GOOD SHAG METE ME OUTSIYD THE OFF LISENS TOMOROW, sined CAROLYNE GREEN, he added with a flourish.

I grabbed the marker off Trev and made my contribution, WANK WANK WANK.

A torchlight's beam flickered across my words. I dropped the pen and turned around quickly. A large, ugly, uniformed policeman stood in the shadows, shaking his head – slow Sergeant Conway.

"Well well well, hello boys," he said. "What have you been doing? It's not very pretty, is it?"

Trev looked at him defiantly. I cast my gaze down towards the damp concrete slabs of the pavement. Pogo shook and shivered, his dreams of an academically successful future dissolving.

"Now what am I going to do with you lot?" the policeman asked rhetorically. "Shall I run you in? Or shall I give you a bloody good clip round the ear?"

We remained silent.

"You little bastards," he said, smiling cruelly. "I've got a better idea. Meet me back here in half an hour. You'd better show up or else..."

"I can't wait any longer," Pogo complained, nearly an hour later, after we'd expended every curse and swear word we knew on the big ugly copper. "I've got to get home or my mother will kill me."

"Conway will do worse than that if we don't wait, so shut your stupid gob," ordered Trev.

The sergeant strolled up whistling, carrying a large bucket of soapy water and three worn scrubbing brushes. "Get to work, you lot," he ordered, plonking the bucket and brushes on the floor at our feet. "I'll be back in an hour and I want to see the whole bus-stop sparkling clean."

"But it's not fair," I said. "We didn't do all this, most of it was here before."

"Would you prefer it if I ran you in then?"

"It's OK," Trev said. "Come on boys."

We scrubbed and cursed, getting wetter and angrier, for the next hour, but still couldn't shift some of the more ingrained graffiti.

"Well that's all he's fucking getting," Trev said, throwing his scrubbing brush into the last half inch of filthy water in the bucket.

Trev had half a Woodbine in his pocket, it was damp but we crouched in the corner of the shelter and got a couple of puffs each out of it. Sergeant Conway returned and examined our work, shaking his head in disappointment.

"You lot are nothing but trouble, if it was up to me I'd lock you up for good, but even I have to abide by the law." He sighed. "And I'm sure you little gits had something to do with the murder of that poor woman, Mrs Johnson. You think you're proper villains, don't you? Well let me tell you, there's some real villains in this town who'd have you for breakfast."

I could see Trev getting riled up. I touched his arm, warning him to control his temper. You can't mess with the law.

"Don't be surprised if you find yourself getting pulled in again. Watch your step in future or I'll really let you have it." He examined our work again, rolling his eyes upwards. "It'll have to do I suppose, but let me warn you, if I catch you doing something like this again it'll be straight down the station for you, now bugger off."

We didn't need any more encouragement and left the scene quickly, cursing the policeman again only when we were sure we were well out of his hearing range.

A couple of days after Sergeant Conway forced us to clean the bus shelter and Trev's anger still showed in his moods.

"They just make you feel so bloody powerless," he said, as we gulped the remains of a flagon of strong cider in the alley behind his house.

I belched. "Forget it Trev, there's nothing we can do."

"Maybe, but it just pisses me off so much. It's the same in school, bloody teachers, always on my back about something or other. What's the point? I'll be leaving in a couple of years at the most, I can't wait. Give me that."

He grabbed the bottle and drained the last inch of alcoholic liquid.

"Fuck 'em," he said angrily, and smashed the bottle on a concrete fence post. "Come on, let's go for a walk around and see who's about."

It was still quite early, too early to go home and hibernate for the night and yet it was getting dark. The character of the Backfields Estate changed in the dark. It became not a more dangerous place, but a safer one – at least for kids like us who might be regarded as the danger anyway. I suppose we must have scared a lot of 'normal', respectable people at the time, but we didn't feel evil or anything, we just got on with the serious business of extracting the maximum advantage out of a bad situation.

We walked and talked and swore at each other as we searched for something to do. The alcohol had smothered the boredom a bit but it also made us more reckless.

"I'm starving," Trev said as we passed a baker's van parked in the street near Jennifer Jones's house.

"Hang on a minute," I said. "See, the baker's just put some bread in that box by the front door of that house. Perhaps the owners are out. When he drives off we'll be able to nick it."

"Bloody good idea," Trev said, a little drunkenly. "Let's hide behind that car until he goes."

We hovered by the car trying to look nonchalant in the cool damp darkness. The van pulled away. We moved towards the house with the bread. There was a light on in the hallway that cast a pool of amber on the path and the bread box. Trev walked on to the end of the row of houses and kept watch while I dashed down the path. I bent down and lifted the hinged lid of the home-made wooden box. Inside were two loaves of sliced bread, and best of all a paper bag, which, when I opened it, revealed 4 large jam doughnuts. Not believing my luck I made a grab for the doughnuts. Trev would be proud of me.

Just then the door opened and I looked up in shock, adrenaline pumping, ready to run, my hand still clutching the bag. It was the girl, the one with the golden hair. She was smiling and shaking her head. I felt like a worm, not worthy of her glance. I let go of the doughnuts and stood up speechlessly.

For a few moments I stood there, awkwardly embarrassed, not able to figure out what to do next. The girl motioned with her eyes and a slight tilt of her head for me to make a run for it, so I did.

I ran up to where Trev was waiting and still breathless said: "Come on, quick, let's get out of here."

As we ran Trev asked: "Where's the fucking bread? Did you get caught?"

"Someone came to the door; I had to leg it. Never mind though, I'll go home and get some chip-money from Ralph."

"Nah, bugger it. Don't worry."

We ran for a few hundred yards and when we stopped for a rest it happened to be in the bus shelter we'd had to clean up two nights earlier.

"Fucking bastard cop." Trev's anger came back with the reminder of the bus shelter.

I felt like I owed Trev something after failing with the bread and doughnuts, I wanted to make it up to him. One of the boys from the bottom site, in one of his friendlier moments, had once told me how it was easy to break the wire-reinforced glass of the type found in bus shelters.

"Watch this," I said with bravado, punching one of the panes of glass hard in its centre. Nothing happened except I got a sore fist. "Ouch," I said, shaking my hand to try and relieve the pain.

Trev laughed: "No, watch this," he said, pulling his head back and butting the glass pane hard.

To my surprise the glass crumpled. Trev pulled his head away without any apparent ill effects.

"That must have been a fluke," I protested. "Anyway, I

must have weakened it first when I punched it."

"Fluke, my arse," he said. "Watch this then." Trev repeated his feat on another pane. "Now it's your turn," he challenged me.

I hesitated before I did the same thing to the third and final pane. What if Trev had some sort of super strong bone structure? What if I did myself some permanent brain damage? What the fuck, I thought, let's do it anyway.

I'll never forget the power I felt when that glass gave way to the blow delivered by my head. Perhaps years of weather and thousands of people pressing against it, had weakened it, but I didn't think of that at the time. It was like, me, the oppressed, the boy at the lower end of the social scale, hitting back for once.

"Brilliant Mick, that was brilliant. Fuck Conway, fuck the law, fuck them all."

We ran off again, we weren't bored any more.

CHAPTER 5

After that night in the bus shelter Pogo became withdrawn and hardly ever came out of the house, always finding some excuse, like schoolwork, or helping his father with the garden. I began to wonder if he'd ever really fitted in with the rest of the gang at all. It didn't really bother me, because I'd always found him to be a bit boring, yet ironically, the only time I sought him out was when I was bored myself.

It was early spring. My mother flung open the bedroom windows and binned everything that wasn't tucked away or didn't move quickly enough. I escaped quietly through the back door, hugged the hedges of the alleys and went to search for my mates.

Trev wasn't in. His father said he'd gone out early, probably hunting, but wasn't sure. I walked around for an hour or two wondering if it was safe to go home. That part of the Backfields sat on the side of a south facing hill, and from carefully selected vantage points, like the red-brick chapel, there was a beautiful calming view of the estuary.

I approached the low wall surrounding the chapel, intending to sit for a while and absorb the peace that some higher power bestowed even on the Backfields from time to time.

Pogo was already there, his stubby legs swinging an inch or two from the ground, his head hanging heavily as he contemplated the pavement below. I sat down next to him.

"How's it going Pogo?"

"Hiya Mick. It's all right I suppose."

"I'm bored," I said. "Have you seen Trev?"

"Tell me Mick, do you think Trev's all right? You know, is he a good person to know?"

"What do you mean? Trev's brilliant, a great bloke."

"Yes, I know. But do you think he's nothing but trouble?"

"Well, not really. Take Snobby now – he's trouble. Why do you ask then Pog?"

"It's my old man, he's told me not to hang round with him anymore."

"Why?"

"He wants me to concentrate on my studies. If I carry on hanging round with Trev and the rest of you, I'll end up in jail, he's dangerous, he says."

I laughed. "Trev's not like that, he wouldn't harm a fly. He would skin a rabbit, or gut a fish, might even mince a cow, but he wouldn't harm a fly."

Pogo managed a smile. "I'm serious," he said. "I really like you and Trev, even Snobby's alright sometimes, but I get scared about the future."

"That's up to you," I said.

I was getting distracted. The future, apart from the next day or two, was something I never really considered. Perhaps it was something to do with the daily uncertainties of my early childhood, when we never knew where the next crust of bread was coming from. If we could see as far as the next meal it was enough.

"What are you doing now?" I asked. "Fancy a wander?"

"No, I have to go in for tea soon, then I'm not allowed out tonight because my auntie's visiting."

I stood on the wall and stretched my arms akimbo, beat my chest and howled at an imaginary moon. I hadn't seen him coming, but my primitive display startled Jacko's father, who turned up, drunk, as usual.

"Little bastard." He was swaying from side to side, trying to light a damp roll-up with a dead match.

"Do you want a light?" I asked, taking my brother Ralph's Ronson from the pocket of my trousers and holding it just out of his reach.

The squint-eyed alcoholic reached up for the lighter. I jumped backwards off the wall, landing in the grounds of the chapel.

"Give me a fag then," I demanded.

"Bugger off, give me a light."

"Fair's fair, give me a roll-up and I'll give you a light."

The man grunted and reached into the side pocket of his greasy suit jacket.

"Here you are then, make your own bloody fag."

He handed me a packet of some strong tobacco and a crumpled packet of papers, making a feeble attempt to grab the lighter off me.

"Make one for me at the same time you bloody bastard."

He sat down heavily on the wall, the still unlit roll-up hanging from his lips. I sat down next to him. On his other side Pogo shuffled further up the wall, holding his nose, and waving his hand to disperse the smell.

I turned my back on the drunk and made two cigarettes, lit them both up and swapped the thinnest with the damp one in his mouth.

He let the cigarette dangle, and sucked on it a few times. It went out, but he didn't seem to notice. I smoked half of mine, saving the butt for later.

I wanted something to ease the boredom that hadn't quite dispersed. Jacko's father was an easy target. I knew from Trev that he was one of the locals pulled in for questioning in the immediate aftermath of Betty Fish's murder.

"They couldn't pin it on you then?" I asked, making sure to keep out of reach of a drunken back-hand.

He looked at me with a blank expression. "Uh?"

"You know. Old Betty Fish – you did it, didn't you? You're the murderer."

He pushed himself off the wall and lurched towards me, his anger clearly visible on his scowling face, despite the alcohol that was numbing his brain.

"I know you, you fucking little bugger, you're that clever sod from Meadow Road, think you know it all. Well you know nothing. One day you'll grow up, then you'll see."

Pogo edged closer protectively. I shook my head at him, warning him to stay back, I could handle it myself. The idiot drunk took a swing at me. I dodged him easily and we ran towards one of the back alleyways that infested the estate.

"What riled him up then?" asked Pogo breathlessly.

"Oh, he's just a piss-artist."

"Do you think he had something to do with the murder? Did you see the way he went for you when you mentioned Betty Fish? It's as if he had something to hide."

"I don't think so, he's incapable most of the time, doubt if he can hold his cock straight to take a piss. Anyway, we saw the way the killer moved, remember. The killer looked younger, or at least more agile."

"But wouldn't it be exciting if it was him and we found out. We'd be in the coppers' good books for sure then."

"Wouldn't do no harm to investigate a bit I suppose. We could spy on him, or get him even more drunk, see if we can force a confession out of him. Even if he didn't actually do it, maybe he knows something about the murder."

"Ooh, I don't know. I mean he could be dangerous, you never know with that sort, they're like dogs. They can turn on you at any time. My father says..."

"For Christ's sake, don't bring your bloody father into this. Just shut up about your bloody father will you."

"Sorry," he said.

"All right, forget it. I'm going."

I walked home in a distracted mood, kicking at every loose pebble, spitting at every gatepost. I felt bitter. The afternoon had started out fine, I'd been a bit bored, that's all. On the bright side I had enough tobacco to last me a couple of days, even if the stuff did stink of old socks. What the hell, I thought, perhaps my mother would have finished her burst of cleaning energy and managed to put some food on. I was starving.

In the end I got fed up of waiting for Mam to make something to eat. She was too obsessed with the cleaning. So I stole a few pence from her purse in the kitchen and went to buy some chips. It was going on for 8 o'clock and was already dark.

I passed Jacko's father on the way, but he didn't seem to notice me. He'd obviously gone home, had a scrub and put on a clean shirt ready for the evening session. God knows what agonies his family had to put up with just to get rid of him for the night.

When I got to the chip shop I joined a long queue. Jacko was in front of me. He turned and grinned at me in his inane way.

"Hello Jacko," I mumbled.

"What you buying? Some chips?"

"Nah," I said. "I've just come in to keep warm."

"I got a dog."

"Oh yes, what sort of dog?"

"It's a sheepdog puppy. My old man got it down the pub. When Shep's older I'm going to take him hunting rabbits, just like Trev does with Smokey."

"Sounds great. Where's Shep now?"

"He's at home, in the shed. My old girl says he can't come into the house, because he'll shit on the carpet."

"Can I come and see him?" I asked.

The conversation I'd had with Pogo earlier came to mind. Perhaps this could be an opportunity to get closer to Jacko's family and investigate the possibility that his father was involved in the murder of Betty Fish.

After ten minutes of queuing, and nodding at Jacko's babblings, I finally arrived back outside the chip shop with my prize. Jacko was waiting with his two portions of fish and chips wrapped up neatly in old newspapers. I ate my chips open from the packet on the walk to Jacko's house.

Jacko's mother was a well-spoken, intelligent, and gentle woman. She seemed pleased to see me, glad her son had a friend to talk to. I couldn't help wondering how a woman like her had ended up with a moron for a son and a drunken bastard for a husband.

"Robert's a good boy really," she said. "He'll do anything I ask, but he does get a bit upset when the other kids take advantage of him."

I blushed. Underneath that care-worn look she was an attractive woman, and no more than thirty years old, younger than my own mother anyway.

"I'd like to see Jacko's puppy," I mumbled.

She turned to Jacko. "Robert, take Mick to the shed. Then come back for your supper."

I followed Jacko to the shed. I expected to see something like the one in our garden, dirty, damp, and smelly, with ten-year-old cobwebs stretched across every corner. I expected to see rusty tools and rotting blankets with bent nails strewn across them.

Jacko's shed was more like an extension of the house, it even had an electric light hanging neatly from the centre of the ceiling, and the light had a clean lampshade. There was a long solid bench fixed to one wall, and above the bench, tools were placed in regimented rows in order of size, and grouped according to functionality.

Under the bench lived Shep, the perfect puppy, a small fluffy ball of black and white, bright-eyed, affectionate and trusting, warm and cuddly. I fell to my knees and lifted him out of his basket. He licked my face excitedly.

Jacko closed the door as he left. "Be careful," he said. "Don't let him out."

I nodded.

Shep was beautiful, but there was only so much wet puppy tongue I could take. My thoughts turned to Jacko's father, Would there be any clues in the shed? I put Shep down and stood up. Somewhere amongst the tidiness there was a clue to the murder of Betty Fish. I was sure of it.

The neat and clean display of tools and objects fascinated me. Something about seeing everything in its place made me feel good. I touched things, moving them gently aside to look behind, lifting them up a little to check underneath. Everything I touched I put back exactly in its original position, afraid that the organised mind that created the display would discover my tampering.

The puppy was sniffing around the bottom of my legs.

"Ouch!"

The little bugger had bitten me with its sharp baby teeth. I bent down to prise him off, even though my first instinct had been to kick the sod across the shed.

As I struggled with the dog's jaws, my eye caught

something underneath the bench. A small bundle wrapped in a white tea-towel was pushed as far as it would go into the corner. I reached for it, my heart pounding, in case Jacko or his mother came in through the door behind me.

I unwrapped the cloth, noting the arrangement of folds so that I could put it back in exactly the same way after I'd examined it. Inside the tea-towel there was a clutch of letters, still in their hand-written envelopes and all addressed to someone called Elizabeth. They hadn't been stamped or addressed, as if they'd been secretly shoved through a letter box, or handed personally to the addressee. I heard the back door of the Jackson's house opening so re-wrapped the parcel of letters as best I could and pushed it back into the corner under the bench.

When Jacko came in I was on my knees playing innocently with Shep. Jacko closed the door carefully behind him and pulled his hand from behind his back.

"Look," he said. "I've got a bit of fish left for Shep."

"Nice," I said, looking longingly at the white flesh and crisp golden batter.

"My old girl would go spare if she knew, she told me not to feed him except at the proper times, otherwise he'll get greedy."

I stood up and nodded. "He's a brilliant animal. I'd love to have a dog like that myself."

"You can come with me and take him for walks if you want. I'd like that."

Paddying up to Jacko was all right if it served my purpose of digging up dirt on his father, but the thought of becoming close friends with him made my scalp tingle.

"Um," I said. "Listen Jacko, I've got to go."

I turned the handle of the shed door and escaped outside before he could protest.

"Make sure you look after that lovely dog," I said, as I walked quickly down the garden path.

The excitement of my detective work made me feel more alive and energetic, so I ran through the Backfields towards home. So much for boredom.

CHAPTER 6

It was a calm Sunday morning A smattering of sudsy white clouds hung motionless in the deep blue sky above my world. I took a walk to Old Joe's to buy a loaf of bread so I could have toast for breakfast.

The name 'Old Joe' suggested that Joe was a benign old man, providing a much-needed service to the residents of the estate, but Joe was in fact a middle-aged businessman, who mercilessly exploited my mother and people like her. He let most people run up a bill on tick, to buy now and pay later, so keeping them locked into paying over the odds for some pretty ordinary merchandise.

The streets were quiet and empty, the milkman and the paper boys had been and gone. A few dogs and small children played quietly in front lawns and I could hear the calls of crows, and the occasional low of a cow from the dairy farm that bordered the top end of the estate.

Inside the small shop at least a dozen people were queuing for service: young children jangling pennies to buy tins of processed peas to go with their Sunday dinner, old women stocking up on white sugar to make apple pies, washed-out men clutching ten-shilling notes, grunting and pointing at tins of tobacco, and at the front of the queue, a now familiar figure, Jacko's mother.

Mrs Jackson turned away from the counter, a small bag of potatoes cradled in her arm. I couldn't believe the change in her appearance from the night before. She looked hurt and distracted, her eyes dull, her head bowed. There was obvious bruising on her face, despite her attempts to cover it with make-up. Her features were puffed up, as if she'd been crying all night. I was too shocked to do anything but stare. She looked through me as she walked past out of the shop.

I took the long way round and walked home slowly with the bread. As I passed the outer edge of the estate where an open field led to the electric cattle fences of Valley Farm I saw a black and white dog bounding over the rough clumps of grass towards me; a hundred yards behind it a boy followed, walking briskly. It was Trev and Smokey.

Smokey greeted me enthusiastically. I patted him as I waited. Trev was carrying a shotgun. They frightened me, but Trev, he could handle things like that. That's one of the reasons I admired him.

"Hiya," I said, glad to see my confident friend, an anchored buoy to cling to in the disquiet I felt after seeing Mrs Jackson like that.

"Hiya Mick, what's that you've got? I'm starving."

"Just a loaf of bread. Here, do you want some?"

"Nah, it's all right, we're going home for breakfast. We've been hunting. I would have called you to come but we went before dawn, best time."

"Did you get anything?"

"Nah, didn't bother in the end, not much about. What you been up to?"

"Not a lot, been a bit boring really. You want to come out later?"

"Probably, I'll give you a shout after breakfast."

"See you."

I turned down towards Meadow Road while Trev and Smokey ran on ahead.

Ralph was still in bed when I got back.

"Leave him there," my mother said. "Sunday's the only day he gets a chance to have a lie in. Besides, he was late coming in last night. Do you want jam on this toast?"

I nodded. "Tell me," I asked, "do you know Jacko's mother, Mrs Jackson?"

"Why do you ask?"

"Oh, nothing really, it's just that I went to Jacko's house last night and she seemed like a nice woman."

"She's had a hard time of it, poor thing. Still, she was always a bit stuck up."

"What do you mean?"

"You know, she always thought she was better than everyone else."

"No, I mean what sort of hard time?"

"That waster of a husband of hers, and her boy, I know he can't help it. Why are you so interested in her anyway? Go on, eat your toast before it gets cold. I have to start on the dinner soon."

After breakfast, I got fed up waiting for Trev to come and call me, so I went out to find him. He was in his garden with Smokey, using an old air-rifle to shoot at a target he'd drawn on the shed door with the edge of a crumbling brick.

"Here, do you want a go?"

I took the rifle from Trev, loaded it, and aimed at the door. The lead pellet embedded itself in the door with a satisfying thud.

"Good shot," Trev said.

I handed the gun back to him. I wasn't really interested in shooting the door.

"What do you know about Jacko's family?" I asked.

"His father's a silly bugger, I know that. His mother's a bit of all right though, for her age, I mean. I hear she's a bit of a one, you know what I mean."

"Jacko's had a new puppy, I saw him last night, he's a bit like Smokey. I wish I had a dog like Smokey."

"Haven't you heard? Jacko's puppy is dead."

"What? Shep is dead? How come?"

I found it difficult to put the two images together in my mind. Here, a beautiful cuddly puppy, full of life, bright sparkling eyes, and overflowing with affection – there, a soggy lump of dead bones and fur, flies buzzing around its open mouth, and staring dead dull eyes. Added to that was the image of a lively attractive woman, intelligent and charming, perceptive and sexy – and there, a defeated bloated bruised face, dulled eyes, and robotic movements, merely going through the motions of living – like a zombie. I wondered if the two incidents were related, the dead dog and the lifeless woman, both beauty and innocence gone.

"Sorry Mick, I can't tell you any more than that, I saw Snobby after I left you earlier and he told me about the puppy. Fancy coming to the shop to buy a packet of fags?"

We walked towards Joe's shop together but when we came near to Meadow Road I decided I'd rather go home.

"Maybe I'll see you later Trev," I said.

When I got home my mother was busy in the kitchen boiling cabbage and potatoes for the Sunday lunch. Ralph was in the living room drinking a cup of strong tea. He looked rough, as if he'd had too much to drink the night before. I sat down next to Ralph on the threadbare sofa.

"What's up Mick?" Ralph croaked. "You look a bit upset."

"It's Jacko's dog, Shep. He's dead."

"Oh." Ralph didn't look very surprised, perhaps he already knew.

"What happened to it?" Ralph asked.

"I don't know he's only just had it, his father got it for him down the pub or something. He was a lovely puppy. Do you know his mother, Mrs Jackson?"

Ralph mumbled: "Yeah, and that bastard of a husband of hers."

I whispered: "Ralph, I saw Mrs Jackson in Joe's shop earlier on, she looked like she'd been beaten up or something, her face was all bruised."

Ralph flinched. He composed himself, glanced at the clock on the mantelpiece and rose quickly off the sofa. "I've got to pop out for a few minutes," he shouted to my mother in the kitchen.

"Don't be long," she said, "dinner will be ready in less than an hour."

Before I could protest in any way Ralph had gone.

My mother came in. "Where's Ralph going?" she asked.

"I don't know, he didn't say, he just got up and went suddenly."

"Never mind, I expect he's gone for a quick pint in the club before dinner. He deserves it poor soul, he works hard enough. Now are you just going to sit around all day doing nothing? Come on, you can help me wash up the breakfast things."

Ralph came back just in time for dinner, he didn't smell of beer. He remained silent throughout the meal and excused himself afterwards saying he had to go and sort a few things out with his mate Ken.

After dinner I went out again, I wandered around hoping to bump into Jacko so that I could ask him about Shep, but all I found was Pogo. He was sitting on the chapel wall again, in almost the exact spot he'd been sitting the day before. He looked a bit happier.

"Hiya Mick, how's it going?"

"All right." I sat down next to him. "Did you hear about Jacko's puppy?"

"I didn't know he had a dog."

"Well he hasn't any more, it's dead." I said. "I saw it last night – poor bugger. I wonder how he died, he looked so healthy to me."

I sat in silence with Pogo. I could still feel Shep's cold nose on my face and the back of my hand. Lost in my thoughts I didn't notice Snobby arriving until it was too late. The little shit crept around behind Pogo and me, and screamed in our ears. We both jumped off the wall with the surprise.

"Stupid bastard," I said. I had no time for Snobby's silly games right then. "Fuck off."

Snobby ignored my anger and joined us on the wall.

"Have you heard about that idiot Jacko's dog?" Snobby asked, smiling gleefully. "Stupid moron only gave it chicken bones didn't he."

Despite the urge to push the evil little git off the wall I restrained myself for the sake of gaining more information about the Jacksons.

"What do you know about it?" I asked.

"The stupid dog choked to death on a bone because its even stupider owner gave it some chicken last night."

"Chicken?" I asked. "It choked on chicken?"

"Well maybe it was fish or something, I don't know. His father went berserk, half-killed him."

"How do you know all this?" I asked.

"I heard my old girl telling my old man this morning. My old girl and Jacko's old girl know each other quite well. And that old alcy thumped his wife too. I wish I'd been there, it would have been a right laugh. Can you imagine that?"

"I'm off," I said.

I walked quickly towards Jacko's house. I didn't know what I would do when I got there, but I couldn't stop myself.

I hovered around in the alley at the end of Jacko's garden, unable to bring myself to open the gate and approach the house. The back door opened and Jacko and his mother came out. Mrs Jackson had her arm around her son's shoulders comforting him. They walked towards the shed. Jacko looked up and saw me. He detached himself from his mother and ran down the garden path towards me.

"Mick, Mick," he said, his face swollen with crying, "Shep's dead, I killed him, it's my fault."

Mrs Jackson called out: "Robert, come here, you can see your friend later. Come back here now."

"But, I want Mick to stay, please can he stay?" Jacko sobbed.

"Oh all right then."

Mrs Jackson disappeared back inside the house and closed the door firmly behind her. I followed Jacko to the shed.

"Where's your father?" I asked.

"I don't know, he went out late last night after all this, and we haven't seen him since. I'm glad too. He's a big bully. Poor Shep, it's my fault." Jacko's face welled up with tears again.

I felt so sorry for him. I put my arm around him as we walked up the path. Jacko stopped and pointed at a little mound of freshly dug earth against the hedge.

"There's where we buried Shep. Come and look at the shed."

The scene inside the shed shocked me even more than the sight of Mrs Jackson's bruised face had earlier that day. Where there had been neat rows of tools on the wall there was only broken plaster. The bench across the length of the shed had been torn from its supports. The puppy's basket lay upside down like a dead tortoise. It was covered in spilt paint

47

from the tins that were strewn open and bleeding all over the shed. Some maniac had taken that tidy comfortable world and destroyed it like some Hindu God of decay would do to the world at the end of time. I stood silently staring at the chaos.

"What happened?" I asked.

"It's my old man, he went mad last night when he came home from the pub. I brought him out here to see Shep but he was dead. My father saw the left over fish in the basket and said I'd killed him. He gave me a good hiding and shouted and threw things around. My mother tried to stop him but he hit her as well. We buried Shep this morning."

"I'll help you tidy up," I said. "Come on, it's not your fault, how were you to know what would happen, and perhaps it wasn't the fish that did it. Puppies die all the time you know. You can always get another one."

"There'll never be another Shep," Jacko whimpered.

"Come on," I said, "let's get started."

We went about the sad task of trying to make sense of the destruction. Bit by bit we managed to make the shed look better again. The damage was mostly superficial, a couple of hours with the right tools would sort out the more serious damage, but we restricted ourselves to simply tidying up. I tried to be very careful, avoiding the spilt paint as I helped Jacko put things right, but I noticed I'd got several splodges of white gloss on the black wool jacket I was wearing.

"Your old girl will go spare when she sees that," Jacko said.

"Nah," I said. "It's only an old coat, she's been on at me for ages to get rid of it. Don't worry about it."

We carried on cleaning for a while, then Jacko went in to go to the toilet. While he was away I spotted the parcel of letters that I'd seen the night before. I grabbed them and stuffed them in the inside pocket of my jacket just as Jacko and his mother came back into the shed. I stood up red-faced.

Mrs Jackson looked a little more alert than she had earlier, and she'd applied fresh make up more judiciously so that she almost looked normal. The despondence in her voice though, carried the pain she felt.

"Look at your jacket, Mick, it's ruined. What will your mother say?"

"It'll be all right," I reassured her. "Honest."

"I still think you should go home and put it to soak, try to get the paint off. Robert and I will finish clearing up. Thank you for your efforts." Mrs Jackson spoke kindly but firmly, and I didn't bother protesting.

On the way home I decided that I would go to my bedroom and examine the letters in peace, maybe later I would find a way of putting them back in Jacko's shed. That stupid old drunk of a father of his wouldn't notice they'd gone, he didn't even know what day it was half the time. Perhaps the letters would give me some clue about Betty Fish's death.

I walked quickly, patting the letters in my inside pocket to make sure they were safe. As I approached the chapel I noticed a lot of people standing around, talking excitedly. In the back of the crowd were Trev, Snobby, and Pogo.

"What's going on boys?" I asked, forgetting about the letters for a moment.

"Dunno," Trev said, shrugging his shoulders. "The cops won't let anyone get close. There's something fishy going on at the back of the chapel, you know, by the outside toilets."

I laughed: "There's always something fishy going on in those toilets, they don't half stink."

We pushed ourselves to the front of the crowd, and sure enough, several big policemen stood like sentries around the low wall at the front of the chapel.

"Let's try and see what's going on from the back," I suggested. "Perhaps they're not guarding there."

We sidled nonchalantly around the outside of the chapel walls until we came to the high brick wall that protected its rear.

"Give me a stump up," I said to Pogo, who as usual appeared to be holding back from full involvement.

Pogo stepped forward reluctantly and cradled his hands together so that I could stand on them and haul myself up to peer over the wall. Trev ordered Snobby to do the same thing as Pogo, and he too hauled himself up. We looked over the wall at the graffiti covered toilets, built as an afterthought against the back of the chapel. Several policemen, some in plain clothes, were gathered, talking earnestly and pointing into the open toilet door. By the way they were shaking their heads and making tutting noises, it looked as if they had found something terrible inside.

"Shit," I exclaimed.

One of the policemen looked up.

"Bugger off," he shook his fist at us. All the other coppers turned around and give us an evil look.

Me and Trev jumped from the hands of our friends and we all ran back to the front of the chapel again. The crowd had grown, but more police arrived and made a huge fuss, so we all had to get away from the scene.

After about ten minutes of speculating amongst ourselves I got bored and went home to see if my mother or Ralph had heard anything. I went into the house breathless and full of questions, forgetting about the paint on my jacket.

"What the hell have you been up to?" my mother asked angrily, when she saw the ruined jacket.

"You said it was an old rag, so why all the fuss?"

"It's not even fit to be a rag now, take it off, it's not worth trying to save it."

I took the coat off and hung it on the inside of the back door.

"Listen," I said, "the police are crawling all over the chapel, something's going on there, have you heard anything?"

"No, what are you talking about? Now get upstairs and have a wash, you're filthy, then you can have some tea and sandwiches. Go on, move now."

After supper I went out again, it was dark by then and a crowd of kids had gathered on the walls of the houses across from the chapel. I found my pals amongst the crowd. Trev, Snobby, and Pogo were sitting in the shadows under a broken streetlight. Trev and Snobby were sharing a Players.

"Put that rubbish out," I said, "I've got some real stuff here."

I pulled the clump of dark tobacco I'd nicked off Jacko's

father from my pocket.

"Have you heard?" Snobby said gleefully. "They found a body in the bogs, it's Jacko's old man."

I was too startled to respond.

"Yeah," Trev said, "bound to happen one day, stupid old git."

"Idiot probably got too pissed or something then went in for a piss, and croaked. Serves him right, bloody piss-artist has pissed his last piss." Snobby chuckled, amused by his own cruel words.

CHAPTER 7

I went fishing with Trev one morning. The tide was just right, but we had to get up early to dig worms before it came in. We walked to the muddy river that flowed up the estuary and plonked our fishing gear on a grassy bank above the worm beds. The short wellington boots I'd inherited from Ralph were not quite high enough to protect me from the smelly black mud and it soon oozed itself over the rims and down into my socks.

We laboured away for an hour or so and half filled a biscuit tin with the pink-bodied ragworms. Trev found a lump of peat in the mud and crumbled it over the worms to keep them plump and easier to handle.

When we took our fishing positions on the small beach below the railway bridge, the tide had just turned – perfect timing. I baited up and laid my rod to rest on the stand I'd made out of a fresh willow branch. I took the wellies off and washed my feet at the water's edge, before settling down on the damp sand to watch the tip of my rod for any sign of fish biting. After ten minutes of no activity I got bored and reeled my line in. The hooks were bare.

"Bloody crabs!" I exclaimed.

Trev had a bite. The end of his rod jerked rapidly. He snatched it from the stand and yanked it towards him so that the hook would take hold in the mouth of his prey. He reeled the line in rapidly and as the trace came out of the water it brought with it a small flounder, the hook buried deep in its body. Trev picked the fish up and tore the hook from its mouth, pulling half its guts out.

"Ah, it's only a tiddler," he said, shrugging, as he threw it over-arm back into the rising tide. "The crabs can finish it off," he chuckled. "Perhaps then they'll leave our worms alone."

We baited up again and cast out. Another fisherman arrived and parked himself a few yards downstream from us. The bloke was one of those Sunday morning types who spent a fortune kitting themselves out with all the right tackle. He wore thigh-length waders and a cosy corduroy coat. He had a wicker basket with compartments for different sizes of hooks, floats and lead weights. He carried a separate basket which no doubt contained a packet of sandwiches and a flask of tea, and a collapsible chair which he assembled next to the deluxe collapsible stand, on which he rested the biggest and most expensive looking fishing rod I'd ever seen.

"He'll catch fuck all," Trev whispered against the light wind that hustled up the estuary from the sea. "I've seen his type before, too much money, but he won't catch a cold."

I chuckled. "Yep," I agreed.

I rolled up a couple of cigarettes and handed one to Trev. We lit up and stood facing the water smiling at the folly of the older, richer man, who was still fastidiously organising his tackle just along the beach.

For the next half hour or so we settled into the ritual of fishing. The hard work of getting up, getting there, and getting bait was over, it was time to enjoy the fruits of our actions.

The posh bloke next to us seemed to be using some kind of commercial bait, removing regulation sized pieces of flesh from a polished container, threading them carefully on his hooks and lobbing the lead-weighted trace far into the tide without effort.

I had a couple of bites and grabbed my rod excitedly but didn't succeed in bringing any fish in.

"Look at that," I said, as Trev's rod dipped sharply and sprung back up with a jerk.

"Now that's what I call a bite," he said calmly. "That's a bass," he proclaimed confidently, "a big bugger, I'll bet."

Trev's rod bent over in a shallow arc as he wound the line in, pausing now and again to make sure the fish was still on the hook. The middle-aged man moved closer to us and watched as Trev finally brought the fish into the shallows and landed it on the sand.

"It is a bass," I said. "A tidy one too."

"Nah," Trev said. "It's less than a pound, still, it'll feed me for a meal at least."

"Can I have a look?" the stranger spoke in an accent that I didn't recognise as local.

"Sure," Trev said. "Be careful of the spikes on its back."

The man leant down and examined the flapping fish. "It's beautiful," he said longingly. "What bait are you using?"

"It's just ragworm," I said. "We dig them up over there." I gestured in the general direction of the worm beds.

"Can you show me how to get there?" he asked. "This stuff I'm using is useless."

"Sorry mate," Trev said. "It's too late, the tide will be coming in over the gullies, you won't be able to get at them."

"That's a shame. Oh never mind," the fisherman said. "I don't suppose you could, er – sell me some of yours?"

I exchanged suspicious glances with Trev.

He spoke up: "It's OK, we got plenty, we always get too much anyway. Take as many as you need, there's no need to pay for them."

"That's very generous of you, thanks a lot."

"Good luck mate," Trev said, as the man jaunted back to his position clutching a handful of peat-covered worms.

"He still won't catch anything, you watch," Trev whispered. "People like that never do, he's a loser."

The day, which had begun for us very early, now brought more and more other people into its snare. The small stretch of beach began filling up with people pursuing very different aims. A few fishermen arrived and set themselves up on our side of the sand. To our left a family of four and a young couple sat down on the dry dunes. That part of the estuary was a mecca for day-trippers, nature lovers, and simple fishermen like us. More groups of people gathered on the opposite shore, across the two hundred yards of rising tide water. There, the beach was much more conducive to a family day out.

Trev didn't like it at all. "What's the time?" he asked.

"Don't know, about nine o'clock, I suppose," I replied.

"You wouldn't think that all these people would be here at this time of day, it's not exactly high summer. It's not even an official day off school," he complained. "They'll frighten all the fish away. It's not worth staying any longer."

"Suppose you're right," I said.

"Let's pack it in and go home, perhaps we'd better come back when it's raining or something. I felt lucky today as well."

We reluctantly pulled our lines in for the last time. Trev took the worms over to the middle-aged man, who still hadn't had any luck.

"Here you are," he said, "you may as well have the lot now, and good luck."

We were walking up the beach towards the main road and the way home when we saw Jacko coming towards us in a distressed state.

"Mick, Trev, I knew you were here, I ... I ..."

His chest expanded and contracted in fast bursts as if he'd been running so far and so fast that he was in danger of collapse.

"Calm down Jacko," I said, putting my arm around him.

Since he'd shared his love for his puppy and I'd visited his home I'd developed a lot of sympathy for Jacko. It was as if I had come to assume some sort of responsibility for the weaker-minded boy.

In between bouts of sobbing we learned more about how his father died. It turned out that Jacko's father had probably been in a fight, he had bruising around his head as if someone had hit him with a heavy object or very hard fists. It looked like he'd staggered to the toilet in the chapel and collapsed and died.

"I didn't do it. I didn't do it. It wasn't me, it's not my fault," Jacko whimpered.

Back on the beach a great commotion started up. People were shouting and a woman screamed hysterically. We all turned to look for the cause of the problem.

"What's she on about?" asked Trev.

"Dunno," I said, "let's take a look."

Forgetting about Jacko's fragile state of mind we ran down the beach towards the family of four we'd seen earlier. Now the family had become a family of just three. The other family member, a young boy of about eight years old had disappeared.

"Nigel, Nigel," the woman called out, and turning to her husband, she said angrily: "You were supposed to be looking after him, I told you not to go over to the sandbank."

I looked out into the middle of the tidal river. At low tide there was a large sandbank visible, but as the tide came in the turbulent water gradually covered it. It was a well-known danger spot and I knew that one or two tourists had drowned there in the past.

"Silly bastard," Trev shrugged. "There's always some idiot."

Smokey barked frantically and ran towards the water's edge. I looked in the direction his nose was pointing, and just caught a glimpse of what could have been someone struggling with the currents. The dog bounded straight into the water and swam towards the boy.

Jacko panicked: "Oh no, Smokey, come back, you'll drown – not you as well."

Jacko ran in after the dog, and soon the water was up to his waist and he was struggling to stay upright against the tide.

I dropped my fishing tackle and walked quickly to the edge of the water. I shouted at Jacko to come back, but he ignored me. I walked carefully into the seawater, testing each step to see if I could handle the strong pull of the current. Before I knew what was happening I found myself in mid-stream. Jacko was just ahead of me, and getting more disorientated as the undercurrents tried to knock him off his feet.

I too felt the unexpected force of the tide, and Smokey was struggling to carry on, barely holding his head above the swirling waves. I felt myself being pushed and pulled in all directions, like in a rugby scrum. I got scared, why hadn't I thought more carefully before following the fool Jacko into such extreme danger? I turned my head back towards the shore. A large crowd were hovering on the sand, gesticulating and shouting, I was about 75 yards out into the channel, and surprisingly the water only just came up to my stomach. I was on the sandbank. I stopped and looked around, I had to walk against the undercurrents with a great effort just to stay in the same place.

The dog seemed to give up his struggle and let himself be carried along with the current, floating past me and out of my reach. Jacko followed him, frantically threshing in the salt water, and crying desperately. A small head bobbed up from the waves, just in front of me and a terrified face spluttered water skywards. Instinctively I made a grab for the boy. My hand found the back of his jumper.

I turned back towards the shore and willed myself to overcome the force of the undercurrents against my chest and thighs. It was hard to keep a grip on the boy and he went under a few times. I was relieved when he became limp.

After that my progress was much easier. The water got shallower and less turbulent. Someone grabbed my free arm and helped me over the last few yards to the sand. I fell on the beach, exhausted, struggling for breath.

When I could breathe again I looked around. The boy was lying motionless on the sand, his family gathered around, while a woman leant over him pushing his chest. He shook and started breathing. The crowd of people were moving away from us and along the shoreline. I looked across. The fisherman that we'd given our worms to was wading out of the water, like a great monster emerging from the depths of the ocean. Under one arm he carried the almost lifeless Smokey and under the other a limp-looking Jacko.

Over the next few minutes police and ambulance men arrived on the beach, and despite my insistence that I was alright, I found myself in the back of an ambulance on the way to the hospital for a check up.

In the hospital I was treated like a hero, it seemed as if the whole population of the town wandered into the cubicle, where I was sitting, dressed in nothing but a clean robe. Everyone wanted to shake my hand and congratulate me. I didn't feel like a hero. I felt like an idiot. I just wanted to go home and snuggle up in bed.

"Well, well, young man." The voice came first followed by the figure of the large angler who had saved Jacko and Smokey. "You were very brave, if a little foolish. If it hadn't been for you, that little boy would surely have drowned."

I blushed and looked away.

"You'll be glad to hear that your mate Robert Jackson is going to be all right. He swallowed a lot of seawater but there's nothing serious. And the boy you saved is sitting up in bed demanding a bag of chips and a bottle of pop. Your other mate, the boy with the worms, what's his name?"

"Trev," I said. "Trev's all right isn't he, and Smokey?"

"Absolutely fine as far as I know, him and that dog of his took off rather quickly when the police arrived. He hasn't got anything to hide has he?"

"Trev? No, he's just a little bit touchy about cops, that's all."

The man had an authority about him. He was big but not too fat, with greying hair and a tough yet kind face. His nose was hooked slightly, the sort you'd imagine a Roman Emperor would have. His eyes, a deep blue, showed a hawk-like intelligence and perception that made me want to curl up in my bed even more. His accent was hard to pin down, not posh exactly, but clear and almost universal. He spoke positively, every word pronounced and easy to understand. He reminded me a bit of my Latin teacher in school except I don't think we'd have been able to make quite so much fun of this one.

"You're Mick, aren't you," he said. "Not as bad as they say, after all."

"What do you mean? Who says?"

"I'm James Phillips, I grew up around here too. Moved away when I joined the force." He held his hand out.

Awkwardly, I shook his hand, "Is Smokey OK?"

"You mean the dog? I suppose so. As I said, your mate went off with him. I love dogs, I've got two of my own, back home in London – that's where I live now. I'm just down visiting what's left of my family in these parts. That, and of course

I'm helping the local boys out on a case."

So, the man who we'd taken to be a loser was in fact some kind of senior policeman. He did have that air about him.

"You're a policeman then?"

"That's me, Detective Superintendent James Phillips of the Metropolitan Police."

"Um, what case are you working on?"

"Something that happened not very far from where you live," he said. "In Meadow Road in fact, the murder of Mrs Johnson. The locals are a bit stumped, the Super is an old friend of mine, we did our training together. He knew I originally came from around here, so he asked me to help. It's a bit quiet on my patch in London at the moment."

I nodded apprehensively. Why was he telling me so much?

"Yes," he said, "you have something to do with this case, don't you?"

"Me? No, not really, we were just..."

"Picking blackberries, I know, there's a lot I know about you."

"Do you know what happened to Jacko's father?" I asked.

"Who's Jacko?

"That boy, Robert Jackson, the one who went after the dog."

"Him? Why? Oh I get it, he must be Jackson's son. The alcoholic who was found dead? That's just routine, probably one of his drunken mates beat him up for a cigarette and went too far."

"Oh!" I said.

"Do you know something more? Is there some kind of connection?"

"No, I'm not saying that."

Now I'd done it, I'd gone against all the best advice I'd been given and spoken to a policeman.

Just then my mother rushed into the cubicle, "Mick, are you all right? I thought you were in school. What have you been up to?"

The Superintendent withdrew slowly: "We'll talk again," he winked at me as he left.

"Who was that?" my mother asked.

"He's the man who pulled Jacko out of the water."

"What's Jacko got to do with all this?"

I sighed. I knew she wouldn't stop nagging until I told her the whole story, so I started at the beginning.

When I finished, my mother smiled, and to my surprise she hugged me. I would have been very embarrassed if anyone had been watching.

"My little hero," she said contentedly. At last I'd done something that made her proud of me.

By the time the local paper came out a couple of days later, I'd been transformed into someone even I didn't recognise. The headmaster ignored the fact that I'd been skipping school that day and used the occasion to brag up the achievements of the establishment. He seemed to forget that only a few weeks earlier he'd slippered me vigorously for smoking behind the school canteen.

Over the next few days my mother's spring cleaning frenzy finally abated and I gave up asking where all my things were, they'd either been tidied away or thrown out. The old jacket with the letters stuffed in the pocket disappeared as well, another victim of my mother's periodic obsession with tidying up. At least she wouldn't get like that for another year. During the same period the police activity around the estate grew to a fever pitch again. I kept a low profile and kept away from Jacko's house. Anyway, I thought, they were better off without the old bastard.

CHAPTER 8

A few days after the incident in the estuary, James Phillips called at our house without warning. I answered the door.

"Oh, it's you," I said, taken aback.

"Hello Mick, can I have a word with you? It's nothing important, just a few details."

Without resistance I led him into our bleak living room. His distinguished presence highlighted the shabbiness of our house. I felt self-conscious and ashamed at the relative poverty we lived in. The floor covering of old brown linoleum had curled and cracked around the edges. In the centre of the lino was a cheap thin carpet handed down from Mrs Painter next door after an allegedly big win on the bingo. Ralph reckoned the Painters had got themselves in debt with Hire Purchase, and he should know, their daughter was one of his ex-girlfriends.

At least I didn't have to show the copper into what passed for our parlour, which was basically an undecorated junk heap. My father's early death had left its mark on our lives and my mother found it enough of a struggle to keep us in decent food without worrying about small things like furniture. The policeman sat down tentatively on the threadbare sofa and pulled out a packet of cigarettes. He offered one to me.

"No thanks, I don't smoke," I said.

A good move considering that just then my mother walked in from the unkempt garden.

"Mick, come out here and help me clear up, the place is a disgrace," she said, as she came into the room.

When she saw Superintendent Phillips she stopped and stared, her eyes agog. It embarrassed me a bit because there seemed to be an instant attraction between them.

"Jimmy," she said finally.

The spell broke when he rose from the sofa and held his hand out in greeting. "Lizzie, I thought it might be you. I almost met you the other day in the hospital. I left as you came in."

My mother lifted her arm awkwardly and almost curtsied. "Oh, I see. I didn't realise it was you. If I had..." she blushed.

"It's been a long time," he said.

"I hear you and my son saved a few lives that day. You must be very proud of yourself. I know I'm proud of Mick."

"If you can count the dog then yes, it was a few lives. But it's not me who's the brave one. I'm trained to behave like that. All part of the job."

"Are you working locally now then?"

"Not really, just visiting, and helping out. I'm still with the Met. It's been a long time Lizzie."

My mother blushed. "Yes," she said quietly.

I was getting more embarrassed. "Um - shall I go out for a bit?" I asked.

Jimmy laughed. "No, it's you I've come to see, but I must admit, this is a nice surprise. We used to know each other, before I went to London to work."

"You've done well for yourself by the look of it," Mam said. "Sit down. Would you like a cup of tea?"

"A cuppa would be great thanks."

My mother went to the kitchen, grateful for the time to collect her thoughts I imagined. Jimmy sat down again and I sat on the arm of a chair.

"Well, well," he said smiling. "Lizzie Long-Legs, that's what your mother's nickname was then – oops, I've put my foot in it now. She'll never forgive me."

I was getting a bit annoyed with all the attention the policeman was giving my mother. I didn't like to think of her as an attractive young woman. I suppose I wasn't mature enough to accept her as an individual with her own story to tell.

"Um, what do you want? Why have you come?" I was nervous but felt I had to make an effort, his manner made

me feel guilty, even though I knew I hadn't done anything
wrong.

"As I said, just a few details. I'm supposed to be on holiday,
but I do know a lot of people around here, at least I used to.
So I'm just helping out a bit where I can."

"What do you want to know?" I asked.

"Well, I'm a little puzzled..."

My mother returned with the tea. She'd dug out an old
enamelled tray from somewhere in the back of the cupboard
and had arranged the only two decent cups we had in the
house next to a small plate of cheap digestive biscuits, along
with a chipped sugar bowl and a pint bottle of milk. I noticed
there was no cup of tea for me. I didn't protest.

My mother put the tray down on the small dining table we
had against the wall furthest from the coal fire.

"Sugar and milk?" she asked.

"Just milk please." James Phillips looked at my mother
with more than a professional eye. She put milk into the cups
and I noticed she didn't put her usual two spoonfuls of sugar
in her own tea. She handed him the tea and sat down with as
much decorum as she could manage, on the opposite end of
the sofa.

"Thanks. Now, as I was saying to Michael here..."

I interrupted, "It's Mick, not Michael."

My mother gave me a look that threatened one of her
famous backhands.

"Sorry, I was telling Mick, I'm puzzled by some of the
details of the two murders. There are some things that
appear to link them together. It's important that the local
police get a fuller picture of the circumstances surrounding
the deaths. I can't tell you too much about the investigation,
but I'd like Mick to go over what he knows."

I nodded.

"Go on then Mick, by some coincidence you were around
when both of these murders occurred."

"Hold on," my mother looked concerned. "Is there
something you haven't told me Mick?"

The policeman replied: "Don't worry Liz, er Mrs Matthews.

I'm sure your son is as eager to clear this up as we are."

I told him everything, about Trev, and Snobby, and Pogo, and the blackberries. I told him about Jacko and the puppy – he seemed very interested in that. I told him about the torn-up shed and Mr Jackson's violence. I even told him about stealing the tobacco from the old drunk, forgetting for a moment that my mother was listening to every word I said. I'd pay for that later. By the time I remembered about the letters I'd found in the Jacksons' shed, the detective was getting up to leave. It didn't seem worth telling him then, besides they were long gone.

The policeman stood up. "Thank you Mick," he said. "You've been very helpful, and thank you Lizzie, for being so hospitable."

He held his hand out to her again. She took it, just as awkwardly as she had the first time.

"It would be good to catch up sometime Lizzie, don't you think?"

Mam blushed. "Maybe," she said.

I led the copper to the front door. Mam collected the cups and went to the kitchen.

He paused on the doorstep. "Thanks again," he said. "I know it's hard to trust the police, but we're not all the same. Some of us do it for the right reasons."

I nodded.

Ralph was coming down the path. He eyed the policeman suspiciously before pushing past us into the house.

The big man looked puzzled.

"My brother Ralph," I said. "He can be a moody git, but he's all right."

"Ah! I see. Goodbye then. I'll see you soon no doubt."

After he left, and before she remembered about the tobacco, my mother wandered about the house in a thoughtful and distracted mood, she even gave me two, two shilling pieces when I asked her for some long overdue pocket-money.

I used the money to go to the Saturday Morning Cinema Club in the Odeon in town. I used to be a Marshall there until I got fed up with the responsibility and the aggressiveness from the local hard boys. As a Marshall it was my job to make sure the young boys and girls, who were dumped at the cinema by parents seeking a couple of hours peace, were kept safe and behaved themselves. At first it was a laugh going around with a torch and ordering people to take their feet off the back of the seats, but it soon became a chore – and dangerous when the so-called child turned out to be older and bigger than me.

I sat down in an empty seat on the bus amongst a crowd of other kids heading for the same place, and spread myself out to discourage anyone from sitting next to me. I hadn't considered Snobby.

"Hiya Mick," he said, as he sat down on my leg.

"Ouch!" I said, "Thanks."

"Going to the Flicks?"

"I suppose so."

"Great, we'll sneak in together."

I resigned myself to the banality of Snobby's company. He no longer threatened me, but he still got on my nerves.

We stood outside the emergency exit of the cinema with 7 or 8 other boys. A few minutes after the main crowd had paid and gone in through the front, the exit doors creaked open. A small fat man poked his head through the narrow opening and beckoned to us.

"Two at a time, just two at a time."

It was the custom to give the fat doorman at least one cigarette and a couple of coppers for the privilege of being let in through the back door. I pushed a fat cigarette butt and a halfpenny into his chubby hand. Snobby ran past laughing.

When we got into the auditorium the lights went down before we could find a seat.

"Shit," I said under my breath.

Snobby grabbed my arm and guided me to a row about halfway up the aisle. We forced our way to the middle of the row and displaced some younger kids so that we could get a good view.

The screen lit up with the giant colourful images and a

thousand young voices said a 'hush' that rolled through the cinema leaving silence in its wake.

"Watch this," Snobby whispered, retrieving a full box of matches from his pocket.

He pushed the box open and pulled out two matches. He put one halfway back in the box, with the live end protruding out. He lit the other match against the side of the box and used it to light the one that was poking out. Then he put the matchbox carefully under the seat in front of him and turned to me.

"Quick," he hissed. "Let's move before that lot goes up."

We clambered over disgruntled kids until we got to the back row and found seats near the exit. Just as we settled into the seats a loud whoosh came from where Snobby had placed the matchbox. There was a flash of flame and a puff of smoke.

"Fire! Fire!" he shouted loudly.

The little fat bouncer came running up the aisle shouting: "Lights, let's have some bloody lights on then. Come on."

Many of the kids were already out of their seats and making frantic attempts to get to the exits.

"Fucking bonkers!" Snobby chuckled. "Perfect."

The film stopped, the screen went blank, and the cinema lit up. In the light the damage looked laughably unremarkable, a few puffs of smoke still hovering above the matchbox, otherwise nothing. Snobby's loud shouts of 'Fire!' had caused the panic.

For a few minutes more the noise and confusion continued until everyone realised that the danger had gone, or was never there in the first place. Apart from standing up to get a better view we didn't move from our seats. Snobby was ecstatic, laughing and pointing, and nudging me to look at the desperate antics of the younger children.

The hubbub quietened down and from the area of the fire a child began to cry. The pitch of the crying raised gradually until it became a plaintive sob. I looked over at that terrible noise, as did everyone else in the cinema. Everything went quiet. The fat doorman, who had been running up and down the aisles trying his best to calm things down, stopped and stared.

The child, a boy of about nine years old, continued sobbing hysterically. No one else dared speak until Snobby laughed and clapped at the results of his own mischief. I looked at Snobby's triumphant expression and all I could see was myself as a naïve four-year-old suffering at that monster's whim.

"Shut it Snobby," I said quietly. "Shut up."

Snobby ignored me. I would have flattened him then if the doorman hadn't broken the spell.

"Come on boys," he said, "play fair, can't you see the poor bugger's scared stiff."

The doorman grabbed Snobby by his arm and pulled him violently

Snobby stopped laughing then. "Get off you fat bastard, I'll report you to the police."

"Get out," the doorman said, red with anger. "Come on, don't muck me around. Get out of here."

"All right, I'm going, get your hands off me."

"And don't come back, you're banned, all right."

Mercifully, the fat man was too slow to connect me with Snobby, so I managed to get out quietly and unobtrusively.

Because of the volume of people leaving the cinema in a hurry, the traffic had stopped in the road outside. After a few minutes the police and the fire brigade arrived and order returned to the scene.

Later, when I returned to The Backfields, I learned that no one had been hurt, though I knew at least one young boy had been severely terrified.

When I got home I found Superintendent Phillips coming out of my front door.

"Hello Mick," he said in a too familiar way. "You look as if you've been dragged through a hedge backwards."

He laughed, patted me on the head, which infuriated me, and turned to my mother: "See you later Elizabeth," he said.

She blushed.

He winked at me and said: "Behave yourself now Mick,

won't you?"

I pushed past them and into the house. My mother came in a few seconds later.

"What did he mean, 'see you later'," I asked, already knowing the answer by the look on her face.

She took a deep breath: "We're going out, just for a meal. We thought we'd go into town to that new Indian restaurant."

"Hmm," I said, trying to hide my embarrassment. I'd have to get used to my mother and men, though why did it have to be a policeman, especially that patronising bastard?

I couldn't stay in the house for long with my mother in that smug mood, especially when she rummaged through the washing basket and every drawer and cupboard in the house looking for 'something to wear'.

"I'm off out," I said.

She was too preoccupied to notice me anyway.

The rain drizzling on the Backfields in tiny soft drops didn't improve my mood as I walked aimlessly, head down, cursing and spitting.

Seeking some peace to analyse my anger I went into the school grounds and crouched in the corner of a doorway. Maybe it was something to do with that man, and the chance he would take my father's place.

After about half an hour I calmed down and stood up, uncurling my limbs ready to face the world again. I emerged from the doorway still uncomfortable from my extended crouching to find Snobby coming towards me.

"Oh, there you are Mick, I've been looking for you for ages, your mother said you must have gone out."

I felt my temper rising again, why did the horrible little git have to follow me around everywhere. I hated him. I grunted and tried to control my hatred.

"That was a laugh earlier on, wasn't it? Did you see that stupid little kid?"

"Look Snobby, I don't care. Why don't you fuck off, I'm just not interested anymore."

His eyes opened in disbelief at the easy-going Mick

behaving so aggressively

"Cool down," he said. "What's the matter with you? It was only a bloody laugh – a joke. No one got hurt."

"You just don't understand, do you? You never will. You're just too fucking daft."

He frowned and tried to lighten the situation by punching me gently on the arm. "Come on Mick," he said. "Lets go and find the boys, we'll have a laugh down Death Row."

That punch on the arm sparked off a ferocious response. I hit back, and not with a gentle, friendly punch. I laid into him, punching and kicking, with an energy drawn from some primitive reserve. I forced him into the corner of the doorway and kept on hitting until he started to cry. He did try to fight back and he was stronger than I thought, but my anger overcame his slightly more mature physique.

I stopped only when he was crouching in the corner, arms above his head, begging me to back off. I stood back breathing heavily and spat at him before I walked slowly and deliberately away.

The beating I'd given to Snobby made me feel both guilty and elated. I almost went back to see how he was. I realised I hadn't attacked him because of what he'd done in the cinema, my motives were more selfish than that. Although the Backfields gave me my life, my personality, my home, I hated the place for how it branded me as just another delinquent loser. I resolved then that one day I would get out of the hole and make something of my life.

CHAPTER 9

The next year or so was a bit of a blur to me, I don't remember much about it at all. I suppose I carried on with the task of growing up, getting into little bits of trouble and getting out of them without too much damage. My schoolwork became less and less important to me, not that I'd ever bothered much with it anyway.

During that time Ralph showed the first signs of great dissatisfaction with his lot in life. He became agitated and morose. Sometimes he'd disappear for days at a time, returning home mumbling about staying with some unnamed friends somewhere. We got used to it. I became less dependent on him, his role in my life diminished as I got older.

I still hung around with Trev and the boys, though not as much as I used to. Trev seemed to be drifting away, growing up perhaps.

The hammering I'd given Snobby was never mentioned. I had mixed feelings about that. I didn't want to acknowledge that I was capable of such violence, yet I'd wanted to hurt him so hard that he never came near me again. It didn't work anyway, it wasn't long before he became as much of a pain in the arse as he'd always been.

"Honestly," Snobby said. "They got loads – thousands."

"Bollocks," Trev said, "They wouldn't have that much in a pickle factory."

"It's true, I saw the money. I know."

"You're a fucking romancer. You know fuck all."

"But..."

"Fuck off Snobby."

"I was going anyway. You'll be sorry when I get my share."

The way Snobby sauntered off grinning, got me thinking he

was telling the truth after all.

"Do you really reckon he's talking crap then?" I asked Trev.

"Does Smokey shit on the pavement? Of course he's lying, fucking loser, he's going nowhere. Come on, forget all that shit, let's go and have a fag."

Trev obviously had something on his mind. We walked slowly and aimlessly around the estate, as we had done many times before. We stopped on a breeze-block wall around the front of a house next door to the plot where a new grocer's shop was being built. The building already had a roof on, and the upstairs windows had been newly glazed. The front door was secured by three padlocks and the big downstairs front window was boarded up. I realised that we were just a hundred yards or so from Jennifer Jones's house. Something stirred in my loins.

I noticed Trev was still distracted: "What's up Trev?" I asked

"Oh, forget it, I'm just being chucked out of school that's all, I'm glad I'm leaving the shithole to be honest. Fucking place never did me any good at all."

"What'll you do?"

"Get a fucking job I suppose. They've got vacancies at the rubber factory. At least I'll be earning. Pay's good."

We wandered through the estate until we found ourselves near the main road, rooting through the bins behind the shops in Death Row.

"Nothing doing today," I said. "Fancy a walk back up? See if Jennifer's about."

Trev laughed. "Randy git."

Someone came rushing around from the front of the shops. We braced ourselves. It was only Walter Swift, a pale irritating boy who, it was rumoured, tortured cats.

"Boys, boys," he wheezed. "There's a gang coming up from the bottom site. You'd better go home, or hide."

"You can fuck off too," Trev said.

"No, straight up, Look, come here."

We followed him to the front of the shops.

"Over there," he pointed towards the junction at the end of

Death Row that connected the bottom site to the middle.
There was indeed a large gang of boys heading towards our territory.

"Fuck me!" I said. "Thanks Walter."

Walter smiled with pride. "What shall we do?" he asked.

"Go home like you said of course. You go first, it's better we all go our separate ways."

"Oh, all right then."

After Walter left, Trev laughed. "You're not really going home to hide, are you?"

"Heck no," I said. "Come on."

We walked casually after the gang, making sure to keep enough of a distance between us so that if it came to it we could leg it down one of the side streets or alleys.

I recognised some of the boys but most were strangers. In their midst was a girl. The boys and the lone girl wandered around the Backfields in a mad spree of recklessness: throwing stones and smashing milk bottles, pushing bins over and running up and down paths to bang the hell out of front doors. They threatened everyone they came into contact with and terrorised the stray dogs that dared to challenge their right to be there. The girl behaved worse than any of the boys – she swore and spat, smoked, and shouted in a loud hoarse voice.

We had fun following them around. Because we knew the estate intimately we were able to keep out of their way and even predict their next move, nipping down an alley or through someone's garden to get ahead of them. It had to happen, we got a bit careless and walked out in front of them just as they approached the half-built shop near Jennifer Jones's house. The girl spotted us first.

"Well hello, it's two little willies isn't it? Look boys," she said to her companions. "Look what I've found."

I backed off but Trev held his ground. The girl came right up to me and pushed her face upwards into mine. She was short and a bit rounded with a pale greasy complexion. Her hair was the colour of dirty pond water and her eyes were small and mean. The breath that escaped from her thin pink lips smelt of stale tobacco smoke.

She hissed: "Looking for a shag boy? We're all going for a shag, do you know a good place round here? You can have one too if you want. Gimme a fag boy," she commanded.

She scared me, not because she herself was physically threatening, not even because she had the support of a big gang of boys, most of who were bigger and looked tougher than I was, but there was a lack of something in her eyes. They had a deathly quality about them, blank and lifeless, except for a lurking malignancy. I couldn't look into those eyes for long and averted my own, mumbling excuses. I felt as if I was in a dark cloud. In the mists behind the girl I could just make out the crowd of boys, who were laughing cruelly.

The girl turned to Trev. "I know you, don't I?" she said to him, "I've seen you around. Do you know this one," she said, turning to her followers.

"Leave them alone Diane," said one of the boys, who I remembered had once bought a ferret off Trev. "That's Trev and his mate, they're all right. Come on, let's move on."

"Pah!" she said. "Where shall we go?"

Another one of the gang, a small, scruffy boy with rotten teeth, said in a high croaky voice: "What about this place, it's as good as anywhere."

He pointed at the half built shop.

"Come on then," Diane said. "We'll get in around the back. Are you two coming?" she glared at me and Trev.

We both shook our heads and retreated along the pavement. The gang rushed around the back of the shop.

"Who the hell was that?" I asked Trev.

"Just some slag from the Tophill Estate. And those boys are a bunch of wankers. They'd run a mile if there was any chance of a real fight."

We walked away from the shop. Snobby was coming towards us.

"Hiya boys," he said smiling.

He looked happy, perhaps he'd just wrung the neck of one of his father's dud pigeons, a task he'd often described with relish. 'You have to get rid of the runts and the deformed birds,' he'd say. 'It's no good paying good money to keep them alive. They're better off dead.'

"What's happening?" he asked. "Anything exciting?"

Trev told him about the gang and the girl who had just gone into the new shop. He smiled wickedly.

"Come on then, let's get in there after them, we don't want to miss our turn."

Trev hesitated. "Why not," he said.

The more curious side of me won the inner struggle that occurred then, and I must admit that I even considered for a moment if I should join in. I followed them.

The upstairs of the new building consisted of one large room, probably destined to be the storeroom. Enough light came in through the newly glazed windows to give a duskily unreal atmosphere to the proceedings. The group had gathered on the far side of the room, away from where the wooden stairs emerged. I stood back by the stairs, ready to make a quick exit if it proved necessary. Trev and Snobby edged forward.

All I could make out from that viewpoint were the backs of the boys. They were all worked up to fever pitch and several of them were on the floor in various positions around what I assumed was the girl, Diane.

I moved closer, despite my misgivings. What I saw shocked me. The girl was lying on her back resting on some empty cement sacks. Her legs were spread open and she was holding her arms out at right angles to her shoulders. In each hand she held the stiff penis of one of the gang and she was wanking them off with great enthusiasm. Another boy was kneeling behind her head and she'd arched her back to reach his penis with her mouth, she was sucking it like a lollipop. Another boy lay on top of her thrusting in between her legs, his trousers tangled around his ankles. Yet more boys dipped in and out and pulled her jumper up to her neck while they kissed and fondled her large white breasts.

Snobby jumped up and down excitedly waiting for his turn while I just watched open-mouthed. Trev was standing to the side, laughing uncontrollably. The scene was so confusing that I couldn't make out who was doing what to who. I felt sick and headed for the stairs, physically repulsed by what was happening.

Trev shouted. "Stop, stop it. This is fucking crazy."

His voice was so loud, urgent, and commanding that everything stopped. He dived into the mess of bodies and pulled them apart like a maniac. No one resisted, even the girl looked chastened.

Outside afterwards, when the gang had dispersed, I had a quiet cigarette with Trev.

"Are you all right?" I asked him.

"Yes, don't worry about me. Did you see the way those boys treated that girl? I just couldn't let it carry on. That's not how you treat people. It's just not right."

"She didn't seem to mind," I said. "She asked for it."

"Asked for it? How can you say that? No one wants to be treated like that, unless they're mad or something."

"Perhaps she is," I said, remembering the look in her eyes.

"Bollocks, no one's that mad, besides she didn't know what she was doing. People like that need help. Just because someone acts hard it doesn't mean they don't feel it inside."

I had the feeling then that Trev was losing his confidence. Lately he just hadn't seemed like the same strong person I admired so much.

One day, Ralph came home drunk.

"Lisshen Micky old boy," he mumbled, "You're a good lad and I want you to know that I think you're OK. You are you know, you're OK."

"Yes Ralph," I said, humouring him. "You're OK as well."

"Leave the bastards alone, bloody women, they're nothing but trouble. Take me for inshtance – there I was having a bloody good time, with my mates, then this silly little cow comes in and starts shouting the odds at me. I told her where to go, I did. I've had enough, I'm getting out of it. You'll be all right, you will, you'll be leaving school soon, get a job. And Mam, well she'll cope, she always has."

Ralph dropped backwards onto the couch. He landed heavily on the arm and it broke.

"There," he said angrily. "Every fucking thing is falling apart: my life, this settee, this fucking town, every fucking thing. Except you and Mam of courshe – you're all right, you are. Where is she? Where's Mam?"

"She's next door, Mrs Painter called her in, for a sherry or something. She won't be long now."

"Make me a bloody cup of bloody tea or something."

I complied with my older brother's request and added extra sugar with the vague idea that it would help to sober him up. When I returned from the kitchen with the tea, Ralph was fast asleep and snoring on the broken sofa.

"Ralph, Ralph." I shook him hard. "You can't sleep there, Mam will be home soon, come on, get to bed."

Ralph roused himself. I helped him off the sofa and he staggered off upstairs. Mam came back a few minutes later.

"Is Ralph home yet?" she asked.

Ralph had always been such a strong person in my life and my mother depended on that strength, ever since my father had died. I didn't want to disappoint her.

"Yes, he came in just now. He was tired so he went straight to bed."

"He's overdoing it at work again," she said. "He should have a break." She noticed the broken sofa. "What the hell? What happened to that?"

"I'm sorry, it's my fault," I said. "I sat on the arm and it just broke."

"Never mind," her voice softened, "it should have been thrown out years ago. It's about time you went to bed as well."

The next evening my mother went round to Mrs Painter's again, I think our neighbour was having some man trouble and needed to talk to someone sympathetic. I sat with Ralph watching television.

"What did you mean last night?" I asked. "When you said you were getting out, you'd had enough?"

"Did I? I don't remember. I was a bit drunk, you don't want

76

to take any notice."

"Oh, all right," I said.

Despite the drink there was something in the way he'd behaved that worried me, as if he really had had enough; he really did want to get out. I shrugged and put the thought aside.

Ralph stood up suddenly, "That's it," he said, "this bloody settee is getting on my nerves. We can't afford a new one so I'm going to fix it."

Ralph went into the small kitchen and rummaged frantically through the contents of the cupboards. Eventually he found the hammer he was looking for. In another cupboard he found a box of long rusty nails. He came back into the living-room and attacked the broken couch with the hammer and nails. A few minutes later he'd repaired it. It looked solid enough and when he leant on the arm to test it, it stood firm.

"There," he said. "It's not that fucking difficult to sort things out, all you need is a bit of muscle."

Ralph looked very pleased with himself, it was the biggest smile I'd seen on his face for a long time.

The day after bonfire night, November 6, I was scouring the field checking out the spent fireworks. Across the grass I noticed the blonde girl from Rosehill Crescent. She was scouring too, and had a bundle of rocket carcases in her arms. I picked up a big one and worked my way closer to her.

"Here," I said, "Do you want this?" I offered her the damp shell.

"Get lost."

"Sorry, I didn't mean ..."

Suddenly, I felt very nervous and exposed, raw.

She relented, "Oh all right then, give it to me. Thanks."

"Wait," I stopped her. "What are you going to do with those?"

She hesitated. "Oh all right, you can come and see."

We walked slowly along the streets, heading towards her house I presumed.

"I've seen you around," I said.

"I know. You're Mick."

"Yes. Sorry, I don't know your name."

"My name is Angel, and yes, that is my real name."

"Great name," I smiled.

At the bottom of Angel's garden, behind a rotting wooden shed, she showed me a pile of burnt-out fireworks.

"Here," she said, holding out her hand. "This one's still live. Do you want it?"

I took the proffered banger. "Ta, I'll dry it out later."

"I'm making a sort of collage, a sculpture. It's supposed to represent the waste of modern society and the temporary nature of enjoyment."

"Fascinating," I said. And I was fascinated, but more with her than with her so-called sculpture.

She tilted her head and narrowed her eyes. "Are you making fun of me?" she asked.

I laughed. "Well no..."

"I'll show you something you won't laugh at, come on."

She grabbed my sleeve and tugged. I followed her through the alleys and across the main road where there was a crumbling building surrounded by tall hedges and iron railings. It was the sort of place me and the boys would have taken apart. Why hadn't we? There were some places that had that feeling, some force that put an unspoken fear in us, as if we didn't belong. Keep out it said, and we did.

Angel didn't have that fear and I felt safe in her company, so I didn't hesitate to follow her through a skinny gap in the railings, and through the dense hedge, into the overgrown grounds of the building.

We pushed our way towards the ruin through dying brambles and the overhanging branches of the trees, the ground littered with fallen rotting fruit. Angel led me around the side of the house to the back where the jungle opened up into a lovely green clearing, surrounded by thick undergrowth. In the centre of the clearing was a thick old tree, its branches dead and dry.

"There." Angel pointed up into the upper branches of the

tree. "It's up there."

"A treehouse?" I said.

"Sort of," she said. "It's more of a platform really."

"Did you make it?"

"Yes," she said, smiling proudly.

"Wow!"

"Come on up," she said. "The view is fantastic from up there, you can see most of the Backfields, well, the roofs of the houses anyway."

I laughed. Angel was fun.

We clambered up by holding onto broken old stumps of branches and arrived at the platform exhausted. I sat down next to her to get my breath back.

"Bloody hell," I said. "That was quite a climb. Do you come here often?"

Angel laughed, the low November sun glinting through her fine hair. She stood up and reached her hand towards mine. I took her hand and pushed myself up. We stood hand in hand tip-toeing to see over the branches. I could just about see the rooftops of the houses in the top site.

"The trees have grown a bit since I first came here," she laughed.

"Fair enough," I said.

I was still holding her hand but it felt awkward, so I turned around and let it slip away.

Angel sighed.

"What's up?" I asked.

"Nothing," she said. She shook herself. "It's great isn't it?"

"Well yes," I said. "But what do you do up here. It must be boring, all on your own."

"Not really," she said. "I think, and read, and sometimes do my homework. I lose track of time, even fall asleep occasionally."

"So, nobody else know about this place?"

"No."

"Not even your parents?"

"No, especially not them, they're mad as bats, in their own little world they are. They don't even know I exist."

"That's sad. But, I am honoured."

"Yes," she said quietly.

I could see tears welling in her eyes.

"What is it?" I asked.

"Sorry Mick. I'm not sure if this was the right thing to do. I've never brought anyone here before. Now it doesn't feel the same anymore. Sorry, I don't mean..."

"Ssh!" I said, taking her in my arms. She felt so thin and fragile, and vulnerable. "I will never tell anyone else about this place – I promise. You can trust me – honest."

"Enough of this." She pulled herself away and gave me a kiss on the cheek, then spun herself around in a pirouette and bowed to me. "Now," she said. "Would the audience please take their seats. The performance is about to start."

All right, I thought, I'll play along. Whatever she was going to do, it should be a laugh. I leant back against a branch.

"Be careful," she said. "Some of this tree is rotten."

I nodded. Angel moved to the opposite end of the platform.

"OK," she said, clearing her throat. "It's a poem ..."

They come with terror
In the night
And go with fear
In the light

"Vampires," I stood up and shouted, without thinking.

"Ssh, it's not a guessing game."

I laughed and leant back on the branch. I heard a cracking sound and the branch gave way against my weight. Instinctively, I jumped forward, and stumbled towards Angel. I tried to stop myself but tripped and fell into her. We both fell with a thump onto the platform.

"Shit," I said. "Sorry."

The platform shifted underneath us.

"It's breaking up," she said. "Quick."

We crawled to the edge of the platform as it continued to rock.

"You go first," Angel said. "You're the heaviest."

I eased myself over the edge. The platform tilted suddenly and I almost slipped and fell off. I swung my legs underneath and found the trunk of the tree with my feet. I took my left hand off the platform and wrapped it around a small branch stump. My feet found some more stumps and I ducked under the platform, grabbing around the trunk with my right arm.

"That's better," Angel said. "Might be better if you went all the way down before I have a go."

When I got to the ground, Angel was already hanging onto the edge of the platform looking for handholds. The platform jerked and tilted so that she was clinging onto it with her hands while her legs dangled above my head.

"Don't move," I shouted. "I'm coming to get you."

"Quickly, please."

"Hang on."

I climbed until my head and shoulders were above the level of her feet. I wrapped my arms around the trunk.

"Right," I said. "Let's think."

"I'm coming," she said. "My hands are slipping."

I braced myself. Angel let her hands slip away from the platform and fell on me as she slid down. Her hands grabbed my shoulders. She wrapped her arms around my body. Despite her small size I knew I couldn't hold her forever so eased myself down the trunk. It was an agonising descent and we landed in a heap at the foot of the tree, bruised and scratched.

"We can't stay here," I said. "Come on."

I stood up and took Angel's hand. We limped to the edge of the clearing before sitting down exhausted against the thick hedge.

"Fuck me," I said. "That was close."

"Thank you Mick," she said. "You saved my life."

"Don't be silly, it was my fault in the first place."

"No, it wasn't, I shouldn't have brought you here. I'm sorry, I'm so sorry." She was crying.

"Ssh," I said, putting my arm around her. "It's all over now, it's finished."

"Yes," she said. "It's finished."

81

We sat in silence for a long time, huddled against each other. I knew that whatever it was we'd shared, it would stay with me forever.

Following the incident with the tree, I spent a lot of time with Angel and less time with my old gang. We talked about everything, from the time when as a five year old, I'd locked my mother out of the house, to the story she told me about her piano practice and a tape recorder.

At first she shied away from talking about Betty Fish's murder and her visit to the house on that day. Then I found out that Betty Fish was in fact, Angel's aunt. After the murder, the house in Meadow Road had remained empty because of legal things concerning solicitors, probate and that sort of thing.

"We're moving in a couple of weeks," she said to me one day. "We're moving into my Aunt's old house in Meadow Road, so I'll be living opposite you."

"It's been sorted out then," I said. "It's taken long enough, hasn't it?"

She shivered.

"What's up?" I said.

"Nothing. I don't like the idea of living in a place where someone has been ... you know. But my parents are insistent. She left it to them in her will. My cousin Kenny, Betty Fish's son, says he doesn't want the house anyway, they never got on. My parents say it's the first good thing that's happened to them in years. I don't mean, sorry..."

I put my arms around her and hugged. "It'll be all right," I said. "It will be fun to have you living so close, we could chat more often. I think I'm a little bit addicted to your company."

Angel smiled and hugged me back. "I'm going to have the big bedroom at the front." she said. "The light in there is good; perhaps it will inspire me to do great things with my sculpture."

Angel moved in across the road about a month later but as time went on I found her less and less welcoming, until I saw her no more than once a week, and then only for a quick update on our respective lives. I felt as if she was holding back, trying to disentangle herself from our relationship. Ralph finally prompted me to stop seeing her altogether. "Bloody women." He was in one of his female-hating moods again. Some girlfriend or other had done the dirty on him and gone off with one of his mates.

"I'm fed up of girls myself," I said, trying to sound as grown up as he was. "Take Angel, for example, one minute she's all friendly, then the next time I see her she doesn't want to know. It's as if we've never been friends."

"Doesn't surprise me, now that she's living in the posh houses across the road, she won't want anything to do with you. What fucking chance have you got, you'll never wash away the smell of the Backfields."

I thought about what Ralph had said. It made sense, ever since she'd moved across the road our relationship had got weaker and weaker, and I'd noticed she spent more and more time with her friends from the Girls' Grammar School.

Eventually my relationship with Angel was reduced to nodding at each other when we passed in the street.

CHAPTER 10

Things were going on in the world that history would tell us were important. The Beatles and all that of course, and the shoots of the flower-power scene were just starting to appear through the heavy covering of bullshit that too many years of consumerism had already laid on society. It was more than that, decades, centuries even, of oppression and suppression were being exposed and challenged.

In our tiny piece of the planet the momentous news finally began to have an effect. Some of the older boys in the Grammar school let their hair grow a little longer than usual, and there were rumours of purple heart pep pills and even pot being available if you knew the right people.

I ventured out from the Backfields and into the bigger arena of the town itself. I made quick forays into back street pubs where the licensees were happy to sell a pint of beer to anyone, whatever their age. I found a small dirty pub in a street behind one of the cinemas. The landlady was a big-haired bleached blonde and the only drinks she kept were brown glass bottles of bitter or mild ale, though as a concession to the new age she had a crate of coke under the bar for those awkward customers who didn't drink alcohol.

I drifted away from the influences of the old gang in my search for something better, or merely different. On one of my lone trips through the back door of The Sycamore I got talking to a boy who became a huge friend.

"You on your own?" he asked, sitting down opposite me on the small table, pint bottle of bitter, and glass already half full of the brown liquid as he poured it in.

"Yep," I replied, trying to sound hard and mature.

He was vaguely familiar, though I couldn't say that I knew

who he was. His hair was longer than any I'd seen. He ha
full beard and yet his face was young, younger than I was, 1
suspected.

"I'm Steve," he said.

He had a kind expression, I liked him immediately.

"Mick," I mumbled.

"Fucking boring here sometimes," he said. "Where are you
from? I haven't seen you in here before."

"I'm from the Backfields," I said. "Do you know it?"

"Aye," he said. "I know it all right. My old man lives there. I
used to, until he got fed up of me and my old girl, and kicked
us out a few years ago. Not a bad place to grow up. Where in
the estate do you live?"

"Meadow Road, not far from Good Stores."

"That's where the private houses are, isn't it? Do you live
on the posh side of the road then?"

"No, worse luck, but it's all right."

"I used to hang around with a bloke from that way
somewhere, Snobby his name is, bit of a twat. Haven't seen
him since we left. Do you know him?"

I laughed. It just about summed Snobby up, that expression
'bit of a twat'.

Steve pulled out a chrome-plated tin of rolling tobacco that
had a special device for keeping the cigarette papers tidy
under the lid. The outside of the tin was engraved with the
initials SM.

"Do you want a roll-up?" he asked, offering me the tin.

"Ta," I said, and pinched a small clump of the dark tobacco
between my index finger and thumb. I took a paper from the
lid and rolled up a cigarette.

We lit up with a Zippo, in the same chrome and engraved
with the same initials as the tobacco tin.

"Do you smoke?" he asked.

"Uh!" I said, pulling on my cigarette.

"No," he laughed. "Not tobacco, not straights, do you smoke
shit?"

I must have looked perplexed again, because he laughed
some more. "You know, shit, dope, cannabis, marijuana, that

said, not knowing whether to feel shame or

to turn on, man. You're just the sort of person who'd enjoy it. You'll love it, I know."

"OK," I said, not knowing whether that conversation would lead to my first experience of illegal drugs, and feeling scared and excited at the same time.

"Tell you what," Steve said. "Come back to my flat after this drink and I'll roll a joint. We'll put some sounds on, it'll blow your mind."

I dived in, hoping for something to lift me above the terrible blend of banality and fear that dominated life on the Backfields. That night in Steve's flat was the first time, and I'll never forget it, because it did absolutely nothing for me.

As I left, Steve handed me a small lump of dark-brown cannabis resin wrapped in the silver paper from a cigarette packet.

"Do you remember what to do now?" he asked. "Not everybody gets high the first time."

"Yeah, thanks," I said, unimpressed. "See you round."

The next day I went for a walk on my own in what passed for countryside in the isles of Britain. The sun shone and the clean air blew away the slight hangover I was carrying from the night before.

I avoided the regular paths and the farmers' fields and walked through the rough brambles and spiky yellow-flowering gorse bushes, along a muddy river bank, and through a small dense forest. I imagined badgers snuffling through the undergrowth, snaffling slugs, slowworms, and small lizards on their nightly trek for food.

I felt in touch that day, in touch with a part of me that I hadn't recognised before, a part of me that had always been there but lay just beyond the limits of my perception. I hid in an empty tumble-down farmhouse and clumsily rolled my first joint.

I laid the cigarette papers on a stone, stuck together in the way Steve had shown me the night before, broke a cigarette open and sprinkled the tobacco on the paper. Then I cooked the cannabis in the foil from the cigarette packet and crumbled the warm resin over the tobacco. Finally I rolled the joint, licked the paper, and pushed a rolled up piece of cardboard torn from the cigarette packet into the end.

I sat on a big stone and sucked carefully, holding the smoke down in my lungs for a few seconds just like Steve had done. I threw the stub into a hedge and stood up, thinking I'd never get to feel this wonderful high I'd heard about. I walked a few steps and realised something was taking effect.

At first I felt a little unsteady, like the way I felt after my first glass of sherry. As the effects of the cannabis travelled around my bloodstream I found myself laughing at the beauty and the ridiculousness of everything. I walked until I came to the top of a small hill. I looked down towards a gate at the bottom of the big field. The grass appeared more lush, and greener than I remembered. The sky was bluer. The air caressed me like soft fingers of silk.

I ran down the hill laughing and leaping. It was good to be alive, on this planet, in this galaxy, in this universe. When I got to the bottom, I fell on the damp grass and lay flat on my back with my limbs spread-eagled, laughing at the feel of the sun on my face. I rolled onto my stomach and took deep breaths, inhaling the pungent aroma of the sweet grass.

I passed the field where I'd seen Trev shoot a fox with his shotgun, and the farmer's house where he sold the brush for a few shillings. I blew that thought from my mind. I didn't want to think of that poor creature then, its eyes staring as its life faded with its slower and shallower breaths.

I found my way across the main road and past the red phone box, where we'd phoned the police the day of Betty Fish's murder. I didn't want to think about that either. I breezed through the top-site and ducked down an alley to Meadow Road to arrive at my front door, my eyes still staring in awe at the revelations of my inner life.

Then the paranoia began.

Ralph was reclining on the broken settee smoking a 'straight'. My mother was busy in the kitchen, and the television was blaring out some weird children's programme, which took on new depths of meaning as I analysed every nuance of the presentation. Clever stuff this, I thought.

"Where have you been Mick?" asked Ralph, in a sloweddown drawl.

"Just out," I replied nonchalantly, but felt as if he'd sussed me out, his penetrating eyes exposing my inmost thoughts.

I closed my eyelids. "I'm tired," I said.

My mother came into the room.

"Food will be about half an hour, I hope you're hungry, I've made some rabbit pie. Mick, that's all right isn't it? You like rabbit, don't you?"

So many questions, my muddled mind couldn't take it all in at once, and yes, I did feel extraordinarily hungry, the thought of a nice savoury rabbit pie made me lick my lips in anticipation.

I don't know how I managed to survive the next thirty minutes that felt like a month, batting off nonsensical sentences from my brother as he watched the television, and more from my mother on her brief forays into the living-room from the kitchen, where she seemed to be opening the door of the oven every second to check on the progress of the pie.

For a change my mother served the food on the fold out table in the living room. She made a great effort to make the meal special, even to the extent of having fresh salad to go with the pie, and I spotted a large paper bag full of oranges as I peeked into the kitchen. I wondered what the occasion was.

The pie looked delicious and when my mother cut into the thick crust a puff of steam escaped, carrying with it a mouthwatering smell.

"Mmm," Ralph said, "this looks nice."

I bit into the first forkful of pie and chewed it with wonder. I'd never tasted anything so good. Soon I became so involved in the food I lost track of time. Ralph was saying something.

"Sorry Ralph. What?"

"I said, wasn't it good of Mr Macdonald to give us the rabbit?"

"Mr Macdonald? Oh yes, I suppose so."

My mother often made rabbit pie. There was always some bloke with too many shotgun cartridges or an overworked ferret who needed to offload a fluffy bunny or two. I think it made them feel like the great hunter, providing food for the tribe.

When I was younger I used to stand in the kitchen next to the draining board while my mother peeled the skin off the poor dead rodents. I remembered the skinny pink bodies lying next to the sink, headless and totally exposed.

I looked at the fork hovering near my mouth, a small piece of cooked flesh stuck on its end. Suddenly the spell broke. I put the fork down.

"I'm feeling a bit sick," I said. "I don't think I can eat any more. Do you mind if I go and have a lie down?"

"Poor thing," my mother said. "Of course you can, but first I have something to tell you."

Ralph put his fork down too and we waited patiently while my mother composed herself.

"I'm going on a little holiday," she said. "I'm going to London to stay with James for a few days."

"I thought that was all over," Ralph said, narrowing his eyes.

I couldn't speak, afraid I wouldn't be able to finish a sentence sensibly, so just grunted.

Since the incident at the estuary when we became heroes and he started seeing my mother, we'd come to learn a lot about the ex Chief Superintendent James Phillips. He wasn't a bad man, just a mixed up human being with a mess of motivations and loyalties like every other human being on the planet.

I thought back to that time when he'd first appeared in our lives. A few weeks after he'd arrived in the area I'd wondered why he seemed to be taking such a long break from his job in London? Surely, I'd asked myself, if he was such an important policeman he'd be needed in his own job, instead of poncing around in our little backwater.

I remembered approaching my mother one day, they were

going out together quite a bit at that time.

"I thought Jimmy would have gone back by now," I'd said. "Why is he still here?"

"Um, he's helping the local police with the murder investigations," she'd replied.

I thought about that time again, the evasiveness, the late night chats they had in our living room while I lay in bed upstairs, straining my ears to make sense of the bass tones of his voice. He'd been around a lot then, but lately we hadn't seen him, or heard my mother talk about him at all.

I don't know if Ralph and Mam talked much more about her and Jimmy, because I left the room and went to lay on my bed, where I fell asleep and dreamed intensely for a few hours about fluffy bunnies, and pink flesh, and dead staring eyes, all swirling in a kaleidoscope of colours.

I went back to the Sycamore at the same time the next night and met Steve again. We sat down in a corner table with a pint of bitter each.

"Well?" he asked. "Did you smoke it?"

I nodded, grinning.

"Thought so," he said. "I knew you'd like it. I've got some better stuff tonight, it's Mexican Grass, blow your fucking head off."

An older boy came in with an acoustic guitar and sat down at our table.

Steve greeted him enthusiastically. "Will," he said, "haven't seen you around for a bit, what you been up to?"

"Just this and that," Will said.

Will's hair was long too, but not as long as Steve's, it was lighter and he didn't have a beard.

"I'm thirsty," he said. "Get me a coke, will you Steve?"

"Sure. This is Mick by the way. Mick meet Will."

I nodded at Will with a smile. He put his guitar down and sighed.

"I'm fucking bored," he said. "What have you been doing? Anything interesting?"

"I've only just got here," I said. "It's early yet."

"Too fucking late for me," he said. "I'm knackered. Have

you got a straight?"

I retrieved a packet of cigarettes from the pocket of my jeans and put them on the table. He picked the packet up and took two cigarettes. He put one in his mouth and one behind his ear.

"One for Ron," he said smiling.

"Oh," I said.

"Later Ron," he laughed.

I was beginning to like Will.

"Have you got a light?" he asked.

I handed him a box of matches. He lit his cigarette and put the matches in his pocket.

"Where's Steve with that drink?"

Steve came back to the table and handed Will the coke.

Will took a long gulp and put the bottle on the table. "Fancy a smoke afterwards?" he asked. "I've got a little bit of hash."

"I've got something better." Steve handed over a cigarette packet.

Will opened the packet and peered inside, sniffing.

"Looks good, smells good. What is it?"

"Mexican."

"Bloody hell, not the same stuff we had last month?"

"Better if anything."

Will nudged me. "I lost four days last time, didn't know what hit me."

The grass turned out to be extremely strong. Will had a theory that it was laced with opium. My mother had already gone off to London so we went back to my house to smoke more. Ralph was out getting pissed again. Luckily, when he came home Steve and Will had already left and he was too drunk to notice the state I was in.

"Make me a cuppa Mick?" he belched.

Somehow I made a cup of tea for Ralph. In the kitchen, in the living room, out the back, in the toilet, cup, kettle, tea, teapot, milk, sugar, water, Steve, Will, guitars, drink, cokes, big Mexican hats – all jumbled up and out of sequence. Unreality, time, space, the stars, mice running over the rafters, worms in the grass, and giggling – lots of giggling.

I handed Ralph the tea and sat down relieved.

"Well I hope she's enjoying herself in London," I said.

"Huh," Ralph said. "You don't know the half of it."

"What do you mean?"

"Working with the local boys my arse. That fucker James 'kiss my feet' Phillips is a bent copper. He got thrown out of the police force before he even came here. My mate Kevin, his father's a sergeant, told me ages ago. When the local boys eventually found out they went spare."

"Uh? Jimmy's not a copper?"

"Not any more, he's not."

The planet spun a little too fast. I nearly fell off. It was probably the grass rather than the revelation.

Ralph continued: "When you first saw him at the estuary he'd already been here a few weeks. He was poking about where he shouldn't have been. They're keeping it all quiet because of the embarrassment. Stupid bastards didn't bother checking with the London cops."

Ralph said a lot more that night. He talked about the murders, Betty Fish and Jackson. He talked about Jimmy, and he talked about Mrs Jackson and Snobby, he talked about our mother a lot.

I didn't take much in, but the gist of it was that around the time of the murders, the Detective Superintendent had arrived back in the area under a cloud of suspicion. Apparently he'd been suspended from his job because of some internal investigation. Since then he'd been asked to leave without any fuss and he'd complied.

I couldn't quite figure out where my mother fitted into all that, but I assumed that they'd discovered some common bond, perhaps it was love?

CHAPTER 11

I got my first job interview just days after leaving school. The small factory was housed in a single-storey building, the size of half a rugby pitch, under a roof of corrugated metal. The job involved operating a metal lathe. I had a quick interview with Mr Brown, a miserable man in a blue suit. Afterwards he took me into the factory and waved his arm around.

"This is where you'll be working," he said. "When can you start?"

"Um, I don't know."

"Tomorrow?"

"OK then."

"You'll settle in soon enough I'm sure. What do you think of the place?"

I looked around. There were dozens of lathes and small machines crammed against each other on the shop floor. Each lathe was occupied by a man. Other men moved between the machines, dragging or pushing trolleys and bins, depositing the raw metal and removing finished objects.

"It's a bit noisy at first, but you'll get used to it," Mr Brown said.

I arrived for work at ten to eight in the morning, after catching an early bus and running half a mile down a dirty road to the factory. I waited in a cold cloakroom, as instructed. Just after eight o'clock a large, fat man in a white coat came in.

"Ah!" he said, scribbling in a small notebook. "You must be the new boy. Mick Matthews?"

"Yes," I nodded.

"I'm Bill Evans, your foreman."

"Right." I said.

"Well, come on then, follow me, you've got work to do. Have

you ever used a lathe before?"

"Um, er, I don't know."

He shook his head and sighed. "Never mind, it's not difficult, you'll be trained up. We're good like that," he chuckled.

"Thank you."

"Come on boy," he said. "Chop-chop, or you'll be having the sack before you start work."

He thought he was funny but there was no humour in his voice, it was too loud and too brash. I didn't like him at all, and he scared me. He was the sort of bloke I wouldn't have given a second glance to had I met him in the street, but there, in that machine shop, he was the king; he had the power of life and death. I followed him meekly.

The foreman guided me to my machine and after ten minutes of shouted instructions that I barely heard above the noise, mostly about the emergency stop button, he left me to work. The noise was hellish, the temperature unbearable and two hours later when the hooter blew for our mid-morning ten minute break I staggered to the small canteen to gulp down a cup of weak tea, served by an old woman with a cigarette dangling from her mouth. I had to pay for the tea of course, and that left me with too little money for the bus fare home.

Another two hours of torture at the lathe deposited me in the paltry twenty-minute lunch break. The canteen was full of blank-faced men munching sandwiches. I leant against the doorframe and held back the tears of despair. A short middle-aged man in a blue overall bumped past me as he entered the room.

"Sorry," I said.

He looked at me with a puzzled expression: "You're new, aren't you?"

I nodded.

"Get yourself a cup of tea, and follow me."

I shook my head.

"What's up?" he asked, "You're going to need some refreshments if you want to survive the afternoon."

"I'm all right," I said.

"You're broke aren't you?"

"Yes," I said quietly.

"Come on, you can have a cuppa on me."

We pushed our way through the crowded room to a door at the back. It led into a small storeroom. He flicked a light on and pushed the door shut behind us.

"Sit down," he said, pointing to one of the two small wooden chairs crushed against a tiny table.

I sat down with relief.

He fished a thick hessian rucksack from under the table and extracted a flask and a packet of sandwiches wrapped in greaseproof paper.

"Here."

He shoved the sandwiches and a cup tea across the table and sat down opposite me, lighting a roll-up which he'd pulled from behind his ear.

"Where are you from?" he asked.

"From the Backfields," I said, as I sipped the too-hot tea.

"Uh-uh," he said pensively. "What are you doing here? You're younger than our usual."

I shrugged. What was I doing there? I didn't know.

"Listen son," he said. "You don't want to be in this dark place, I'm sure a bright young man like you could find something better. This is a terrible place to spend your youth."

A hooter sounded. The man looked at his watch.

"Was that the back to work sound?" I asked.

He nodded, but made no move to get up.

"Shouldn't we be going back?" I asked nervously. I didn't want to get the sack on my first day.

"You should," he said, "but I don't work on the lathes. I'm the factory electrician. Having a trade does have some advantages."

"I'd better go," I said.

"Finish your tea, don't worry," he said.

There was something familiar about the way he pulled on that cigarette and the way he flicked his greased hair away from his face as he spoke. I gulped the tea down and stood up.

"Look," I said. "I really should get back to work."

He nodded. "Think about what I said."

As I pushed past him in the cramped room, he touched my arm.

"Here," he said, handing me a ten-shilling note. "Take this. There are far better things waiting for you in your life, don't waste your precious breath in this shithole."

I looked into his brown eyes, there was an intense kindness and caring there that stirred something deep inside me, but also a sadness for something lost.

"Good luck," he said softly.

I hurried through the then empty canteen and re-entered the factory. The second I closed the canteen door behind me the noise of the infernal machines returned and filled my whole being with dread. I couldn't move forward. I recalled the electrician's benevolent sad smile and realised who he reminded me of. It was my father – my father who had left me so long ago. How could it be? I stood transfixed, stuck to the wall of the factory.

Bill, the large fat foreman, approached me: "Oi, you," he shouted. "You, the new boy. Chop-chop, get back to work. You're paid to do a job, not hang around like a bloody stupid bat."

I moved forward, back towards my station at the lathe. The door behind me opened and the electrician came out. He reached up and patted the big man on the head, winking at me. The foreman seemed to diminish in size and power after that pat. He glared at the smaller man and his face went red. I felt my whole being getting lighter. I suppressed a chuckle.

A resolve grew in me then, a resolve that I was not going to settle for that kind of hell any more. I didn't care what the consequences would be, nothing could be worse than having to work in such a black hole.

My heart pounding with excitement and fear, I walked past the foreman and out of that factory forever.

During the next year or so I tried out at least half a dozen other jobs, finally settling as an assistant in a trendyish men's clothes shop. After a few weeks I developed a very lucrative sideline. Spurred on by Steve, I threw pairs of denim jeans out of the toilet window to where he waited in the lane behind the shop.

The money we got from selling the jeans financed the drugs we got more and more involved in during that time. We didn't stop at just plain cannabis, we took anything we could get our hands on, and when we couldn't find anything to buy, Steve would steal sleeping tablets from his mother. Will discovered that a certain brand of cough medicine, when drunk in quantities of at least half a bottle, would send him into a nether world of half-hallucinations and sogginess.

Then Will found a new girlfriend who nagged him so much to stop taking drugs that he went straight and cut his hair. He even stopped playing his guitar, which was a shame because he was very talented.

All the drug taking had an effect on my work and I took days off on the sick. My boss, a gentle but naïve middle-aged man, warned me time after time to sort myself out. I went to work on a Monday morning after a heavy weekend when a combination of drugs and alcohol had robbed me of an entire Sunday. Mr Jenkins, my boss, called me into the storeroom.

"Mick," he said. "I've heard some disturbing allegations about you and your friends. Have you got anything to say?"

"About what?" I asked, puzzled. There were so many things he could have been referring to.

"Jeans, amongst other things, does that mean anything to you?"

I looked down and kept quiet.

"Right," he said. "I want you to go. You will not get your pay for last week and you will certainly not get a reference from me. If you want to dispute that then I will have to call the police. Now get out please."

I scuttled out of the shop, sorry I'd be losing my income, but relieved I wouldn't have to get up for work anymore. I wondered how Mr Jenkins had come to find out about the jeans. Someone must have dobbed us in. I went to see Steve in the flat he shared with his mother above a shoe shop, not far from where I'd worked.

Steve came to the door rubbing his eyes.

"What the fuck time do you call this? It's Monday morning for fuck's sake."

"I know," I said.

"You'd better come in."

"Is your mother here?" I asked.

"Yeah, but she's sleeping like a baby, as usual. Too many sleeping pills probably."

I laughed.

"What's up Mick?"

"I just got the sack," I said.

"About time too, you lazy bastard, I wouldn't give you a job if you paid me."

"It's not that, my boss found out about the jeans."

"How come?"

"Somebody must have split on us."

"Hmm, I think I know, hang on a minute."

I waited while Steve changed into his going out clothes of stolen jeans, check shirt, and a long black wool coat he'd nicked from a charity shop.

We walked a mile out of town to the electrical wholesaler where Will worked. He was at the counter when we walked in.

"What are you two doing here?" he asked.

Steve came straight to the point: "Did you tell Mick's boss about the jeans?"

"What do you mean?"

"Mick's just had the sack, for stealing jeans."

Will looked indignant: "I didn't even know you two were still at it," he said. "You were bound to get caught one day, fair's fair."

I was puzzled, why had Steve seemed so sure?

"Listen Will, did you ever tell Judith about our little schemes?" Steve said.

Will shrugged. "I suppose so."

Steve continued: "My mother said something. It puzzled me at the time, but it makes sense now."

We waited.

"Yeah, she cleans sometimes, at the place where Mrs Robinson works, you know, Snobby's mother."

I was taken aback, Snobby's name coming up again, whenever there was trouble in my life.

"Hey, come on Steve, get to the point," Will said. "Or I'll be getting the sack as well."

"My mum reckons Snobby's mother's been gossiping about us lot, about how you were lucky to have got away from us, about how Snobby's girlfriend works with your girlfriend, and Snobby told her it wouldn't be long before Mick had what was coming to him."

I gasped.

Steve continued: "I didn't take much notice at the time; my old girl's always coming up with crazy stories to make me 'come to my senses' as she puts it."

"So, do you reckon Snobby's split on us?" I asked.

"Maybe," Steve said. "You've always said he's capable of anything."

"That would mean," Will said, "that Judith has been talking to Snobby's girlfriend and telling her things she shouldn't."

"Don't jump to conclusions," Steve said. "Anyway, people talk all the time, it's natural."

"Tell you what," Will said. "I'll see you two tonight, in the pub, I'll talk to Judith before I come, and find out what she said to Snobby's girlfriend, if anything. I've got to get back to work now."

Later, in the pub, Will arrived looking angry and upset.

"What is it?" I asked.

"Get the drinks in Steve." Will sat down heavily. "The bitch. Not only did Judith tell Snobby's girlfriend about you – us, she did it deliberately so that it would get back to Snobby. She knows what he's like. For my own good, she said. What does she know? Anyway we had a big row. We're finished – it's all over."

"Phew," I said.

"Got any dope?" Will asked, a big grin on his face.

We all laughed.

After that incident Will packed his job in and the three of us became constant companions. Our appearance got even scruffier. Our hair continued to grow. We became outcasts in most areas of town and our families nagged us constantly to get haircuts, or to get a job, or to smarten up. We indulged in some small time drug dealing to supplement the meagre dole money we got.

At one time we even formed a band, the trouble was that Will was the only one who could play a musical instrument and not one of us could sing, so we give that up as a bad idea and went back to getting stoned every day. I moved with Steve into a cramped bedsitter in a run-down hotel on the outskirts of the town centre.

One day in midsummer the three of us took some acid in the flat that Will shared with a bunch of other blokes who I didn't know very well, but where we spent lot of our time lying around listening to records.

We dropped the acid and headed out of town. By the time the drug kicked in we had reached the middle of Old Oak Forest, a hilly wooded area that looked down on the town and helped to create the moderate climate we enjoyed all year round.

I sat down with Steve and Will around the base of the huge ancient oak tree that gave the woods its name. The sunlight sparkled through the leaves of the oak and the surrounding trees, and painted butterflies on the faces of my companions.

We didn't speak. A glance, a smile and a small eye movement carried all the words we needed. We laughed and sighed with the pleasure of the experience. Steve rolled a joint and passed it around. When it got to me I looked at it for a few seconds before deciding that I didn't want any and passed it to Will. He let it drop to the forest floor where it went out unsmoked.

Without speaking we stood up and looked around our environment. It seemed to me that we were in the Garden of

Eden. We didn't need big explanations, we just were. We floated in a timeless, limitless place where the only thing that mattered was just to be. We made our way down the hill, through the woods, and towards the shoreline that bordered the southern part of the town.

We walked along a street of small cottage-like properties, garlanded with luscious green ivy and fronted by deeply-coloured flowers, whose scent wafted in great streams, and bathed us in sweet fragrances. As we passed the gates and hedges we saw small orchards of apple trees, the fruit just forming.

We were passing the gate of one of the cottages. Will reached through the hedge and grabbed a tiny apple. A whooshing sound drew my attention to the path that led to the side of the house. A small dog, something like a Jack Russell, belted from the rear of the house, and along the path to challenge us at the gate – something, no doubt, that it had done a thousand times before. My mind, tripping on LSD as it was, twisted this image. I knew what it was, a small territorial dog, harmless in itself, but what I saw was a long evil serpent. The dog was moving so fast that it was leaving after-images behind, giving the impression of a huge snake shooting from behind the house.

We all ran on rubber legs. My feet were sinking into the road as we bumbled across towards the sandy beach. Before we could get to the safe, natural haven of the seashore, we had one more barrier to cross. That part of the shoreline housed a big sprawling steelworks, with smoke belching from its stacks, and noisy trains ferrying raw material in, and finished goods out. It was a vision of hell.

Where we had been delicate elves in the woods, bouncing between the trees and delighting in the elements, there we were great lumbering old elephants, marching to our graveyard, every step a gigantic effort. Our progress over the railway took an eternity and by the time we reached the beach my head was so big it held the whole universe. At the same time the whole universe was so small I could describe it by turning in a circle with my arm outstretched and my index finger pointing at the horizon.

I threw myself on the damp sand near the rising tide and closed my eyes, but there was no escape, the horror was inside me. We continued walking along the beach, the salt water lapping at our feet, until we found our exit near the railway station, over an iron bridge and back to Will's flat.

Once inside we gorged ourselves on oranges and sugar, put some soothing music on, and took a couple of tranqs each to help bring us down. Throughout the nightmare we didn't look each other in the eye, because when we did, all we saw was a terrible reflection of an inner monster that was our human nature gone wrong.

One of Will's flatmates had been making jam tarts when we came in, but when he saw us he freaked out and locked himself in his room. We were glad of that. We didn't need anyone else to share that dreadful experience.

A smell of burning reached us as we lay sprawled on a mattress listening to Roy Harper and waiting for the sugar and the tranquillisers to take effect. I realised it must be the jam tarts burning in the oven. I got up and went into the small dirty kitchen and switched the oven off. I opened the door and the smoke billowed out, getting in my eyes, up my nose, and in my throat.

Burnt jam. That just about summed it all up. Here was a beautiful gift from god – fruit. Here was man, corrupting that fruit with refined sugar, making a sickly imitation of the real thing, and then burning it.

Thank God, I was coming down at last.

Later, we went out again and sat on a bench near the town hall, relieved to be normal again. When Angel turned up unexpectedly I realised how we must have looked. Three sad, dirty, haggard young men – all the more off-putting because of the way we dressed and the length and scruffiness of our hair.

I looked up and my eyes met Angel's.

"Hello Mick," she said with a look that said: "What have you become?"

I mumbled: "Oh hi, Angel – what are you doing here?"

"I work here, in the Town Hall. I've just finished for the day. I haven't seen you around lately. I wasn't sure if it was you at first."

At that time I was proud of what I was, I believed that I was some kind of pioneer, pushing forward the limits that humanity had imposed on itself. I was a head, my friends and I had it all sussed out. Whatever we looked like I felt that we were better than anyone was from the 'straight' world. But when I saw the tears welling up in Angel's eyes as she felt so much pain at what I had become, I felt deep shame.

"Bye then Mick," she said emotionally, and she was gone.

That night I went home to my mother's for the first time in weeks.

Ralph was out somewhere with his drinking mates, Mam looked drawn and distracted, but that didn't stop her from insisting that I went upstairs and had a long soak in the bath. By the time I finished bathing I felt so much better that when I went down to sit at the table to eat the meal my mother had prepared I actually give her a kiss on the cheek.

"What's that for?" she asked surprised, it wasn't often that members of our family showed that sort of affection to each other.

"Thanks," I said. "You're too good to me, I don't deserve it."

"Don't be silly, you're my little boy, where would I be without you."

"How's it going?" I asked. "How's Ralph? And Jimmy?"

My mother sighed, "Ralph's worrying me a bit, he drinks all the time, I'm afraid he'll lose his job. And I haven't heard from Jimmy for a while now."

"I'm sorry," I said. "Have you two split up?"

"It's not exactly like that, it's … Oh, never mind, eat your dinner."

I was completely knackered, it had been a long and tiring day, both emotionally and physically. I asked my mother if I could stay the night. She'd already made a bed up for me when I was in the bath.

I slept until late afternoon the next day. When I got up, I

had another bath. After a light meal at tea-time I went across the road to see if I could talk to Angel.

Her mother answered: "She's not home yet. I'll tell her you called."

She closed the door rather too abruptly. She won't tell her, I thought, so I sat on the wall outside my house and waited. Half an hour later Angel came up the street from the bus stop.

I stood up to greet her: "Angel," I said. "Stop a minute."

She looked away. "I'm in a hurry, my mother will have food ready."

"Please Angel," I begged. "Just a minute."

She sat down reluctantly on the wall and for a few minutes we both sat and stared at the other side of the street towards her house, the same house where a few years earlier I'd seen her aunt, Betty Fish, being carried out on a stretcher, with her face covered by a sheet.

"Look at me," I said. "I know how it must have looked to you yesterday. But I'm OK really. Look at me."

She turned her head slowly towards me. Her eyes were full of tears again. In that moment I knew I wanted to be with her. I'd do anything for her. I'd even get a job. I wasn't sure how she felt about me, but it was worth a shot.

"How about you and me go for a drink tonight?" I said "We can go to the Carpenters, it's only down the road."

She hesitated, "All right, I'll give you a knock about half past seven."

Angel sighed and crossed the road to her house.

In the pub that night we began on the road to a relationship that promised to be one of the happiest times of my life. I kissed her goodnight outside her gate, walked across the road and knocked the door of my mother's house.

Mam came to the door in tears. "I'm so glad you're all right," she said, hugging me.

"What's the matter?" I asked.

I went through the front door and closed it behind me. In the living room sat two policemen. One was Sergeant Conway, the brute who I used to hate so much. Strangely he looked contrite and subdued, not his usual heavy self at all.

"Where have you been tonight?" he asked.

"Why? What's happened? What's going on?"

"Do you know Stephen Morris and William Jones?"

I thought for a second. Did he mean Steve and Will? "Yes, I think so. Why, what have they done?"

"I'm afraid there's been an accident."

I kept silent, expecting the worst.

The policeman continued: "Apparently they stole a car, it crashed on the bridge over the estuary. They're both dead. We think they were on drugs. Do you know anything about that?"

CHAPTER 12

The shock of Steve's and Will's deaths traumatised me for several months. Angel lived up to her name and helped me to keep together during that time. It might have been some sort of guilt at first, because it emerged that it was her cousin Kenny's car that Will and Steve had nicked, and there were some questions about the brakes, but as the weeks passed we became proper lovers for the first time.

I got a place on an electrical engineering course at Elchurch College and studied as best I could. I moved back in with my mother permanently, it was cheap of course, and convenient for my relationship with Angel. Ralph was still drinking too much, but somehow he managed to hold on to his job.

Mam gave up the part-time job she'd had in the school canteen for over ten years and found a job in a haulier's firm as a general office dogsbody. She didn't rate the job highly but she enjoyed the pay packet at the end of every week.

I got a small grant for my course, so our financial situation improved enormously. The old sofa finally got thrown out and we all pitched in to redecorate the living room and the kitchen. The parlour, that had shamed me for so long, was gutted and decorated as well.

Despite all these apparently good things that our little family enjoyed during that period, I still felt that under the surface something was not working quite as well as it should be. Ralph's drinking was one thing of course, and I still felt the shock of the deaths of my friends. But there was more. Sometimes when I caught my mother in a quiet moment, I noticed her eyes were bloodshot, as if she'd been crying, but despite my entreaties, she refused to acknowledge that there was anything wrong.

I went out with my older brother one Saturday night. It

made me feel completely adult for the first time in my life; even Ralph treated me like an equal and not some irritating little runt. We were going to a nightclub for his best friend's bachelor party.

We caught a bus down to town and intended to walk home in the early hours of the morning. On the bus, Ralph talked to me like an old mate, something I enjoyed.

"How's it going with you and Angel, Mick? Any signs of wedding bells?" Ralph joked.

"Me married? Never," I said instinctively, but maybe he was on to something.

"You're a lucky man," he said. "There's not many like her about, you want to hang on to that one. If only she had an older sister. Mind you her mother's not too bad, if only she was twenty years younger."

I laughed; this was more like the old Ralph.

Ralph's friends bored me. All they talked about was work and cars. Most of them were already married or would be soon. As far as I could tell from the conversation, Ralph was the only one who didn't have a partner.

Jon, the one whose wedding it was the following Monday, got drunk quickly, probably because his mates spiked his beer with vodka. The nightclub filled up at pub closing time. By then we were all quite drunk, and Jon was virtually legless.

Jon lay his head on Ralph's shoulder and mumbled drunkenly. "Mick," he said, "you ought to be very proud of your big brother. He's been a great friend to me. Haven't you Ralph?"

"Shut up Jon, you're pissed." Ralph said.

"I know, of course I'm pissed, it's my bachelor night, isn't it? Wouldn't you be pissed on your bachelor night?"

"Yeah, yeah," Ralph said.

"What about Marie?" Jon opened his eyes and looked up at Ralph.

"Shut up Jon, let it go will you."

I stood up to go to the toilet and spotted Trev and Snobby standing at the bar. I pushed my way through the crowd and approached them. I was drunk but not incapable.

"Hiya boys," I said. "How come you're here, do you know Jon?"

"Who's Jon?" asked Trev. "You're pissed."

"Nah, not really. Anyway how are you two?"

Snobby gave me a hateful look. He hadn't forgotten about the beating I'd given him, even if I had put it to the back of my mind.

"Let me buy you a pint," I insisted.

They didn't object.

I ordered the drinks and put some money on the bar.

"Hang on there a minute," I said. "I'm going for a piss, I won't be long."

In the toilet, I stood facing the enamelled wall, shoulder to shoulder with a crowd of men and boys, most of them swaying from side to side. I swayed a little too far and bumped into the bloke next to me.

"Sorry," I said, expecting a violent reaction. Those nightclubs could be dodgy places.

The short bloke farted. "S'all right. Don't menshun it."

It was Pogo.

"If I'd known you were here with Trev and Snobby. I'd have bought you a pint. I'll get you one when we get back to the bar."

"Don't mind if you do," he said. "But I'm not with them. I'm here with my girlfriend and some other friends."

"Bloody Hell, you're courting are you? What's her name then?"

"Shylvia, her name ish Shylvia, and she'sh gorjuss."

I zipped my flies back up and made a half-hearted attempt to wash my hands. I walked out of the toilets with my arm around Pogo's shoulders. Trev and Snobby were still standing near the bar. They nodded at Pogo, but didn't seem interested in having a conversation.

"Come on boys," I said. "Let's liven it up a bit, find some girls to dance with."

I grabbed Snobby by the arm and led him towards two girls who were dancing together. As we approached them I whispered in his ear: "Mine's not bad, but I don't fancy yours."

Snobby's expression was poison.

We danced with the girls anyway. A smoochy number came on. I held my partner close. She smelt sexy and feminine. I peered over her shoulder and saw Snobby's partner thrusting herself up against him. I winked at him. He gave me a glowering look. My resistance lowered by the alcohol I found myself happily leaving the club with Snobby and the girls. It was still relatively early for a nightclub, so I reckoned that I'd be back before Ralph realised I'd gone.

We went up a lane behind some shops and snogged a bit, but it didn't go any further, because I remembered Angel and felt guilty. Besides, I didn't want anything to jeopardise our relationship.

The other girl and Snobby had some sort of altercation and the two of them went off in a huff. Snobby and me walked back to the club, most of the way in silence. As we got near the entrance to the club, Snobby turned on me, a venomous look on his face.

"You fucking ponce," he spat the words out. "Don't think I've forgotten what you did to me. You and your high and mighty ways, you don't know fuck all, you and that arsehole brother of yours. You're lucky I don't go to the cops, you'd both be sent down for years."

I swung for him but because of my drunkenness I missed and hit a wall.

"Serves you right, fucking twat."

He ran off.

I nursed my sore hand. What did he mean?

When I got back to the club, most of the people had already left. Ralph and his mates were staggering out of the exit.

"There you are Mick. Where have you been? Come on, we've got a long walk home."

The group split up as we left town. I walked on with Ralph.

By the time we got home Ralph was in a stinking mood.

"Leave me alone," he said angrily, when I tried to help him over the step.

"OK, calm down," I said. "I'm going to bed, I'm tired."

When I got up the next morning, Ralph had gone and so had his car.

"Did you have a nice time last night with your brother?" My mother put a cup of tea in my hands.

"Great," I said. "Where is Ralph, by the way?"

"I don't know, he must have gone out before I got up, probably something to do with the wedding."

"Oh," I said, slurping the tea. "Have you got any aspirins? I've got a bit of a hangover."

I'd arranged to go over to Angel's for my Sunday lunch. I got washed and changed and crossed the road at 12:30. I'd never been inside her house before, so it was a big day for us. Her parents would be there. Time to gain official approval on our relationship.

I made for the rear entrance as Angel had instructed me, but found the side gate locked, so I went back around the front and knocked on the big brass knocker. Her mother came to the door. She was a lot older than my mother, and scared me with her overbearing presence.

"It's you, I see. Well, sorry to disappoint you, but you're not welcome here today. In fact you will never be welcome here. I can't say I'm sorry. I never did like you. My daughter could do much better, and now you've proved it."

I was taken aback: "What's going on?" I asked. "Let me see Angel."

"Just get back across the road where you belong. You're nothing but scum." She slammed the door shut.

I banged the door hard and shouted: "Open up, let me talk to Angel."

Angel opened the door and stood above me on the high doorstep. She had tears in her eyes. Hovering behind her was a man I didn't recognise. He was in his late twenties, tall, with a mess of floppy hair the same golden colour as Angel's.

"It's over Mick, go away," she said.

"Who's he?" I asked. "What's he doing here? Is that it, is he why?"

"He's nobody, just my cousin, Kenny. Now please leave me

alone."

Kenny stepped forward: "You've been asked to leave," he said, his eyes narrowed in a cold stare.

Angel turned to him: "Go back inside Kenny – please."

He shrugged and faded into the shadows.

"But why Angel?"

"You know, you bastard."

"Sorry, I don't know what you're talking about."

"Last night, where did you go?"

"I went out with Ralph to a bachelor party, you know that."

"Yes, but where did you go during the party, and more importantly, with who."

I remembered about Snobby and the two girls. "But that was nothing," I protested. "Nothing happened."

"That's not what I heard. Get lost. I never want to see you again."

Angel slammed the door. I retreated to think things over. It must have been that swine Snobby. How stupid I was to get involved with the evil little git again. He nearly ruined my life when I was just a tiny tot with his bullying, now he'd really fucked things up for me.

Ralph came home mid-afternoon while I was still gathering my thoughts and deciding what to do next. He did not have the car with him. He looked distraught.

"What's the matter?" my mother asked him.

"Leave me alone," he snapped.

I was too preoccupied to notice much of what went on next, but late that night a car pulled up outside the house and Jimmy knocked the door. Ralph, Jimmy, and Mam went into the parlour and talked quietly for a long time. I got fed up of waiting for them to come out and went to bed.

I was hoping that Angel would calm down and I'd be able to get back together with her. Give her time, I thought. Without her, my life was empty and pointless.

Jimmy hung around for a week or so before disappearing, back to London, I assumed. I couldn't get any sense from Ralph or from Mam about what had gone on, so I gave up talking to them altogether, limiting our interactions to mundanities such as shopping and eating.

I slouched through the days at college and spent most of my spare time alone or drinking in the Sycamore. Even there I was alone – the gap left by Will's and Steve's deaths was too big for anyone else to fill. I had friends, if that's what they were, some of the regulars, still hanging onto shreds of hope, all that was left of the idealism we had in the recently deceased sixties.

Len White planted himself next to me. "Hi Mick," he said. "How's it going?

I shrugged, Len was all right, if a bit dim, probably on account of all the dope he smoked. It didn't take him long to broach the subject.

"Fancy a smoke?" he asked. "I've got some good shit man, a block of nice Red Leb."

I shrugged again. Why not, it had been a while.

The landlord didn't care what we smoked or where, but we went out the back yard and sat on a bench. It was a cool refreshing night. As the cannabis entered my bloodstream I relaxed. The things that had been bothering me dimmed. It was a relief. I could even think about Angel without crying.

I sighed.

"You all right Mick?"

"Yeah, I guess so."

"It was a shock, wasn't it? Will was such a good musician, and Steve – well he was just Steve, you know."

I nodded.

"This fucking town," he said. "It's shit. I'm getting out."

"I don't blame you," I said. "I wish I could."

"You can – if you want."

"Nah. I've got college, and then there's my mother you know, and my brother."

"You've got to make your own way in this world Mick."

"Maybe," I shrugged.

"You can come with me," he said.

"Where are you going?"

"Me, I'm off to the Big Smoke I am, got a job up there."

"What are you going to do?"

"Vroom vroom," he said.

"What? Driving?"

"Sort of. I'm going to work as a roadie with a big soul band."

"Well done," I said. "Sounds a lot more interesting than Elchurch College."

"Their stuff needs a lot of lugging," he said. "All over the place, three or four gigs a week. I'm going to need help – cash in hand too."

"I can't drive," I said.

"No need – yet. You can be a lugger, a kind of Roadie's assistant, to start with anyway. I know you're cleverer than that, but who knows where it could lead."

I was interested but couldn't find the energy. "Thanks Len. I appreciate the offer, but it's not for me. Not at the moment."

"All right, but if you change your mind I'm off in a couple of weeks, when the new van arrives."

Things got a little easier at home, but I lost all interest in my college work. The lecturer in Electrical Engineering was the most boring bloke on the planet, and on the rare occasions when I tuned into the actual words he was saying I couldn't understand them. I was going nowhere. My brother felt the same way.

We were having a pre-dinner drink in the Carpenter's. Mam had woken up in a positive mood, so she sent us off to the pub while she prepared a rare Sunday roast.

"Sorry I've been shit lately, Mick," Ralph said.

"It's cool," I said.

"I know you've got your own problems," he said. "Do you want to talk about them?"

Another time I might have, but he looked more miserable than I felt. "No, it's all right," I said. "I'm fine."

He nodded. "Listen Mick. Don't tell Mam, but I'm thinking about going away."

"Oh!"

"Yeah, a long way away – Canada."

"Fucking hell. That is a long way."

"They need toolmakers there – good money. To be honest there's nothing left for me here. Of course there's you, and Mam, but you're all grown up now, and Mam, she's all right – thinking of standing for the council, she is."

"I didn't know."

"Yes, some new friend of hers – Louis."

That made me think again about my own situation and when I saw Angel on the street with her cousin, her looking scared of me, and him sizing me up for a beating, I made a decision.

I waited until the night before I was due to leave before telling Ralph and Mam.

"It's only for a few months," I said.

I expected Mam to get angry, to accuse me of wasting my life, giving up college, leaving the Backfields, leaving her. But, instead she gave me a hug. It was an unfamiliar experience, all bones and flesh

"You look after yourself Mick," she said, through teary eyes. "I'm very proud of you, both of you, my boys."

She pulled Ralph into the hug. We looked at each other over her shoulders and raised our eyebrows.

Later, when Mam went to the off-license to buy a bottle of wine, Ralph patted me on the back.

"Good on you Mick," he said. "I hope it works out."

"What about you?" I asked. "Canada?"

"I'm not sure about that yet. Keep it quiet – for now."

I nodded.

Len White arrived early the next morning, driving a sparkling new big blue van. I chucked everything I needed into a large duffle bag and climbed into the passenger seat.

Len twisted the van through the streets of the estate and we headed towards the M4 motorway.

He nodded at the parcel shelf. "There's a few ready-rolled joints under there," he said. "Light one up for me please."

Ah! This was the right thing to do, I thought, relaxing into my future.

CHAPTER 13

I'd forgotten to ask Len where we were staying in London
and he hadn't bothered to tell me, so it was a nice surprise
when we pulled up in a lovely tree-lined street close to
Paddington station.

The street was wide enough to house rows of large multi-
storey red brick buildings, pushed up against each other to
form an upmarket terrace. The flat was on the fourth floor,
near the top, accessed via an antique lift with collapsible
doors and a black metal grid.

"There's five bedrooms," Len said, "or is it six? Anyway,
you'll be sleeping on the floor of mine for the time being. Is
that all right?"

"Of course," I said.

"There is a mattress though, so it won't be too bad."

"Who else lives here?" I asked, wondering why there was no
one about.

"Well there's Granddad of course, well, he's not really a
granddad, he's only thirty-odd, he's up North."

"Who's he?"

"He's the bloke who gave me the job, the head honcho. He's
from Elchurch too as it happens, the Backfields as well. You
should get on. Then there's Carl and Simon – they're a
couple, away on tour with the band they manage at the mo.
I'm not sure about the others. I think there's someone who
works with Alan Price, or Georgie Fame, or someone. They're
doing something in the Marquee Club."

"So, everyone's a roadie?"

"Just about."

I settled into the flat quickly. I didn't pay any rent and two or
three times a week I'd travel with Len to gigs in places like

Bournemouth and Birmingham, Newcastle and Oxford. My work involved long boring journeys along motorways and 'A' roads, followed by an hour or two of intense physical effort lugging amps, speakers, and leads, through narrow passages and up and down steep steps to the backs of stages.

Granddad usually turned up just as the hard work was finished to ponce about on the stage, arranging leads and fiddling with volume mixers.

During the gigs, we'd hover behind stage, wander among the crowd, or find a bar and drink a few pints. The band were all very skilled and polished musicians, and the lead singer was brilliant, erupting on stage, pumping out a set of pure soul pleasure.

The music was good, but after being present in half-a-dozen identical sets, I blanked it and focussed on my future.

My break came when one day Carl and Simon asked me to help out in a studio in central London. Their musicians were a cult jazzy band, as good technically as the guys in the soul band, but each with an individuality that marked them out as artists.

My job was to fetch coffees and burgers and occasionally help to move a bit of equipment about. I spent most of my time watching and absorbing, getting to know the industry from the ground up. That was until I got distracted by Linda. I made endless excuses to myself and to the others, so that I could visit the reception area where she worked.

The studio gig lasted about two weeks and at the end of it I was part of a couple again. Linda lived in Enfield with her parents. She was tall and dark skinned, a year or two older than me and ready to settle down.

"What do you reckon then Mick?" she asked. "I'd love to visit Wales one day, meet your family."

"Sure," I said, hoping she wasn't going to ask me to visit hers. I was still adjusting to the metropolitan experience, and not ready to get too pally with the locals.

"I was thinking," she said.

"Oh yeah?"

"Just thinking, you know, of moving out from home. We could see each other more often then."

Being with Linda gave me a nice feeling, it was good to be loved, and I knew she loved me. I just wasn't sure if I loved her.

"There's no room in the flat," I said.

"I know that. I was just thinking, maybe we could share a flat of our own."

"I can't afford that. I don't earn enough, just a tenner here and there."

"There's a job going in the studio – Trainee Technician. I could put in a good word, the owner is my uncle."

I don't know if I was persuaded more by my feelings for Linda, or by the temptation of a quick way into the music industry, the studio had intrigued me during the time I'd spent there. Whatever my reasons were, a couple of weeks later we had a nice one-bedroom in Muswell Hill, and I had a proper job.

Things went well at work and over the next six months I was promoted three times until I was elevated to the position of shift studio manager. Apparently, I was a natural at dealing with the artists and could get my head around the technical bits too. I found the work easy, and got bored too quickly, so poked about in other parts of the business. By then Linda was three months pregnant.

"What are we going to do?" she asked.

I shrugged. "Get married I suppose."

Her reaction was just as sanguine. "Right then, I'll tell my parents."

Within a few days, the wedding was arranged and we moved into a large bedroom at her parents' house. My introduction to them was a little fraught but they were decent people and pulled out all the stops to help us get established.

Despite all that I hated the place as soon as I stepped inside, and my feelings towards the situation I found myself in festered. The house was large, so when Mam and Ralph

117

came up a couple of days before the wedding, they stayed there too.

Mam was nervous and out of place. Ralph was more despondent and morose than I'd ever seen him. The only relief came when I took Mam on a pre-wedding shopping trip. I wanted to spend some time alone with her and show off how much I was earning in my new job at the studio.

During the shopping trip Mam was distracted, she obviously had something on her mind. I took her to Carnaby Street but she was too afraid of the clothes there, so we headed for a branch of a familiar chain store in Oxford Street.

"This is a lot of money," Mam said, as we queued to pay for the wedding outfit she'd chosen.

"Ha!" I said. "You want to take a look further up the road, where the pop stars shop – now that's an eye-opener."

"Thank you Mick," she said, with a weak smile.

"What's the matter Mam?" I asked, as we walked to the Tube, making our way back to Enfield.

"Matter? Nothing's the matter. I'm very happy for you."

"I mean, what's the matter with you. You've been very quiet."

She sighed. "Sorry Mick. It's Jimmy. I'm worried about him. He hasn't been in touch for a long time."

"Sorry to hear that. I'm sure he's all right – busy I expect."

"You don't understand Mick, he's fragile."

"Jimmy?"

"Yes, he's not as tough as he looks, he's had some problems."

"Ralph told me he had to leave his job, is it that?"

"Not exactly," Mam said. "Look, sorry, it doesn't matter. I don't want to spoil your big day with my misery. We'd better get back to Linda. There's a lot to do before the wedding."

The thought of going back to that big cold house made me shiver.

"No," I said, "come on, let's go and find Jimmy. He lives in London, doesn't he? Do you know his address?"

"Yes. Are you sure?"

I put my arm in hers: "Come on."

We took a cab to where Jimmy lived in a private mews flat near Tottenham Court Road. I pressed the intercom.

"Hello yes, can I help you?" it was Jimmy's voice, and still strong and confident as far as I could tell.

My mother looked at me and nodded at the speaker.

"It's Mick," I said. "From the Backfields. Mam – Lizzie, is here too."

"Oh good!" he said, buzzing us up.

His flat was comfortable and well-furnished, decorated with what looked like original artworks.

"Nice," I said, looking around.

Mam stood quietly at my side, looking wistfully at Jimmy.

"Thank you," he said politely. "Tea?"

I hesitated, perhaps it would be better to leave them alone together to catch up. It looked like they needed some time.

"No thanks," I said. "Tell you what. I'll pop out, have a look around the neighbourhood. Maybe I'll see somewhere nice for me and Linda when the time comes. We'll need our own place eventually."

"Linda?" Jimmy said.

"I'm sure my mother will explain," I said. "What do you say? I'll come back in an hour or so."

I walked back towards Oxford Street and found myself sizing up all the beautiful girls I passed, assessing them for partnership potential. It was then I realised I didn't love Linda. She was a lovely person, beautiful and caring, but she lacked something, some magic. Angel had that magic, but alas, I was banished from its presence due to the evil intentions of that horrible goblin Snobby. I was not a person who relished revenge, but the thought of smashing Snobby's head in appealed to me. One day, I vowed.

When I got back to Jimmy's, Mam was sitting quietly, looking happier.

I went to the toilet. When I came out I paused in the hall to look at an oil painting. It was a portrait of a pope by the look of it. The face was etched with deep grooves of paint, giving the skin the appearance of ancient tree bark. The eyes stared out from a black void, like he was staring up from the pits of the universe. I touched the surface of the paint, it was cold and clammy. I shivered. That was creepy.

I heard Mam's voice, coming from the lounge. "Are you sure Jimmy? Tell me it's going to be all right. He's been through so much."

"Yes Lizzie," Jimmy answered. "I will arrange it all. Please don't worry."

"I don't want Mick to hear about it, now that he's getting settled, he doesn't need to know."

I walked into the room. "What don't I need to know?"

"Sit down Mick," Jimmy said.

I sat down on the other sofa, opposite Mam. Jimmy sat next to her. I waited.

"It's Ralph," Jimmy said. "He's got problems."

"Ralph? What's happened, what's the matter?"

"It's not his fault," Mam said. "He's leaving the country – going to Canada."

I nodded. "He told me he was thinking about that, but that was a while ago. It's not that big a deal. I mean, he's my brother and everything, but I'm all grown up now, honest."

Mam burst into tears. Jimmy put his arm around her.

"What is it? What's the matter?" I said.

Jimmy stood up. "Please trust us Mick. It's better you don't know. When everything settles down, perhaps then, we can talk again."

I shrugged. I had more important things to think about, like the wedding, and whether I should go ahead with it.

I did get married. Mam went back to the Backfields with Ralph, and a few weeks later I had a letter from her telling me he'd gone to Canada.

I carried on working at the studio, getting increasingly frustrated at the sloppy way they ran things there. They needed someone else to run the whole place, someone who had a clue how to turn that morass of talent into hard cash. Someone like me.

The twins were born in February 1972, two beautiful

healthy girls, with my eyes, and, thank God, their mother's nose. By then, part of Linda's parents' house had been converted into a self-contained flat for our new family, which was nice, but I was still frustrated and unhappy.

I soldiered on for a year, blocked from further promotion by Linda's uncle, fair enough I suppose, his was the only job left in my sights, and he was the owner. My reputation as a creative and technical whizz spread throughout the industry, and finally, I had an offer to head up a studio in LA. I was only twenty-three. It was a once-in-a-lifetime opportunity, but Linda refused point blank. I didn't blame her, the twins were secure and they had a large garden to grow into.

I was going mad with my desperation to get out of there. I needed someone with a brain to talk to, so headed off to look up Jimmy. I hadn't seen him since the wedding.

I pressed the buzzer.

A stranger's voice answered. "How may I help you?"

"Sorry," I said. "I'm looking for Jimmy – James Phillips. I thought he lived here."

"Are you a friend of his?"

"Yes, we go back a long way. It's Mick, from the Backfields, in Wales."

"You'd better come up," the voice said.

The flat was in disarray, what wasn't jumbled up in the chaos was packed in boxes around the room.

"What's happened to Jimmy?" I asked.

The man was plumper and shorter than Jimmy, but he had the same air of authority about him.

"I'm Jimmy's old chum, Jeremy. I'm afraid he's dead."

I felt sick and faint, and had to lean against the door frame. How would Mam react?

"It was a couple of weeks ago, they just released the body; suicide – so they say."

"What do you mean? Don't you believe them?"

"He wasn't the type. He was strong you know, after everything he'd been through, his relationships, losing his job, everything. I thought he was over all that, but what do I know."

"Do you mean the relationship with my mother, Lizzie?"

"Ah Lizzie, he talked about her a lot, and about you Mick, and about your brother, Ralph isn't it? He had a special place for your little family. He was a good man, but it wasn't that."

"But they were so close you know, him and my mother."

"I know, but he was gay, homosexual. Didn't you know? That's why he had to leave the police; things were harder then – ten years ago."

Mam came to London for Jimmy's funeral. She was all right. Her new man Louis was with her and they seemed comfortable together. Afterwards, it struck me that no matter what you thought your life was, in the end you didn't really have a clue. You had to take what you could, while you could.

The split with Linda was quick and amicable, and a few weeks after Jimmy's funeral I was on the plane to LA to start my new job.

2013

Deckchairs don't stay comfortable forever. I was in a ridiculous situation and didn't know how much longer I could cope in the attic, physically or mentally. After all, I was an old man, ancient from that young Mick's perspective. Luckily, my Californian diet kept me fit.

I put the bundle of paper back in its envelope. There was so much I'd forgotten, so many of the details that make a life what it is. But it wasn't enough. I looked at the second envelope, wondering if I had the capacity to read that too.

I needed a piss first. I took the photos out of the box, and used that. I zipped up and remained standing, the top of my head touching the old wooden rafters, my bones and muscles aching to extend themselves in a less cramped environment.

There was movement down below. Angel was coming up the stairs, talking to herself. It took a moment to realise that she was speaking into a mobile phone. She paused on the landing, underneath the hatch I'd crawled up through. I listened intently, trying not to breathe too heavily. I could just about make out what she was saying.

"Don't worry, I know what's at stake ... I've never let you down before, have I? ... Everything is under control, no one is ever going to know the truth ... All right ... Yes ... We'll meet tomorrow then."

Finally, after a bit more bumping and clattering, Angel went to bed. I waited another twenty minutes, it was all I could stand. I allowed the tears to come. I needed to grieve for those lost lives, Jimmy, Will, Steve, even Jacko 's father and Betty Fish – could they really all be victims of that dark Angel? Most of all I needed to grieve for my own lost life, all those meaningless decades. I needed time to think, and plan.

I clambered down carefully from the attic and stretched my bones back into place on the dark landing. I couldn't resist lingering in the house, pausing at every doorway, stroking the banister, staring at my reflection in the bathroom mirror, remembering the other times I'd spent there, all the time aware I could be discovered at any moment.

I snapped out of my reverie and let myself out of the back door of the house. The garden was illuminated with an array of dim solar powered lights, pressed into the lawn. There was a neat wooden shed where the bramble bushes used to be, but it didn't stop me visualising that group of wild boys at the bottom of the garden. That was the day it all changed, the day the Garden of Eden dissolved into the swamp, and I became defined by the black hearts that infested it.

I crept around the side of the house to the front and walked casually into the night.

I wondered if the South Beach Hotel was still operating, and if Matthew still worked there. Twenty years is a long time, but it was a place to start, and I needed somewhere to lay low anyway.

I decided to meander through the site to the main road, where my hired car was parked. The quiet streets echoed with my footsteps and with the newly-refreshed memories of the time I'd spent growing up on them. The old house, rebuilt since the fire, merged almost perfectly with the rest of the houses in the small terrace, distinguished only by the thicker-framed windows.

I turned right, opposite the plot Good Stores used to occupy where a pair of slightly upmarket semis had taken the shop's place. I walked on into the heart of the estate.

I stopped on the edge of the Field, it was still there, but diminished, both by the perspective of my age and by the encroachment of more concrete buildings around its perimeter. It was dark, and although there were plenty of street lamps, most of them were shot out – they had become some other generation's targets.

It was going on for 1am. All the shops in the little row at the top of the field were closed, even the Indian takeaway. I heard voices shouting in the distance, some drunken kids by the sound of it. The old instincts kicked in and I withdrew into the shadows. I was outside a small block of flats. There was a light on in a downstairs window but the doorway was dark.

I edged back into the doorway and looked out at the group, who were travelling quickly and loudly through the middle of the Field towards where I was hidden. They drew closer, jostling and arguing. I was safe in my doorway but pushed myself back tight against the door to be sure. As they passed, a light came on in the passage behind the glass door, and lit up the space I was standing in.

I stepped forward and turned to face the door, someone was opening it. I was trapped between the gang on the pavement and whatever was coming through the door. It opened fully and a girl of about fifteen came out. She looked directly at me and held the door open.

"Well, get in then," she said. "If you're going in, I can't wait here all night."

Surprised, I looked between her and the boys on the pavement, and they were just boys, not one of them older than the girl. What was the matter with me? Why was I afraid of a few teenagers?

I smiled at the girl. "Thanks," I said, edging past her into the building.

"Hey bruvs," I heard her call out to the boys.

"Who you shagging there then?" one of the boys said, as the door swung shut behind me.

It was a bleak corridor, an unadorned concrete stairs leading to the upper floors. I sat on the bottom step and looked around. There were four blank doors, leading into what I assumed were equally blank flats. I needed to get out of there, needed somewhere safe and warm, time to figure out how I was going to deal with the Angel who had turned into a devil.

I got to the hotel at about 1.30am. Luckily they had plenty of rooms spare. I asked the receptionist for the best they had.

The room was perfect. Since my last visit twenty years

earlier, the hotel had been updated and expanded. I was safely and warmly ensconced in the Tudor Harries suite, named after some local rugby hero, according to the framed bumf on the wall near the door.

It was late and I was tired. I helped myself to a small bottle of brandy from the bulging bar, but I still couldn't get to sleep. It wasn't enough. I needed more time, and more information.

I picked up the second manuscript, the account of my return to the Backfields two decades earlier. I hadn't read it since I wrote it down in the weeks following those terrible events.

I started to read.

Book 2
1993

CHAPTER 14

Isaac Newton's laws of physics work particularly well when it comes to road bridges. Engineers and architects use them as a basis for their calculations. For example, how much cement to use, what size supports to build, and how to shape the structure. These are all elements considered in the design.

The forces are worked out precisely before the building begins, so it all hangs together perfectly, unless something extraordinary like an earthquake occurs and produces such immense force that the bridge collapses. Even then Newton's laws apply, it's just that the earthquake's force is greater.

At the quantum level things are different, Newton's laws lose their validity. Particles that exist only in theory whizz about unpredictably. Why then doesn't the universe collapse into chaos?

I didn't know the answer to that question. After all, I'd only read one book on the fascinating paradigm of sub-atomic particles, but I did know the Severn bridge was still standing when we sped over it like a pair of synchronised quarks.

"Everything all right Ramona?" I asked.

She'd been quiet since we landed in Heathrow. It suited me. I was preoccupied, thinking about what was waiting for me in the Backfields. Was Mam really as ill as she'd made out? Was she really going to die? Whatever it was, it would be an extended stay, I'd planned for that.

"How far is it now?" Ramona asked. "I'm tired."

"Hold on, we'll be at the hotel in an hour."

One of the many escapes from the Backfields used to be a muddy path that led from the bottom of the bottom site, through fields and marshes, past industrially-scarred land, and eventually to the South Beach.

Sometimes in summer we used to take all day walking that path to the beach and back. On warm days we'd sneak our bathing trunks out with us and swim in the filthy waters of the estuary. We'd pick cockles, or fluke for flatfish with fat nails hammered into the ends of broom handles and filed into barbed spearheads. We'd trawl through the ruins looking for anything that held value or interest, whether it was a newt in an old drain or a lump of lead that would be worth a few bob to the scrap dealers whose yards hid at the end of overgrown muddy lanes.

That landscape was disappearing. The wasted industrial sites were being cleared up and the land reclaimed. A new building, the South Beach Hotel dominated the horizon. That's where we were heading in the hired car we'd picked up on our arrival in Britain. I knew that changes were taking place of course. I'd read about the redevelopment in the local paper my mother still sent me now and again, but I wasn't prepared for the scale of it.

The coastline was under development, proclaimed the billboard. Forward to the next millennium. No more rusty rivers, no more pits of death. The people shall have their playground back. Abandoned by the barons of coal and the lords of iron, the folk will have their clean seas, their green grass, their golf, and their ice-cream. They shall serve in the leisure complexes and shop in the supermarkets, they shall doff their caps to a different master.

"My father died there, when they built the steelworks, the first time. That's where he worked and where he died."

We were driving parallel to the sea along a neat black-tarmacked road, painted with fresh white lines. The South Beach Hotel loomed, the only substantial building after the shiny stainless steelworks.

"But it looks so peaceful, so pleasant and harmless. It is only grass and sand and birds now," Ramona marvelled. "It is beautiful. I think I like your Backfields, Mick."

"This isn't the Backfields, that hasn't changed so much. We'll see the estate tomorrow. Look there's the hotel."

Ramona looked at the clock on the dashboard of the Mercedes. "You were right. It's an hour since we crossed the bridge."

"Here we are."

The car responded predictably to the light touch on the power steering as I guided it into a convenient parking space in front of the hotel reception. We got out and stretched.

The hotel had only been open a few months. It was just what I'd expected, constructed to the same formula as so many hotels I'd visited. It could have been anywhere.

The man at reception busied himself with open hardcover notebooks, and tapped absently at a computer keyboard as we approached. On cue he looked up and greeted us. He was too familiar. Perhaps he was a clone too, like the hotel.

"Ah, it's you Mick."

He wasn't a clone then. I dug into my memory and found him there, with long dark hair and a gringo moustache in the driver's seat of a big blue van. Of course, it was Len White.

"Ah Len, not on the road then?"

"Nah," he said. "Not for a while, you know what it's like, a young man's game."

I laughed: "You're not old."

"Tell my back that," he joked. "I thought it might be you when I saw the name on the computer. It's been over twenty years since I saw you last?"

"Really," I said, not at all surprised. Everything seemed so long ago to me, I wouldn't have been surprised if he'd told me it had been a hundred years.

"Yes, it's been five years since I moved into this game, and I was on the road for at least fifteen. Let the punters come to you, I say, it's a lot less hassle than taking the show to them."

He smiled at Ramona.

I turned to her: "Ramona, this is Len, an old friend."
Len held his hand out to her. She responded clumsily,
dropping the suitcase she was holding to the deep-pile carpet,
which obeyed Newton's laws and absorbed the weight of the
luggage without causing any damage.
"Twenty years," I said, shaking my head as if in disbelief.
"Yes, it must be," he said, sucking his pencil.
I was surprised at how casually he accepted the time
passing, all those years, oceans of experience. Perhaps he too
really felt like I did, ambivalent about the disappearance of
the decades, surprised at how quick it seemed and weary
enough to believe it had been forever.
"I've reserved one of our best rooms, or should I say suites,
it really is something special. Come on, I'll show you up."
We followed Len dutifully. The hotel was certainly grand,
considering where it was, as good as any corporate hotel I'd
ever stayed in.
Len showed us the small suite with great pride. It was
difficult to reconcile that effusive corporate employee with
the anarchic dope-smoking dropout who'd once boasted he'd
dropped five acid tabs in one session and still managed to
drive to work the next day.
We didn't feel like rushing to catch the restaurant so we
ordered sandwiches and wine to be brought to our room.
When the food and drink came, Len had added a basket of
fruit and a bunch of flowers. A note attached to the flowers
read: 'Look in the vine fruits for a special gift from the
management.'
I peeled the clingfilm from the fruit and poked around in
the grapes. Sure enough there was a large perfectly rolled
joint of cannabis hidden there.
"Look," I said to Ramona, laughing. "Len used to roll the
best joints. You can see he hasn't lost his touch. We'll keep it
for later."
Ramona shrugged.
After our meal in the room Ramona decided to take a bath.
She was in the habit of taking long baths, so I went for a
walk outside the hotel.

That part of town was certainly changing. Before, it had been a degenerating industrial area; a place where us kids could practise exposing ourselves to the dangers of life out of view of prying adult eyes. Now it reeked of money and success. Everything was so new, the roads, the street lamps, extra bright, even the grass and shrubs at the front of the hotel looked as if they had been put there earlier that day by an army of landscape gardeners.

I walked away from the bright lights around the hotel to the outer limits of the car park where it met with the new road. I looked over the outskirts of the town in the direction of the Backfields estate, less than a mile away in a straight line. The street lights from the estate were glowing amber in the last vestiges of twilight. In the other direction there were no street lights yet, but I knew from my mother's occasional letters and the local paper that there were great plans for the whole coastal area.

Beyond the dark, undeveloped patch, was the railway station and the area around it that was strictly off limits to us boys from the Backfields, populated, as legend had it, by characters much more dangerous than us mere council estate dwellers.

A car screeched into view from the dark road leading to that part of town. I felt that fear again, the instinct to turn and run from any potential trouble. The car stopped with a cacophony of noise, heavy loud rave music, people shouting and screaming, engine revving. I stepped back into the shadows of the young oak trees around the entrance to the hotel. A small body tumbled out of the car and lay squirming in the road. The car screeched away as abruptly as it had arrived.

I ran into the road, it was a young boy, no more than thirteen years old. I noticed he had a long red scar along his forehead. A scar not caused recently, but by an old wound.

"Are you all right," I asked.

The boy looked at me, defiance and fear in his eyes: "Fuck off, leave me alone."

He stood up slowly, shook himself, and ran off into the

131

darkness from where he'd come. No one else witnessed the incident, at least no one else showed themselves, so I carried on with my walk.

I made my way to the beach, to a section I remembered, where the sewage pipe used to jut proudly into the bay, not one of the more popular spots then, at least.

At the beach it was too dark to see anything other than the phosphorescent tops of the small waves that rolled inexorably against the land. The silence and the darkness enveloped me. I felt at one with the planet.

I stayed for a few minutes intending to return to the same place the next morning when I could see more. I walked back to the hotel slowly, extracting the last remnants of timeless bliss from the peace of that moment, as if I knew it heralded the beginning of another turbulent storm in my life.

In the lobby of the hotel, Len White was nowhere to be seen. In his place was a younger man, no more than a boy really. He reminded me so much of my old friend Trev that I was taken aback at first. I would have to ask him.

"Where's Len?" I asked.

The young man shrugged his shoulders, "Sorry sir," he said. "Can I help?"

"Well, as it happens, I just wanted to ask, you remind me of someone. Are you related to Trevor Thomas?"

"Trev's my dad. For my sins."

We both laughed.

"Do you know him well then?"

Before I could answer, we were interrupted by the entrance of a leather-clad woman, with spiky grey hair, who rushed up to the desk.

"It's Timothy," she screamed. "Have you seen Timothy? That waster of a brother of yours. The little sod went out with that bunch of bastards again, after I told him to stay in and look after his sisters."

The young man looked embarrassed. "Ssh, Mam," he said. "Please be quiet."

"I'll fucking kill him, I'm only trying to earn a living." The woman paused for breath, and looked me up and down disdainfully. "Well," she said, to her son. "Have you seen him or not?"

"No, I haven't, now please shush, or I'll lose my job."

"Pah!" she spat the word out. "You're just as useless as your bloody father."

The woman hurried towards the exit.

"Sorry," the young man said.

"Does Timothy have a long red scar on his forehead?" I asked.

"Yes, that's him, why?"

I ran after the woman. I caught up with her as she was getting into the driver's seat of a taxi. In the back were two young girls in their night-clothes. They were shaking with cold and excitement. They giggled when they saw me.

"Hang on a minute," I said breathlessly. "I think I saw your Timothy a few minutes ago."

"Why didn't you say before? Where was he? How long ago?"

"Just here," I said. "He ran off down that way, fifteen, maybe twenty minutes ago."

"Right then, just wait 'til I catch him."

She was sitting down by then, her hand on the ignition key.

"Thanks," she said, as she slammed the door and drove off into the darkness following her son.

I sat in the bar of the hotel afterwards, sipping a whisky and American ginger. Trev's son approached me, a glass of beer in his hand.

"Is it all right if I sit here for a minute?"

"Sure," I said.

He sat down.

"I'm Mick," I held my hand out. "I used to live around here. I was a good friend of your father's at one time, as it happens."

"I'm Matthew."

"So, I suppose that was your mother, I often wondered who Trev would end up with."

"Yeah, but they're not together, her and Dad. He buggered off years ago. Timothy's my half brother, I only met his father once, so did my mother, I think."

133

I couldn't help laughing.

"It's not that funny," Matthew said, a twinkle in his eye.

He had the physical appearance of his father but I could see something of his mother's spirit in him.

"So are you Trev's only child?"

"God no, he's got loads. Let me see."

Matthew started counting on his hands and gave up when he reached ten.

"Oh bugger it," he said smiling. "It's twelve, my dad's got twelve children. Sarah's the oldest, but we didn't know about her until a couple of years ago, then there's me, and my sister Kate. We're the only two from my mother, though she's got four more. After my Dad left we lost touch for a bit, but when I was about ten, I found out about some of the others. The youngest is three, I think, or is it four? Anyway, there's loads of us, it's a laugh."

He seemed to enjoy talking about his family. I imagined all his brothers and sisters loved him.

"Where do you live?" I asked.

"On the Backfields Estate," he said.

"That's where I lived, not a bad place to grow up I guess."

"It's all right I suppose, but it can be a bit rough, and it's not really the best place to bring kids up nowadays. I'm not thinking about myself. I can handle it, it's my little brothers and sisters I worry about. Take Tim now, we thought we'd lost him once. You saw that scar on his forehead."

"Yes."

"Marked for life he is. I can't wait to get out of there to be honest."

"Sorry," I said. "Sounds grim."

"Anyway, I'd better get off home."

"I've kept you talking."

"No no," he said. "I thought I was boring you."

"Not at all," I said. "Let me get you a drink. If you're alright with that?"

"Yes please. I've just finished my shift. I've been working in the restaurant most of the evening. They only pay you for the hours you actually work, and then only when they want you in. There's no guarantees or anything. Last week I only got twenty-one hours, not enough to live on, but then I am still living at home I suppose."

For the next half-hour he talked about his family. There were so many of them to keep track of my brain went numb. He painted Trev as a loving father, but also as a hopeless provider.

Eventually I went back to the room and found Ramona sitting in an armchair watching television, she looked morose and distracted.

"Sorry," I said. "I got talking to someone. From the Backfields actually, I didn't realise the time."

"No problem," she said. "I have only just finished bathing."

Before we went to bed, we smoked Len's joint. Ramona seemed to relax a bit then. We watched television and laughed a lot.

In between the giggling we talked about Matthew, and about Len, and I went on too much about my childhood on the Backfields.

Smoking the weed reminded me of the freshness and excitement of the sixties. I imagined that all over the world ex-hippie types were finally ascending to positions of influence, and our naïve dream of world peace would finally come true.

Flower power at last!

CHAPTER 15

In the morning, of course, the world was still the same, the same few lucky bastards had everything, and I was one of them. I didn't know if that was a good thing or a bad thing?

It was early. Ramona was lying beside me in a deep sleep, her face clear and smooth. I was ready for a first look around some of my old hangouts.

I eased myself from the bed and dressed quietly at the other end of the room. I drove the short distance from the hotel to that part of the beach I'd visited briefly the night before.

The rocks, the sand, the sea, the low bright sun, and the morning air, combined to create a sense of timelessness and belonging, but the feeling dissipated as the reason for my visit to Elchurch came to mind.

I drove to the Backfields and parked in a bay near the cluster of shops we used to call Death Row when we were boys. The butcher's shop was still there, all cleaned of blood, with scrubbed stainless steel trays and bright green plastic parsley sparkling in the early morning light. The sweet shop had become a hairdresser's, populated by rows of brain-shrinking space helmets waiting for their next set of blue-rinsed victims to rouse. The chip shop had been transformed into a Chinese take-away, a menu of pork and beef and chicken and shrimp, a hundred times more choice than there was the night I met Jacko's ill-fated puppy.

I locked my car and walked towards the primary school where I'd shown such early promise. Like so many other boys from the Backfields, my eventual lack of academic success disappointed the teachers there.

'Look at me now,' I whispered to the moss-stained brick buildings as I took a short cut across the playground to emerge in the street behind my mother's house. 'I haven't done too bad, have I?'

I paused outside the plot that had once been Good Stores, where I'd said goodbye to Trev the day that Betty Fish was murdered but I couldn't find the strength to walk the few yards to my mother's house, I wasn't ready.

I sat on a wall, looked up Meadow Road and remembered the naïve adventures of my childhood. A woman came running towards me. I could have been back in California, no one jogged in the street I remembered. As she drew level with me I looked up, our eyes made contact, she was small and pretty.

She stopped. "My God – Mick."

"Angel, you look good, it must be..."

"A long time, it feels like decades, it is decades. You look all right yourself."

Angel sat next to me on the wall.

"You must do this sort of thing all the time," I said, slightly awed at how good she looked.

"What do you mean this sort of thing? Chat up men with funny accents at 7.30 in the morning?"

I laughed. I'd forgotten how good Angel made me feel.

"I hear you're doing well there in the good old US of A, your mother used to give me regular bulletins, before she got ill."

"Yes, I've come back to see her, haven't had the guts yet, we only got back last night. I'm afraid to face her, what's she like?"

"Come on." Angel grabbed my hand. "I'll make you coffee, breakfast if you like. You haven't had any have you? Then we'll talk."

Angel still lived in her aunt's, Betty Fish's old house. I stood side-by-side with her in the front room and looked across the street at the house I grew up in. It was disorientating being on the other side of the road looking down at my past, my memory filling the street with familiar scenes and faces. My childhood home looked so small and plain from that perspective.

"This is a nice house," I said.

"Thanks."

"So, have you seen much of Mam lately?"

"Not really. I work away a lot, but she used to pop in for a chat now and again. I don't see much of her now though. Shame really, we're both on our own."

"It's probably the illness, these things affect people."

"I do notice Linda and your children visiting sometimes. They're beautiful girls."

"Thanks. They love their granny. They were over in the States with me a couple of months ago. They come over once or twice a year. They get the best of both worlds."

"They're very lucky," she said.

"Do you remember?" I asked, "When we first met, those damp fireworks, the tree house?"

"We met before then, the doughnuts, remember?"

"Ha! Sorry about that."

"You should have taken them."

I laughed.

She handed me the coffee.

We sat at a small table in the bay window.

"Where are you staying?" Angel asked.

"We're in a hotel, the new one on the South Beach, that's me and Ramona, my new partner in life, she's Mexican, an actress, sort of."

"Good, Mick. I'm glad. I hope it works out."

"What about you?"

"Like I said, I work away a lot, I haven't got the time for all that. Anyway, what's it really like in Hollywood?"

"Same as anywhere else, a bunch of fucked up people trying to make sense of it all, there's a few Prima Donnas, but what do you expect."

"There's a few of them around here too, there's a woman in the post office, thinks she's Shirley Bassey," Angel laughed.

"I know her," I said.

"Shirley Bassey?"

"No, the woman in the post office."

Angel smiled, but looked down. "Anyway, I'd better get ready for work."

"All right, I won't keep you. What do you do?"
She hesitated. "Oh, it's too boring for words,
Angel stood up to clear the coffee cups away.
"I'd better get off myself, don't tell anyone you've seen me.
We'll be back later to see my mother. I need to psyche myself
up first."
"See you around then Mick," she said.
I left Angel's feeling as if I'd missed something. She didn't
look happy, but then she was always like that, some secret
she didn't want to, or couldn't, share. It saddened me.
When I got back to the hotel, Matthew was on duty again.
"You seem to be getting plenty of work this week anyway,"
I joked.
"Don't you believe it," he said smiling, "I've had to come all
this way just for a couple of hours."
"Did Timothy find his way home last night?"
"He always does, eventually. When I got home he was
already in bed. Then, my mother had a late call to a night
club. Tim crept downstairs as soon as he heard the car
pulling away. He was on his way out again."
"He sounds like a proper handful. I don't know how your
mother copes."
"You've seen her. She's a tough old bird, at least that's what
Dad always says."
"What's your father do, by the way?" I asked.
"He's a tryer. I think he's just started a new job, I haven't
seen him in a couple of weeks, so I'm not sure."
"Where does he live? I might look him up."
"He's shacked up with some old girl from the Tophill,
someone he's known for years, off and on. You won't find him
at home much though. Your best bet is the Poacher's Rest, or
the Carpenters, do you know them?"
"Thanks. Yes."
"By the way, your friend left you a note."
He reached under the desk and handed me a sheet of
notepaper folded neatly into a small square.
"She said she'd ring you later to explain."
I took the note and opened it slowly.

139

Derec Jones

Dear Mick, sorry, I had to leave suddenly, will be in touch. Love Ramona.

"Thanks," I mumbled.

I went up to my room, my head numb. What could have happened to prompt her sudden departure? I thought about the last few days: the flight from America, the faltering drive along the motorway, the hotel, our intimacy, and the love I thought we shared.

I checked the bedside cabinet, her passport had gone and so had one of the return air tickets. There must have been some kind of family crisis. Why didn't she tell me? Perhaps I'd become so self-obsessed I was taking her for granted.

I telephoned the airport to check the flights back to America. The earliest one she could get would be at half past three. I needed a drink so I could think, so I raided the mini-bar. I soon fell into a drunken sleep. When I woke I looked at the clock on the bedside table, it was gone one o'clock, too late to catch Ramona up.

I had the unexpected feeling that I was glad she'd flown out of my reach, it was as if she'd served her purpose, a dear friend on my journey back. Perhaps I didn't need her anymore? Then I realised that something had woken me up. The telephone was ringing. I fumbled the handset to my ear.

"It's reception, there's a gentleman to see you. He's a detective. Shall I send him up sir?"

I hesitated, what could the police want with me? No one knew I was there.

"Give me five minutes," I said. "I'll be down."

The woman on reception sent me into the bar, where the policeman was waiting, sipping a glass of cola. He stood up. He was big, in his early-twenties, dressed in what the police still regarded as civilian clothes. He looked like an off-duty security guard, with his perfectly pressed dark blue trousers, and black shoes with a little too much shine on them. His blond hair was too short and tidy.

"Sorry to bother you sir," he said. "Mr Matthews, is it?"

"Yes, that's me."

"I'm Detective Constable James Conway. I'd like to ask you

140

a few questions about last night if you don't mind."

As if I had a choice. I seemed to have developed a habit of answering to detectives named James. What would the future hold for this Jimmy? I wondered.

"Of course," I said, "I'll just get a drink."

I got a double whisky and ginger from the bar and sat down opposite Detective Conway at the small round table.

"I hope you don't mind me asking," I said, "but your name – Conway, when I was young, there was a..."

He nodded. "Yes, my grandfather was a Sergeant, back in the sixties."

"Ah!" I said.

"I know he had a bit of a reputation, old school he was, but he's a good man, retired now. He taught me a lot."

"He was a character," I said.

"We've had a report from a young boy's mother. Apparently you witnessed an incident outside the hotel last night. The boy in question is Timothy Roberts. Do you remember the incident sir?"

"Yes, of course, but it didn't look that serious to me, and I thought he'd got home all right afterwards. His brother Matthew works here."

"Well it seems that after thinking about it, his mother wasn't satisfied with his explanation, so she demanded we act. To be honest, there's not much we can do about the way he was allegedly treated, he's a bit of a tearaway anyway. We're more interested in the people he's associating with. What can you tell me? What did you see?"

"Not a lot really. A car came speeding up. The door opened and the boy tumbled out. Then the car sped off again, down along the beach road, towards the railway station."

"What sort of car was it?"

"Well, it was noisy, loud music, I didn't notice much else. It was dark."

"Do you remember the colour?"

"Blue, or black possibly, and it had sporty wheels, low-profile tyres, oh and it wasn't very big, but then after being in California most cars here look small anyway."

He scribbled in a notebook. "Can you remember how many other people were in the vehicle?" he asked.

"It was difficult to see. Let me think, quite a few, it was probably full. I'm sorry, that's all I know. What's it about?"

"It's all part of an ongoing investigation, there's not much I can tell you I'm afraid. Let's just say it's important to us and to the good people of this town that we get as much information as we can about this crowd."

Detective Constable James Conway stood up to leave: "Thank you for your time sir, we may need to talk to you again. Will you be in the hotel for long?"

"Just a few days probably, but I'll leave a forwarding address if I move on."

"That would be appreciated, thank you once again."

I finished my drink and got a taxi into town.

The town centre had become very much like any other – the same pack of national chain stores selling the same collection of mundane goods to the same group of brain dead people. I decided to walk around the back streets to remind myself of the real Elchurch, and found myself heading towards the railway station.

I'd run out of cigarettes so called into a small convenience store squashed between a massage parlour and a funeral director's. I bought a pack of twenty, lit one up in the street outside, and read the postcards in the window while I thought about what I was going to do next.

The door of the massage parlour opened. I expected to see some sad, fat old businessman emerging red-faced and guilty looking. Two men came out into the street, laughing and joking. One of the men got into a large black car parked just outside the massage parlour and the other stood on the pavement and waved him off with a grin. The man on the pavement had to be Snobby, older, greying hair, and fatter, but definitely Snobby.

"David," I said. "David Robinson."

The smile fell from his face and then I knew for sure it was Snobby, there was that same cruel turn of the lips, the same eyes seeking an unfair advantage over his fellow human beings.

"It's me, Mick," I said. "Do you remember – Mick from the Backfields?"

"Oh, you," he said unenthusiastically. "I thought you were in America or somewhere."

"I was. I mean I still am. I'm just visiting. How are you? You look like you've done well for yourself."

Snobby squinted his eyes, as if thinking up some horrible torture for me. I was regretting attracting his attention at all.

His face brightened, he smiled in his sly way. "Well, well, I hear you're doing all right too. Come into my parlour and have a drink, we'll have a chat about the old days."

He put his arm around me in an avuncular way that give me the shivers, and led me inside.

We went into an office at the back of the massage parlour and he poured out a lavish dose of some expensive bourbon for each of us. We chatted a bit about generalities, but all the time I felt as if someone was hovering behind my back with a dagger drawn. I made my excuses and left after ten minutes, but not before he insisted I accepted an invitation to a big function later in the week, to celebrate the reopening, after refurbishment, of The Majestic Hotel.

"Everyone will be there," he said. "It will be a laugh."

CHAPTER 16

I lolled about in the suite, still not ready to visit my mother. Len turned up with music and weed. He put on a Santana record. I closed my eyes. The music was all there was, until a fog of memories seeped into my awareness.

Dreamlike vivid images came into focus and drifted away again. Good things were there, Angel reciting her poem in the tree house, Will with his guitar. Bad things too, Snobby's taunting, Betty Fish, Jacko's dog, but they were vague and greyed out, the details hidden.

Somebody was shaking me.

I forced my eyelids open. Len's face filled my vision, his reddened eyes smiling.

"Good shit, eh?" he laughed, handing me a joint.

I waved it away. I shivered, thinking of Snobby's leering face in that dark fog.

"Are you all right?" Len asked.

"Did you ever know Snobby, in the old days?" I said.

"Who? Snobby. Let me think. What did you say?"

"Snobby, do you know him?"

Len was bewildered. "What the fuck are you on about?"

"David Robinson, do you know him?"

"Name's familiar, hang on, let me think. What did you say again?"

"Robinson," I said slowly, "David Robinson – Snobby."

"Robbo," Len said, screwing his eyes in the effort to remember. "Do you mean Robbo, the jerk who owns half the bars in town?"

"Could be."

"He's a nasty piece of work, didn't get where he is by being a nice guy, or so I hear."

"Sounds like the same bloke. I used to hang around with

him when I was a kid. He was just a pratt then."

"Yeah, well he's a bit more dangerous now. I hear he was very upset about this hotel. He couldn't compete with the big money from out of town, even though he's got dirt on most of the local worthies."

"Because of the Majestic?"

"Yeah, he owns that too. It's been done up, he's spent a fortune on it."

I rested my head on the arm of the sofa. I woke at three in the morning. Len had gone. I crawled to bed and promised myself I'd make the effort to go to Mam's early in the morning.

I woke again at ten, too late for breakfast in the hotel dining room. I took a shower and drove to Meadow Road. The door was unlocked.

I took a breath. "Hiya," I said, going into the living room.

My mother surprised me by walking briskly out of the connecting door to the small narrow kitchen. The place was neat and clean, much fresher than I remembered.

"Mick, it's you," she said smiling, wiping her hands on a newish looking pink housecoat. "I expected you yesterday."

I hugged her and stood back.

"You look well," I said, relieved she wasn't tucked up in bed playing out the last few weeks of her life.

It had been five years since my last brief visit, yet within a minute I was sitting down waiting for Mam to make a cup of tea, feeling at home.

She came into the room carrying a tray of unchipped china cups and a teapot, with a circle of chocolate covered biscuits arranged neatly on a matching white plate. She winced with pain as she bent to place the tray on the coffee table.

"Are you warm enough? I'll put the gas fire on," she said.

"I'm fine," I said.

She sat down carefully on the armchair opposite mine.

"Have you heard from Ralph?" I asked.

"Yes, yesterday. He's coming home soon, in a day or two."

"So, how are you?" I asked, fearing too explicit an answer.

"Good, I'm feeling good Mick. You look well. Been jogging

again?"

Somebody knocked the door.

A surprise – Linda and the girls on the doorstep. Linda looked relaxed, but she still had the way with her glance that made me question who I was. I opened my arms to the girls. They didn't say anything, but hugged me with a tightness that said they loved me. Jodie, the youngest by ten minutes, stood back first.

"Mum said you'd be here."

The girls walked over to their grandmother to say hello.

Linda whispered to me: "How is she? She looks better today."

"She's putting on a brave face, I think." I whispered back. "Where's Bernard?"

"Gone bird watching down the estuary. Where's Ramona?"

"It's a long story."

It was done, the first contact. The only person that mattered I hadn't seen was my brother Ralph, and I was used to our infrequent meetings, so I relaxed.

The two girls went out for a walk and we settled down in the living room. My mother produced an old metal biscuit tin from the side of the sofa.

"Here are all my papers," she spoke clearly, though with effort. "I want to sort out a few things while I still can."

Linda gave me a pained glance. I coughed.

"Do you mind if I smoke?" I asked, reaching in my pockets for the pack of cigarettes.

My mother ignored me and Linda gave me her evil eye. I lit up using my saucer as an ashtray.

"I saw the doctor a few days ago," my mother said softly.

Linda fidgeted with her watch. I puffed on the cigarette.

"I've had a good life, all things considered. I don't want to leave things in a mess. There's the house, it's all been paid for, bought off the council. And there's a bit put aside."

She looked directly at me.

"Mick, I know we weren't very well off when you were young, but you're all right now, so the girls will get most of what's left. And when I've gone I don't want a big fuss."

"What about Ralph?"

"He's got everything he needs."

Sounds of banging and crashing came from the house next door and a deep voice penetrated the walls.

My mother looked up: "He's a nasty sod."

A woman screamed and a child cried.

"It happens all the time," Linda said. "You should complain to the council."

"They can't do anything. At least he's not as bad as that lot up the road, the Carters. The other day she ended up in hospital, said she'd fallen over."

Linda sighed: "This estate has gone downhill. And the drugs, the place is riddled with them."

"It's not that bad," Mam said. "It's much worse in America, isn't it Mick?"

"I'm sure it is, in parts," I said.

The noise from next door subsided. The girls came in from their walk. Mam went to make lunch. Over soup I got up to date on the girls' progress at college. I left soon after, promising to call back later that evening when I could have a private chat with Mam.

I walked around the estate for a while and didn't see any widespread child abuse, or drug taking, or alcohol abuse. Everything looked calm and peaceful, hardly anyone was on the streets, I was disappointed, I wanted to see gangs of boys, roaming like we did in my memories. Perhaps everyone was on holiday?

Later, Mam was tired so I drove across the estate to the Poacher's Rest to see if I could find Trev. I bought a pint and sat in a dark corner to wait. After nearly an hour Trev walked in. I watched as he got himself a pint and stayed at the bar. I drained my glass.

Trev still had the same tousled fair hair and bony frame. He looked downcast.

I nodded to the barman to refresh my glass.

Trev looked around, his eyes dull. "Well, Mick, it's you."

"Sure is pardner," I used my best American accent. "Will you come and sit with me."

Trev shrugged.

He started to loosen up after his second pint: "You've been lucky," he said, "I wouldn't wish this life on anyone, thirty years of hell. I've seen my own kids making the same mistakes as me, you were lucky, you got out."

"But this is what life is all about, the estate, the Backfields, the daily struggle to survive. Sitting pretty in a Californian mansion isn't all it's cracked up to be you know."

"Don't give me that crap. Do you think I've enjoyed being banged up, crying myself to sleep in a cell? I thought I knew it all, but you know what, that bloody little wimp Pogo, he had it sussed it all the time. Have you seen him now? He's a solicitor, doing well, and he deserves it. Why didn't someone tell me then?"

"Hey, don't be so hard on yourself, you're a cool guy. Have you read the Admirable Crichton? It's about a butler on a desert island, and how he becomes the leader, and his master becomes his servant. I've always thought of you that way."

"That's not real life, that's a story. There's no such person as that Admiral. We're here to be shat on and that's it. I've lived here all my life. How many of those boys of our age are still left with any hope? Oh fuck it!"

I was getting a bit fed up with Trev's self-depreciating manner. He didn't understand he was still that boyhood hero, always knowing what to do, where to find the snakes under the tin sheets, never being afraid to climb the tallest tree to get the rare bird's egg. Why couldn't he see it?

Somewhere along the way he'd been damaged, he'd become a pale ghost of his potential self. I suppose someone's got to be the underdog so that the overdogs can have their day, but why him? Why Trev?

"All right Trev, I guess I've just been lucky."

"Nah, you always were the clever one. When we were kids, you always seemed to know when to say 'enough is enough'. Me, I just went for it like a mad dog. I never had any brains."

"Bullshit," I said, perhaps too sharply.

He flinched. It was a shame. I felt an immense debt to Trev, in many ways he'd contributed to what I'd become, to all the successes I'd achieved. I couldn't do anything but shrug and sigh He was a hopeless case.

"Drink up," I said, downing the last dregs from my glass. "I'll get you another."

"Just a half then, I've got work in the morning. I don't want to get the sack from this job as well."

There were two men at the bar, dressed in regulation business suits. I hovered behind them.

"And a glass of house red please."

I knew that voice. It was a chubbier and older version of the Pogo I used to know three decades earlier. I tapped him on the shoulder.

"Mick," he said, "I heard you were back, sorry to hear your mother's not well."

"What are you up to these days?" I asked.

"Oh, you know, still in the same place, still slaving away."

"You're a solicitor, aren't you? You must have met some dodgy characters in your time. Don't they scare you?"

"You used to frighten me Mick, you know that? You took chances. Yet you could have had anything you wanted, you were much brighter than I was. But you know what, it did me good in the end. Look at me now, I've got it all."

I nodded.

"I'll catch you later," he said, dismissing me with a confidence the Pogo I knew never possessed.

I went back to a fidgeting uncommunicative Trev. I got a little too drunk, so I left the car where it was and went for another walk around the estate intending to find a taxi to take me back to the hotel.

CHAPTER 17

The streets were even quieter than they had been earlier, perhaps there was something good on the television? Or maybe everyone was too drunk or too stoned to bother.

I walked slowly, in a pensive mood, until I found myself at the heart of the estate, on the field. I stopped and looked around, listening for the sounds of the night on the Backfields. I edged towards the centre of the field where the light from the street lamps hardly reached.

I remembered lonely nights when I was a teenager, standing in the middle of the field and looking up at the stars, so close to the centre of the universe and so trapped in the cage of the Backfields.

The ground was more uneven than I remembered it, and muddy. My slow walk continued until I began to emerge from the darkness on the other side of the field. The windows of one of the houses bordering the field lit up. There was shouting and the sound of doors slamming. A small shadowy figure ran straight towards me from the direction of the house.

The boy tried to change direction when he saw me coming out of the gloom, but in his panic he slipped on the muddy grass and slid into me, knocking me over and falling hard on his face as a result.

His eyes were wide and terrified, but held the same defiance I'd seen in Timothy's. I lifted my fist. He looked even more terrified. I realised in time what I was doing, and stopped myself, allowing my body to go limp and roll away from him. He saw his opportunity and ran off across the field

I got up, covered in mud, and moved towards the light. An old man in a paisley dressing-gown was standing near the gate of the house.

"Did you see him?" he asked, leaning on the wall, obviously distressed, breathing rapidly and shallowly. "Dear me, you are in a mess, aren't you." he added.

"He got away," I said, a little breathless myself. "I had him for a minute but he wriggled free."

"Little bastard." He looked pale under the weak light.

"Are you all right?" I asked.

"Touch of angina, that's all. I'll be all right in a minute." He sat heavily on the low brick wall next to the gate.

"Did he get away with anything?" I asked, sitting down next to him.

"Not this time," the old man's breath was steadying, "but he'll be back, or someone else. This place has gone to the dogs."

"Shall I call the police?" I asked, reaching in my pocket. "I've got a cell phone."

"A what?"

"A mobile phone, you know?"

"Ah! No, what's the point, the police can't control things any more than I can. It looks like I'll just have to buy stronger locks – again."

"Does this sort of thing happen often?" I asked.

"Only to some of us, usually the vulnerable, like me, an old man, alone. Most of the time they're too busy fighting amongst themselves. There's no honour among thieves around here – only last week someone got stabbed in School Lane, and God knows how many of them are on drugs."

I shook my head, remembering my own youth, not much had changed really.

"Can I do anything for you?" I asked, still a bit groggy from the alcohol.

I was glad when he waved away my offer of help and went back into his house muttering about satellite television and violent films.

After talking to the old man, I went to see Angel. I couldn't face going back to the hotel.

She flung the door open without hesitation when I rang the bell, something no one would do late at night back in

151

California. I gave her my most appealing puppy dog look.

"Come to the kitchen and get cleaned up," she said. "What have you been up to?"

I explained what had happened and with Angel's help I was soon sitting in the lounge with a cup of hot black coffee, wearing a too small bathrobe. We sat on a long floral-patterned settee together. I was shaking with the cold.

"I'll turn the heating up," she said.

"It's all right," I said. "The coffee's kicking in."

We talked for a while, and as we talked I began to feel closer to her, emotionally and physically.

I shivered again.

Angel got a continental quilt from a cupboard under the stairs. She brought it back into the room as if she was carrying a big white cloud.

"Here you are," she said, throwing the quilt over me.

My head found a gap and poked itself through.

Angel laughed.

She sat down again, closer than before.

Angel shivered.

"You're cold too."

"Just a little."

"Come on, it's big enough."

We snuggled up under the quilt. So much time had passed since we'd last shared an intimate moment, yet I felt completely at ease and comfortable. I realised then that I'd never felt as close to another person as I had with Angel, not even with Ramona or Linda.

"I forgot," I mumbled.

"Mmm," Angel whispered, resting her head on my shoulder.

I turned my head to look at her. Naturally we kissed. It was a warm, clean kiss, sensuous and cool at the same time. We said few words after that.

Later, Angel produced some grass from a small wooden box, carved with flowers, and we shared a joint.

"I have the odd smoke, only on special occasions though," she laughed.

"Me too," I sighed with pleasure.

"I suppose I should go back to the hotel," I said, hoping she'd beg me to stay.

"Don't go," she said. "I won't sleep for a while now anyway. I'll make some more coffee."

We huddled together under the quilt, sipping and talking.

"You do know," I said, "that you've always been special to me, and that time, when we finished, nothing happened, I thought of you. It was only a stupid kiss."

"Ssh Mick," she said. "It doesn't matter now."

"But I want you to know. It was that idiot Snobby. He ruined everything, he changed our lives Angel, spoilt everything we had."

Angel pulled herself away and faced me.

"Listen Mick, nothing is ever what it seems. I'm not stupid, and I wasn't then. It wasn't just that, it wasn't right Mick, me and you – it wouldn't have worked."

"But..."

"No Mick. Life is complex, sometimes you've got to give things up and move on – it's for the best."

"What do you mean? I don't get it."

"Some things are best left Mick, that's all there is to it."

"Someone else said that to me once, I don't believe it. The truth is always the best."

Angel became agitated. "Not now Mick – please."

I relented. "What about us?"

"I don't know, but it's all right Mick. Whatever happened in the past, you are very special to me too."

I kissed her on the cheek.

"I saw him today – Snobby, or Robbo, as he calls himself now." I said.

"Oh!" Angel said.

"Hey," I said, "there's a do on at the Majestic Hotel soon, how about if we went together?"

"The Majestic, that's a bit of a dive, or so I hear. I don't know about that."

"Well, they've done it up, spent a fortune apparently. According to Robbo everyone who is anyone in this town will be there."

"Hmm."

"So, will you come?"

"I don't know. I've heard some stuff about him."

"What do you mean – stuff? I know he's a bit shady."

"You could say that."

"I met Trev and Pogo too, earlier on in the pub. Pogo seems very sure of himself."

"I don't know him very well, though I do hear about him. It's a small town."

"It's the same in LA," I said.

"Really?"

"Well it's a bit easier to keep your head down there, I suppose, but I'm so glad I got out of Elchurch. Coming back has made me realise just how insular and narrow-minded this place is. Though, it is quite entertaining seeing it again, from a distance. It's sort of strange, like looking at a soap opera."

"Oh cut the crap Mick, it's just people getting on with their lives."

"Sorry. Give me a chance. Come with me to the Majestic and we'll see how it goes?"

Angel sighed: "All right then, we'll see. You'd better go now, your clothes will be dry."

I called a local taxi firm. I was pleased when the driver turned out to be Matthew's mother.

"You," she said, when I got into the cab.

"Hello again," I said. "Is Timothy tucked up safely in bed?"

"Matthew's home tonight, thank God. The hotel, is it?"

"Yes please. Do you often work late?"

"It's better paid, so yes, I do. I catch up on my sleep in the day when the kids are in school."

The car pulled away.

"It must be tough, bringing up all those kids on your own. Does Trev help at all?"

"You're very nosey. You want to get a life of your own, you do."

I smiled. "Sorry, I don't mean to pry. I saw Trev earlier on, in the pub."

"Tell me something new," she said.

"No, actually, he left early. He had to get up for work. He seems to be quite sensible, very keen to make an impression in his job."

"How long will it last this time? He's been in and out of jobs as long as I've known him. He's a loser, nothing will change that. Not like you. I've been hearing things about you. Matthew doesn't stop talking about you. I suppose you're a better role model than that waster of a father of his."

"Trev's all right," I said. "He's been unlucky, that's all."

"Huh," she said, deftly removing a cigarette from a packet on the dashboard. "Do you want one?"

"Not now thanks. Where does he work anyway?"

"That's just it, he's a driver, working for a car parts wholesaler. They don't know he's banned from driving or about his record, God help him when they find out. He can never seem to get it right. Nearly there."

We pulled up outside the front entrance to the hotel

"Hang on a minute," I said. "I've always had a soft spot for Trev. Do you think there's anything I can do to help him?"

She turned the engine off and lit another cigarette from the stub of her last one.

"I gave up on Trev years ago, I don't think you'll have any better luck. Others have tried too. Take Robbo for example, that man bent over backwards for Trev, but what does he do? He only gets caught stealing a lorry load of bricks from a builder's merchant. Bricks for Christ's sake. He could have knocked off some fags or something, something useful like that. That's how he went to prison, the first time anyway."

"How many times has he been sent down?" I asked.

"Three times altogether. The second time he ripped a condom vending machine off a wall in a pub toilet when he was pissed. The last time was the best though. He was done for fencing stolen goods – they found a whole load of condemned meat in a garage."

"So how is he mixed up with Robbo? I've heard he's a bit of a wide boy, if you know what I mean."

"Maybe he is, but I'll tell you what, he looks after his own,

God help you if you cross him though. Just because he doesn't have fancy letters after his name and doesn't belong to the right party doesn't mean anything. Some of those council officers and even the councillors are as bent as a dog's dick."

"How do you mean?"

"Come off it, everyone knows how you get on in this town, all you have to do is buy a few councillors and the contracts come flooding in. And what do the councillors do that's any good anyway. They've made a right mess of the Backfields, it's a disgrace. The families they shove on us. They just cause problems."

"Oh," I said, "the place seems pleasant enough."

"Huh, it's a tinderbox, it could go up at any time. Listen, I'd love to stay here chatting all night, but the meter's still running and I've got to get home for a bit of kip before the morning."

CHAPTER 18

Four uniformed policemen in fluorescent jackets moved towards the centre of the road in front of the Mercedes. The nearest one approached the driver's window, which I'd rolled down as I stopped.

I smiled, mentally checking my pockets for illegal substances. The old prejudices hadn't left me.

"Officer," I nodded respectfully.

"Good morning sir, just a routine check. May I ask you where you're going?"

"I'm going to see my mother, she lives in Meadow Road."

"May I ask where you have come from sir?"

"From the South Beach Hotel, I'm only here for a few days."

I'd actually come from the pub, where I'd left my car the night before, but I thought it wouldn't be wise to tell a copper that.

"Thank you sir, sorry to bother you. You can drive on now."

I restarted the engine. "What's it all about?" I asked over the noise.

The young policeman turned. "Nothing to worry about," he smiled, "it's just a bit of high-profile policing, you'd be surprised at the effect it has on the crime statistics in this area."

When I got to my mother's house, she already had another visitor. It was one of the old neighbours.

"Well hello Mrs Mellor," I greeted the old woman warmly.

I remembered her as always being very generous to me on New Year's and Bonfire Night when we went collecting money. She'd also been a very good tipper when I used to deliver newspapers to her house.

"Hello young man," she growled in a deep rasping voice. She turned to my mother: "Always was a charmer, your

Mick. A very nice little boy I remember him as."

"The estate is crawling with police," I said. "I got stopped, but it was only routine, something about high-profile policing."

Mrs Mellor nodded, and smiled wryly: "They're at it again are they? Fat lot of good it will do. It just gives the villains another holiday, as soon as the police are gone, they'll be back, up to their old tricks."

"Is it really that bad around here?" I asked, sitting down on the edge of the sofa.

"That bad? It's worse, believe me."

"It seems such a peaceful place, the residents must be mellowing with age by now."

"Some of them have mellowed too fast, they're six feet under my boy, and look at the rubbish they replace them with. Ought to be evicted, thrown out on their ears."

"I'm afraid you've started Mattie off again Mick, it's one of her pet subjects."

"I didn't mean to go off like that, Lizzie. Anyway it's time I went, Jack will be screaming for his dinner soon."

I offered to make a cup of tea, then I had a better idea. "Get your gladrags on, and we'll go back to the hotel for lunch. They've got a great menu."

"Oh no, Mick, I couldn't."

"Come on Mam, I haven't had lunch there myself yet, it'll give me a chance to try it."

"Oh, all right. I'll come and spend your money for you."

The restaurant in the hotel was virtually empty so we got a good table and perhaps a little too much attention from the waiting staff. My mother only picked at her food and I wasn't very hungry either, but it wasn't really about the food.

"How are things with you, Mick?"

There was something about the way she asked, something about the tone of her voice, the way she tilted her head to one side as she spoke – softly, knowingly. A great sadness welled up from the pit of my stomach and I struggled to stop the tears.

"I'm, I'm all right," I said with an effort.

"There's no need to bottle it all up Mick. It's got to find its way out somehow. Your brother Ralph, now there's nothing I can do for him, he's always been a very inward looking sort of person. But you're not usually like that. What is it Mick, what's the matter?"

I'd love to have been able to explain how I felt to my own mother, but I didn't really know how I felt myself.

"Don't worry," I said. "Everything's good."

She sighed. "I'm getting a bit tired now Mick, have you finished your food?"

I shook my head and brought my attention back to the external world. "Sorry, of course."

I drove Mam back to her house and left her there to rest. I knocked on Angel's door but there was no answer. I drove to the estuary where the river narrowed, and the tide, when it was full out, left the riverbed almost dry.

Apart from two anglers at either end of the beach between the railway bridge and the road bridge the place showed no human activity. I walked down the narrow strip of sand that abutted the rising seawater and stood quietly, staring at the dirty dark tide.

I sensed a movement to my left and looked across. The angler snatched his rod off its stand and reeled the line in rapidly. It was Trev.

"I didn't expect to find you here, half day or something?"

Trev gave me a disdainful look as the end of his trace emerged from the water. It was bare.

"Something like that," he said.

"Is everything all right?"

"I've had the fucking sack." He leant over and took some peat-covered ragworms from a plastic container and threaded them onto his hooks.

"How did that happen?"

"I don't know, someone stitched me up, I reckon."

"What'll you do now?"

"Fucked if I know. Fucking dole again, I suppose."

"Isn't there anything about?"

"Fuck all 'round here, unless you call sucking up lugworms

Derec Jones

something."

"Want a fag?" I asked.

"No thanks, I've got my roll-ups, I prefer them. Anyway, I've had enough of this shit, I'm packing up."

He shook the remains of the worms off his fingers with disgust and rubbed his hands clean in his trousers.

"Where are you parked?" I asked.

"Parked? You've got to have a car to be parked. No, I walked here, it's only a couple of miles."

"I'll give you a lift back if you like. We could go for a pint."

"Ah go on then. I'm sorry I'm in such a bad mood, you know how it is."

"I guess so."

Trev packed his gear up while I finished my cigarette. He dismantled the fishing rod and put it carefully in its canvas case. He picked up the plastic container of worms and hurled it into the sea.

"Feast time for the crabs again."

I pulled into the car park of the Carpenter's Arms and went in with Trev. He paid for the drinks, a pint of bitter for him and a mineral water for me.

"I may as well buy you a drink while I still can. I don't know why I bother trying. I can never seem to do anything right," he said, as he sat down in the almost deserted bar.

"Aren't there any possibilities for work?"

"Well, to be honest, I have been offered something. You remember Snobby?"

"How could I forget."

"Well I saw him the other day and he offered me a job."

"What sort of job?"

"That's just it, I don't know. All he said was he could do with someone like me on the payroll. Said he'd see me right."

"It's up to you, but I don't know if I trust him. Never have."

"What choice have I got? I'll have to give it a go."

"Be careful," I said.

The few men in the pub at that time of the afternoon stopped chattering, leaving an uncomfortable silence, all eyes staring impassively towards the entrance. I looked around

160

and saw two clean-cut men. One of them I recognised as the young detective James Conway. The two policemen walked to the bar and said something to the landlord. He pointed at our table and they came over.

"Mr Thomas."

"Yes," Trev said, nervously clutching his pint.

"We've been looking for you for hours."

"I've been fishing. Ask him."

"That's right," I said. "I met him by the estuary just now. What's it all about?"

He turned to Trev: "I'm afraid it's about your son, Matthew. He's in hospital."

Trev stood up abruptly. "In hospital? What happened?"

"Seems he's been attacked, taken a beating. A gang by all accounts."

"Where? When?"

"This morning, outside a house in Western Street, near the station. We're still trying to establish what he was doing there. The house is well known to us, we suspect it's used by drug dealers."

"My Matthew would never be involved in something like that," Trev said angrily. "I want to go and see him, how bad is he?"

"We'll take you to the hospital. He's conscious but pretty groggy, perhaps you can get some more information about who attacked him. He won't tell us anything."

The three men left me alone in the pub. I sipped the last of my mineral water and drove back to the hotel. Len White was on reception looking harassed.

"I'm a bit short staffed," he said.

"I heard about Matthew," I said. "What do you know?"

"Nothing, as usual. It's me who's got to run this place, what am I supposed to do?"

"I can see you're busy, catch you later," I said.

I went up to my room and took a long shower.

It had been a long day but the evening still loomed ahead. I was at a loose end wondering what to do with myself until I could legitimately crash out for the night. I thought about going back to see Angel but decided that I should let things cool off for a day, we'd be going to the do in the Majestic the next night anyway. I made a few phone calls to my offices in California to make sure that everything was running well in my absence. It was a quiet period and everything was fine.

I caught Len in the hotel bar in a quiet moment and asked him again if he knew anything about Matthew's situation.

"He's a good boy is Matthew. This business is a great shame. He's not too badly hurt, some severe bruising apparently. I don't know if we'll be able to keep him on after this though."

"What do you mean? He didn't do anything wrong did he?"

"Well, I don't know, but he's been arrested."

"Arrested? For what?"

"I don't give a shit myself, but it wouldn't look good for the hotel if we had a drug dealer on the staff."

"Matthew's been arrested for dealing?"

"I don't know, but the police have been here asking questions and I gather the house he was in was searched and a large quantity of Ecstasy and Speed was found. He's been arrested on suspicion. I don't think he's been charged yet."

I left the hotel quickly and drove to the hospital to see if I could find out more. Even though I hadn't known Matthew long I'd grown to like and respect him.

A police constable stood outside a private room on ward 10 of the hospital. He asked me who I was but didn't try and stop me going in. The room was big enough for a hospital bed, a television and a few armchairs. Trev and Matthew's mother were in two of the chairs. Matthew's brother Tim was on the bottom of the bed staring up at the small television. Matthew was sitting up in bed, his face swollen and bruised.

"Sorry to disturb you," I said, closing the door behind me.

Trev stood up and stretched. His ex-wife looked at me in her challenging way and stood up too.

"Come on Tim," she said. "Let's go and get a cup of tea. I could do with a fag."

"What's going on Trev?" I asked. "I heard Matthew was arrested."

"I am here, you know." Matthew's voice was muffled through his swollen lips.

"Sorry. Why have they arrested you?"

Trev answered: "They reckon he's involved with those fucking toe-rags from Western Street. They haven't got a clue. There's plenty of real villains around without picking on a hard working boy like my Matthew."

"I was only looking for Tim, he'd been missing all night," Matthew said painfully. "Some of his mates said I might find him there. I didn't know what sort of place it was. Now they reckon that I went there to buy supplies and got into a fight. All I did was to knock on the door and..."

"Fucking bastards," Trev said. "I'll fucking kill them."

Matthew mumbled again: "And Tim wasn't there anyway, not then at least. He's denying everything and there's nothing we can do to make him talk, he's always been a stubborn little... "

"A stubborn little git, that's what he is. If he was my son..."

"Calm down Dad," Matthew squirmed uncomfortably. "Pass me that glass of water please."

"Have you been charged?" I asked

"Not yet, but they've promised to charge me as soon as I'm well enough to leave here. I don't know what I can do to convince them. I don't know anything about drugs or anything else."

"You need a solicitor," I said. "Have you got one?"

"Never thought of that."

"What about Pogo?" I turned to Trev. "He's a solicitor, isn't he? And quite a successful one at that."

"Pogo won't bother with the likes of us," Trev said.

"What if I had a word with him, I'm sure I could convince him to sort this mess out?"

"Sounds OK to me," Matthew said.

"Why not," Trev said.

"It's a deal," I said, getting up to go. "Do you know where I can contact him?"

Trev thought for a moment. "That's a point, his office will be closed now won't it."

"I've seen him in the hotel a few times," Matthew said. "I think he acted for the developers. That's what Len White told me anyway. Perhaps Len will know how to contact him."

Outside the hospital, Timothy and his mother were sitting in the shadows on a wooden bench.

I sat next to them: "I'm going to try and sort out a solicitor for Matthew," I said. "An old friend of ours, Pogo, do you know him? I think his name is Peter something."

"Wouldn't be Peter Summers, would it?" she said. "Married to Sylvia, two kids – a boy and a girl."

"That's him," I said. "Thanks."

"Yep, he's all right, he is. I've given him a lift more than once, usually from the Majestic Hotel. He seems to spend a lot of time there lately."

Curious, I thought. "Well I'd better go and sort it out."

"Make sure you do," she said, throwing the butt of a cigarette into a hedge and getting up to go back inside.

I drove through town to the hotel and parked in the corner of a dark car park. The hotel itself was floodlit and several commercial vehicles were parked outside. Men hurried in and out unloading furniture. The building was impressive, huge stones locked into each other, like a castle. To its side was a brand new glass extension, lit up like the mothership.

I made my way past the activity, through the deserted reception, and into a large bar area. There were people working everywhere, laying carpets, cleaning, fixing light fittings, and generally rushing about. I noticed Pogo and a smart looking woman sitting in a quiet corner. They had a tray of coffee materials laid out before them on the round wooden table.

Pogo looked surprised and a little alarmed to see me.

"Mick, what are you doing here?"

"It's about Matthew, Trev's son. He's been arrested, and he's in hospital. I was hoping you'd sort it out with the police. He didn't do anything wrong."

Pogo blushed and looked at his wife.

I introduced myself: "Hello Mrs Summers, I'm Mick, an old friend of Peter's."

She smiled and sipped her coffee.

Pogo shook his head. "I don't know Mick, I'm very busy at the moment."

"Oh please," I begged. "Matthew needs your help."

A voice behind me said: "Who needs Pogo's help then? Who is this Matthew?"

I turned and there was Snobby, clutching a brandy glass. He looked so in control, so tough and unflappable that I stammered a little: "It, it, it's Matthew, Trev's son, he's been arrested."

"Matthew, he's a fine boy, what's he been up to?"

"Nothing, that's the point, in fact he's the victim."

"Of course Pogo will help Matthew, won't you Pogo?" His voice carried a vague threat.

It was Pogo's turn to stammer: "Yes, yes, yes, of course I will."

I drove Pogo to the hospital. His wife stayed with Snobby.

"Don't you worry about Sylvia," Snobby said as we left. "I'll look after her. I'll make sure she gets home all right."

Pogo looked uneasy.

On the way to the hospital, Pogo telephoned someone in the police station to arrange to meet him at the hospital.

"It's Inspector John Green," he explained. "We go back a long way, I'm sure we'll be able to sort this out without too much fuss."

"Thank you," I said. "I really appreciate this.

"Who's there with Matthew, in the hospital?" Pogo asked.

"Trev's there, and Matthew's brother Timothy, and Trev's ex-wife, Matthew's mother, I don't know her name."

"It's Ellen, that's her name. Don't you remember her, she used to hang around with that gang from the Tophill Estate, but then she is a bit younger than us I suppose, perhaps you'd left town by the time she became active."

It didn't take long, a few quiet words in a dark corridor, and five minutes later the uniformed officer left his post at the door. Pogo came back into Matthew's room.

"The police aren't going to charge Matthew, but they do want to talk to him again, just to clear things up," he said quietly.

"It's amazing what you can get done if you know the right people," I said.

Trev sighed with relief and Ellen gave Pogo an enthusiastic hug. Pogo blushed with embarrassment.

I dropped Pogo off outside the Majestic.

"Do you want me to wait in case you need a lift home?"

"No, I'll be fine."

"I expect I'll see you tomorrow night then," I said, as he closed the car door.

He looked puzzled.

"In the do, at the hotel, Snobby's big night."

"Oh that, I expect so."

CHAPTER 19

A taxi picked me up from the South Beach Hotel at eight o'clock then drove on to collect Angel on the way to the Majestic.

Snobby's hotel was even more brightly lit than it had been the night before. Red-blazered staff hovered everywhere, some carrying trays of champagne, others offering savoury tit-bits. Each had a white badge showing their name and position in bold black ink.

It all looked so bright, so fresh, so expensive and so professional, that I had trouble reconciling the image I had of Snobby with such an achievement. Perhaps I'd misjudged him, anyone who could put that together deserved respect.

I stood with Angel, who looked classy in a plain dark dress, as we sipped from fluted glasses of sparkling wine. Across the room we spotted Trev, surrounded by red blazers.

He waved at us and came over, grinning. His fair, greying hair had been newly trimmed and styled. He was wearing a black jacket, with a neatly printed badge that read: *'Mr Trevor Thomas: Events Manager'*.

"Wow," I said. "What's happened to you, you look smart."

"It's good isn't it, and Robbo's been generous with the wages as well. You wouldn't believe how much I'm getting paid to look like this."

"It's good to see you smiling. How's Matthew?"

"Much better, a bit battered and bruised, but much better than we expected at first. In fact, he's out of hospital already. I think he's coming here tonight."

Trev's eyes scanned the room. "Sorry," he said, noticing something that needed his attention. "I've got to go."

Someone tapped me on the shoulder as I chatted to Angel. I turned to see Len White's smiling face. He looked the part in a black dinner jacket and dickey-bow.

"What the fuck are you doing here?"

"Ssh," he hissed. "I've got to check out the competition. I'm very impressed so far. There's a lot of the right sort of people here."

Angel smiled and nodded.

"Aren't you going to introduce me to your lovely companion?" Len looked her up and down appreciatively.

"Sorry, this is ..."

"I'm Angel."

"Ah, of course you are."

"This is Len," I said.

"Ah yes, the hotel," Angel said.

Len took her hand and kissed it softly.

"Always was a gentleman," I laughed.

Angel was distracted, selecting nibbles off a tray held by a bored girl with a red jacket big enough to be an overcoat.

Len tilted his head towards Angel. 'Two?' he whispered.

"Ssh! It's complicated."

The place was getting busy. Len was absorbed by the crowd. Angel nodded at every other person who caught her eye. I realised I knew little about who she had become.

"How do you know so many of these people?" I asked.

"I don't really know them that well," she whispered. "See that man over there."

She moved her head in the direction of a large grey-haired man coming from the bar with a pint of beer in his hand.

"Yes."

"Well, he's a high-ranking police officer, and that red-haired man is on the board of the steelworks."

"I didn't realise Snobby had such illustrious friends."

"You'd be surprised," she said, smiling into the distance at some other acquaintance.

"I'm sorry," I said, "Sounds daft, but I don't know what you do for a living."

"I work for the government," she winked.

"Carry on."

"I'm an investigator more than anything."

"You're a spy?"

"Not really. It's a long story."

"Intriguing," I said.

"Maybe I'll explain one day."

People were moving away from the bar and along a corridor that led to a large function room. About a hundred tables were laid out with four or five chairs around each. A red-blazer led us to a table near the dance floor. There were six chairs around our table; two already occupied by Pogo and his wife Sylvia.

"This is a surprise," I said, as we sat down.

We greeted each other.

"Who else is joining us?" I asked.

"I'm not sure," Pogo said. "You can never tell with Robbo."

A few minutes later Matthew and his mother Ellen sat down and solved the mystery. Trev came up to make sure everyone was comfortable and fussed over his son, who winced with pain every time he raised his glass.

Snobby came to the table before Trev had finished.

"Here we all are then, all the old gang. Who'd have thought it eh? Now I want you all to enjoy yourselves. It's all on the house tonight. We've got good food, great drink, and even better entertainment for you. So sit back and relax, let me take care of everything."

When Trev and Snobby left I couldn't help but shiver. I felt very uneasy. There was something about David Robinson that still made my skin crawl.

The evening continued with a local stand-up comedian acting as Master of Ceremonies. Snobby made a long speech about the history of the hotel and his own business successes. Waiters and waitresses circulated continually, handing out food and endless bottles of wine.

We all got drunk. Some people made fools of themselves on the dance floor. It didn't take long for the initial clean professional order to degenerate into a chaotic drunken bash.

"We mussht do thish more often," Pogo said, his big head lolling drunkenly on his small frame. "Isht great, ishint it Mick?"

"Shure is," I replied.

"Ooh, I feel sick."

He lurched from his chair and staggered towards the toilets.

Angel gave me a look that said 'Go on then.'

I saluted her and followed Pogo through the crowd. When I caught up with him he was retching into the urinals. I put my arm around him.

"Come on Pogo, I think you need a bit of fresh air."

I led him outside and around the side of the hotel. We came to a dark area near the back entrance to the kitchens. I lit a cigarette. Pogo sat on a dustbin and held his head between his hands.

"Thanks Mick, I'll be all right in a minute."

"No problem," I said.

The cool night air had begun to sober me up as well.

A young girl came out of the kitchen and emptied the contents of a stainless steel tray into a dustbin. When she saw us she hurried back inside. The door didn't close properly and a chink of light escaped and illuminated the path that led towards the rear of the hotel. Pogo stood up and promptly fell back down on the bin, mumbling to himself.

"Come on," I said. "You need a walk to clear your head."

I supported him as we walked past the kitchen and around towards the back of the hotel. I peeked in. Snobby was having an animated discussion with someone who was out of view, probably a staffing problem.

There was a service area at the rear of the building. An iron stairway led from up from the tarmacked parking area to a half open door. I guessed it led to the backstage area of the function room.

Pogo sat on a bollard. I lit another cigarette

Someone came out of the door at the top of the iron stairs. I looked up and saw Trev leaning on the rail clutching a beer bottle. He lifted the bottle to his mouth, drained it, and threw it onto the tarmac below him, where it smashed.

"Oi, you!" I shouted.

"You bloody bastard," he laughed. "What the fuck are you

doing there?"

"It's Pogo," I said. "He's been puking up, he's overdone it on the free wine."

"Serves him right then. Got any fags?"

"Here catch."

"No, I'll come down."

Trev clanked down the stairs and joined Pogo and me in the gloom.

"How's it going?" I asked.

"Depends what you mean. If you mean is everyone getting drunk and stupid, then I suppose it's going great, for Snobby at least. Me, I'm a bit pissed off to tell the truth. This isn't really what I'm cut out for. I'd rather be in the pub, all these nobs making arseholes of themselves. These are the sort of twats who run our town – no disrespect to you Pogo."

Pogo grunted and retched.

Snobby appeared at the top of the stairs. "What's going on? Who are you lot?"

His eyes adjusted to the darkness: "Well fuck me, if it ain't all the old gang again."

I couldn't help laughing. The whole thing was ridiculous.

Snobby shouted. "What the fuck's so funny?"

I waved him away. "Nothing, it's just the drink."

"You're not on that fucking wacky baccy are you?"

I laughed again, and then, seeing the way his body stiffened, made an effort to control myself. Pogo shivered. Trev stepped away from the rest of us, looking nervous.

There was a commotion coming from behind Snobby; raised voices, muffled by the thick door, the noise of what sounded like equipment falling over and glass breaking.

Snobby went back inside; the door slammed behind him. Trev bounded up the iron stairs and tried to open it.

"It's bolted from the inside," he said.

Pogo was already scuttling out of sight around the corner in the direction we'd come from. I waited for Trev to come down.

"We'd better go round the front," he said. "Find out what's going on."

"OK," I agreed.

It took us a good five minutes to push ourselves through the crowds in the hotel and find our way back to our table. Matthew, Ellen and Angel were still there. There was no sign of Pogo or Sylvia.

"Have you seen Pogo, or Snobby?" I asked.

Angel answered: "Funny, but a few minutes ago Pogo rushed in, then left with Sylvia in a hurry, without explanation. Before that Snobby ran across the dance floor, in that direction."

"Thanks," I said.

"That's the kitchen," Trev said.

We moved around the function room to the kitchen entrance. Snobby came out of the door.

"It's all right boys," he said, shooing us away. "Just a little accident, nothing to worry about. Trev, would you mind going to check on the bar staff? Just to keep them on their toes."

Trev slouched off meekly. Snobby shepherded me away from the kitchen entrance.

"Please carry on enjoying yourself. It's been a good night, don't you think?"

It was pointless trying to get anything more out of him. I made my way back to the table, sat down, and sighed.

"What's going on?" Angel asked.

"Don't bother," I said.

Angel shook her head: "Boys will be boys. Can we go now Mick? I think I've had enough."

We said goodbye to Matthew and Ellen and made our way to the front entrance and one of the waiting taxis.

By the time the cab pulled up outside Angel's house we both agreed we'd had too much to drink and it would be best to call it a night, so I carried on alone to the South Beach Hotel.

The hotel was quiet so I went straight to my room. A familiar sweet perfume greeted me but I was still taken aback when Ramona appeared from the bathroom wearing a large white hotel towel, her dark hair hanging in damp ropes around her beautiful bare shoulders.

Before I had time to think about how I would explain Angel

to Ramona and vice-versa, the phone rang.

"Hello ... yes ... thank you."

"It's my brother, Ralph," I said to Ramona.

She shrugged. "No problem, you'll need some time to talk. I'll lock myself away in the bedroom. You won't know I'm here."

"Thanks, we'll catch up later."

I stood in the doorway to wait for Ralph. How long had it been since I'd even seen him?

A casually dressed man came shambling up the corridor looking at his shoes. He was much smaller than the image I had of the Ralph in my imagination.

He sensed me standing in the doorway and looked up. His face was lined, he looked too old. He always did care and worry too much.

"Mick," he said. "You look good."

"And you," I lied.

We entered the room awkwardly, crushing each other in the frame of the door.

CHAPTER 20

We talked awkwardly about banalities, drunk too much wine, and fell asleep on the furniture. Ramona was sleeping when we woke.

Ralph wasn't ready to visit Mam, so we drove into the mountains and spent the day walking and talking about what we'd each been doing with our lives over the previous two decades. He told me about his work in the factories of Canada. I reciprocated with anecdotes about life behind the scenes in Hollywood. Neither of us was really listening to the other, and we avoided talking about anything important. Still it was nice to feel close to him again.

In the evening we got drunk again and ate too much. Ramona looked a bit pissed off, but didn't say much and kept out of our way.

The next morning we drove to a greasy spoon café in town to get some breakfast and talked some more. Afterwards we walked into the town centre, just as the shops were opening.

"This town's changed, everything's changed," Ralph said.

"Not at its core," I said. "It's still the same old shitheap it always was. The same dirty fingers picking the cherries, just a different generation that's all."

"You're too cynical, you always were Mick. I've travelled remember, and lived in different towns in different countries. It's the same everywhere, it's only natural."

"Yeah, but there are better places to live. I'm so glad I got out. Otherwise, I'd have been buried by now. There's no creativity in this place, just look at the faces of the people, they're living a facsimile of life."

"You don't know anything about them. Who knows what shit they've had to put up with. Each one of these people has a story. People may look like one thing to the outside world, but inside, only they can know."

We stopped in the main square and sat on the low wall around a mock-gothic clock tower.

"Do you think you'll be able to face up to Mam today?" I asked.

"I don't know," Ralph hung his head and shook it slowly from side to side.

"I'm knackered," I said, "I could do with another coffee."

"Don't waste your money," he said. "We will go and visit Mam and we'll have a cuppa there." He sighed with the effort.

We didn't say another word to each other on the way to Mam's house.

Mam cried when she saw Ralph. He cried as well, and when I felt my own tears welling up, I went into the small kitchen to brew a pot of tea. While it was brewing I went out the back for a walk and wandered around the alleys.

A pale skinny man asked me for a light for an equally pale and skinny hand rolled cigarette. I obliged by handing him my Zippo lighter. I waited patiently while he flicked the top open and turned the flint wheel with his thin white thumb. He looked at the lighter admiringly before he handed it back to me reluctantly.

"I used to have one of these," he said, shaking his head and smiling with the pleasure of the memory. "It was gold – real gold, I had my name engraved on the case. But that didn't stop the bastards nicking it off me. Mind you, it was my fault, I was very drunk at the time."

"Oh yeah," I said, wishing I didn't smoke.

"Yeah. I know you, don't I?"

"I don't think so, I'm just visiting my mother."

"Mrs Matthews, that's right. You're Mick aren't you? Don't you remember me?"

He looked up at me and squinted his eyes through the cheap black rimmed spectacles that rested on the end of his nose.

I remembered: "William Swift. Nice to meet you again, sorry but I've got to..."

"Walter, it's Walter. William is my brother. How are you doing Mick? Where do you live?"

"Here and there, in America mostly."

"I used to live there, in New York. It's a great place, but you can't beat the green grass of home, can you?"

"No, I suppose you're right. Listen, I've got ..."

"Do you remember, when we were kids? How we got into all those scrapes. The things we got up to." He laughed at his own false memories.

I dug into my own memories of the Backfields and dredged up the young Walter Swift. He was a pale skinny kid then too, living in a netherworld on the border of reality and fantasy.

"The place isn't the same anymore," he sighed. "It's gone to the dogs. We used to have fun, but we were never violent – and the drugs! This estate is crawling with drug dealers and heroin addicts. They should dump them all on a desert island, without a boat."

"I've got to get on," I interrupted, walking away from him.

"Call in for cuppa sometime. I'm with my old girl at the moment. Lying low for a bit if you know what I mean?" He winked.

I made my back to the house and delivered the stewed tea to Mam and Ralph. They didn't take any notice of me, so I went for another walk. I paused outside the gates of the primary school and looked into the grounds, remembering the toughness of my time there.

I kicked at a stone lying on the pavement and stubbed my toe. I leant on the gate and took my shoe off.

A policeman approached me from nowhere, he was older, shorter, and fatter than he should be.

"Is everything all right sir?" he asked.

"I hurt my foot," I said. "I'll be fine in a minute."

"Well if there's anything I can do for you, just let me know."

"It's unusual to see you lot on the streets this time of day," I said.

"It's this high-profile policing policy, not that I mind, it gives me a job at least. Who'd have thought? Two years ago I was a redundant car-factory worker. Now look at me, poncing about in this uniform. But I do enjoy the job. I'm on my way to visit the school – give a talk to the kids." He looked at his wristwatch. "I'm a bit early, so I'm just walking the streets, showing myself a bit. You'd be surprised at how effective it is. Criminals don't just come out at night you know."

"Do you get a lot of trouble around here then?" I asked.

"I can't be everywhere, you know. I try my best, it's a big estate."

"I didn't mean to imply anything else. It must be a tough job. I know I couldn't do it."

"I'm just the local beat officer, there's only so much I can do. I used to be an electrician, you know. I've only been in the job for two years."

I nodded patiently.

"The beat officer is the central figure on this estate," he said. "I visit the schools – aim at the kids. It's important to get their trust at an early age. Most of the people on the Backfields are decent. We're doing it for them."

"What about the bad guys?" I asked.

"There's just a few small pockets of them. We've teamed up with the council. We've got rid of one or two families already."

"Where do they go?"

"Away from here. If they push their luck they get evicted, they get warned first of course – that makes them voluntarily homeless. That way, the council is under no obligation to re-house them."

A small fat woman of about seventy came out of the house next to the school entrance. She looked angry. I was expecting her to tell me off for hanging around outside her house. As a boy on the Backfields, I'd been harangued many times by similar upstanding citizens for being where I shouldn't have been.

She marched up to the police officer.

"About time we saw your face around here," she said, shaking her finger. "Where were you lot last night when old Mrs Harries got robbed, when she was having her tea?

177

Where were you then, eh?"

The beat officer's face flushed. "Hold on Mrs Powell, Mrs Harries got burgled?"

"Don't they tell you anything at that police station? You come round here, wandering about the estate as if you had all the time in the world, while a defenceless old woman gets mugged in her own home."

"I didn't know. I'll get on to the boys back at base in a minute and see what I can find out."

"This place has gone from bad to worse," she said, still wagging her finger. "Too many people who live here are rubbish, they're all criminals. When I moved here over thirty years ago, it wasn't like this. The kids got up to a bit of mischief of course, but there was no mugging of old people. Children used to respect their elders, there were no break-ins and no violence then."

I remembered the stunts our little gang pulled thirty years earlier, but I'd never thought of what we did as criminal as such – it didn't seem wicked or evil at the time.

"I'd better get on," I said.

Neither the police constable nor the old woman took any notice of me, so I sidled off in the general direction of Mam's house, skirting the south side of the Field. The old man that I'd met a few nights before was sitting on the wall outside his house, smoking a cigarette. Next to him sat a young boy, who looked suspiciously like the boy I'd seen running away, and who'd knocked me over in the mud.

"Hello again," I said.

The old man looked puzzled and the young boy looked sheepish.

"I met you the other night, it was late, I fell in the field, remember?"

"Oh yes, that's right, you were in a right mess," the old man wheezed.

"Who's your young friend?" I asked.

"This is Robbie, he often comes to have a chat with me, runs errands, that sort of thing. He's a good boy, not like some around here. Robbie's a good friend of my grandson

Scott, who's a bit backward, but Robbie looks after him as well. Don't you Robbie?"

Robbie smiled weakly and looked intently at his shoes swinging a few inches above the pavement. A telephone sounded from inside the house. The old man moved surprisingly quickly to answer it.

"Well Robbie," I said, "you have been a good boy haven't you?"

"Don't tell, please Mister. I promise not to do it again. I didn't mean to, honest."

"Why did you do it in the first place? And to a friend of yours as well. That's not very nice is it? Does it make you feel big or clever or something?"

"Please don't tell, please."

"I'll think about it. In the meantime, behave yourself."

When I got back to Mam's, she was alone and in a reflective mood. "Where's Ralph?" I asked.

"Gone to see some old friends. Where did you get to?"

"Just went for a little walk around the site. Is it really as bad as people make out? You know, all the crime and drugs."

"Everyone's on drugs," she said. "The kids aren't the worst by any means. Most of my friends are on anti-depressants or tranquillisers. God knows how many people depend on alcohol to keep them sane. I blame the television. We never had things like that in my day. Children today, they have too much to cope with. Even the news is enough to make you swallow a bottle of pills. You can't blame people, the world has gone mad. Anyway, enough depressing talk, how did it go with Angel the other night?"

"It was a good evening, different, I didn't realise there were so many posh people in this town. The place was crawling with businessmen, solicitors, accountants, and councillors; even the mayor was there."

"But how about you and Angel," she persisted. "How did it go with you two?"

"It's a bit complicated," I said, "Tell me. What is it that Angel does? I never got around to asking her properly. Something to do with the government I think."

"Angel is a very clever woman. She worked away from here for many years. She only came back about nine months ago permanently, or at least until she finishes her current assignment. She used to come down quite often of course during the time she worked away, but her job took her all over the country. It's all very secretive, so don't tell anybody what I'm telling you."

My mind raced through all the possibilities, what could my mother be talking about? "What do you mean exactly?" I asked.

"Listen Mick, I'm only telling you this because I think that you and Angel have got something special, I've always thought that. The only reason I know is because she needed someone to confide in over the years, and you know me – everyone's confidante."

"Go on."

"It's true that she works for the government, she's actually a senior customs officer. She works undercover."

"Angel told me that you and her don't talk so much now. Did you fall out?"

My mother winced with some inner pain that I could only guess at.

"Are you all right?" I asked.

"Yes, I'll be fine. Could you get me a glass of water please?"

My mother sipped the water and continued talking. I had never seen her like that before, she used to be just my mother – a woman who had struggled to keep her family together, on her own most of the time, and someone who lived in an insignificant backwater. Yet here she was, in the throes of what was probably a terminal illness, privy to what I guessed was internationally important information.

"You amaze me," I said. "I didn't think ..."

"You'd be surprised Mick. You haven't been around much. You don't know much about my life here since you and Ralph left. Do you think I've been sitting around on my backside waiting for you to come back?"

"Sorry," I said. "I didn't mean to imply anything."

"Never mind that now..." She winced again.

I leant over and touched her on her arm: "Are you all right?" I asked.

"Not really, the pain is getting worse. The tablets aren't working as well as they used to. I think I need something stronger. Ow!"

"I'll call the doctor."

After the doctor had given her an injection, Mam lay down on the sofa. I went upstairs, got some blankets, and tucked her in.

She smiled at me through the drugs: "You're a good boy Mick."

She fell asleep. I sat with her until Ralph came back about an hour later. He decided to stay with her for a few days and sleep in his old room. I was anxious to get back to the hotel to talk things over with Ramona, so after making sure my mother was comfortable, I left.

CHAPTER 21

Matthew was sitting in the hotel reception area with DC James Conway, the young policeman I'd encountered too many times already.

"Ah, Mr Matthews, we've been waiting for you to turn up."

"What's the matter?"

"I'm investigating the disappearance of Leonard White, the hotel manager. He hasn't been seen for a few days."

Matthew said: "I noticed his car down by the old harbour, when I went for a walk yesterday. It looked abandoned, and he still hasn't shown up for work."

"The last time I saw him was in the Majestic the other night," I said.

"When did you see Mr White exactly, can you remember?"

"Sure," I said. "It was at the start of the evening, before nine. He seemed fine to me then, happy and excited."

"Why do you think he was excited?"

"He said he was going to check out the competition, you know, suss out the Majestic Hotel. He was taking a professional interest."

"Did anyone else see him?"

"My companion, Angel Bright, she lives in Meadow Road."

"Ah, Ms Bright," he said. "Thank you, that'll be all for now. I'll be in touch."

After the detective left, Matthew sat down next to me.

"What are you doing in work?" I asked. "After everything, you're entitled to a few days off."

"I love my job," he said. "Better here than moping about at home."

"Fair enough," I said.

"I'm worried about Len," he said. "I was getting to know him a bit, he's a good bloke. I hope nothing's happened to him."

"I'm sure he's all right." I said. "How's your father? He looked a bit pissed-off at the do in the Majestic."

"I haven't seen him since then myself. It's not unusual for us to lose touch for long periods. Anyway, I'd better get back to work."

"I'll catch you later."

"By the way," he said. "There's some messages for you in reception."

The messages were scrawled on scraps of yellow paper and stuck on a cork noticeboard behind the reception desk. Matthew handed me three slips of the yellow squares. I read them on the way up to my room.

The first one was from my office in California, it read: *'No panic, but please call your PA when you can.'* The second message was from Ralph, it simply said: *'Your brother called – 10:45am.'* It was dated that day. The third message intrigued me, and mercifully, gave me some extra time to sort out the mess in my love life: *'Had to go away for a few days with work, see you when you when I return, Angel'.*

When I got to my room, Ramona was soaking in one of her marathon baths, so I drove over to Meadow Road to find out why Ralph had called. He was alone downstairs in the sitting room.

"She's in bed," he said. "She had a bad turn this morning, the doctor gave her even stronger painkillers. She was better afterwards, but she needed to rest. I thought I'd better let you know."

"Thanks," I said.

"You all right?" he asked.

"I think so. Do you know Len White?"

"Len White?"

"Yes, an old friend of mine, the manager of the South Beach Hotel. I told you about him the other night, remember?"

"Oh yes, why, what about him?"

"He's disappeared or done a bunk, I don't know. The police are investigating, so they must think it's serious."

"I don't know anything about all that. I did hear one

interesting thing though. It's about your other friend Pogo. You sure do know how to pick them don't you Mick."

"Go on," I said.

"Talk is he's on the take. Very ambitious sort of bloke I understand."

"Where did you hear that?"

"It was something Auntie Glenys said. Her friend in the Women's Institute is married to a retired solicitor. It seems the police have questioned him, they're investigating some big case locally It's all very hush-hush. That's all she knew, but you know how she is, she can make a drama out of boiling a kettle."

I laughed, Ralph was right. It wasn't worth taking Auntie Glenys seriously, not until you got the same information from an independent source at least.

"I've got to get back to the hotel," I said. "Maybe I'll call back tomorrow."

"Mam will be all right now," he said.

I got to the car just a few seconds too late, or too early. Walter Swift caught me as he walked past the front of the house. He placed his pale skinny body directly in my path and opened his mouth in a wide smile, showing a set of small pointed yellow teeth.

"Hello there old chap," he said enthusiastically.

"Oh, hello," I said weakly.

"Still here then? I'm off myself in a few days. I'm going back to Australia, to visit some old friends I made when I worked there as a night-club manager ten years ago. Just a flying visit you understand, I'm too busy to stay too long."

I doubted whether Walter knew how to catch a bus, let alone fly halfway around the world. It was pointless challenging him and his lies, because I remembered from the old days how that would only send him into a more complex web of fantasy that could be extremely boring.

"Sounds interesting," I said, as I sat on the wall outside my mother's house, resigned to at least ten minutes of verbal diarrhoea.

Walter sat next to me with a pleasurable sigh: "Do you

remember," he said, "when Betty Fish got murdered? It was just across the road. I know who did it," he whispered, looking up and down the road, checking for hidden cameras and microphones.

"Do you?" I said, feigning interest.

"I've worked it all out. It comes from my time with the Metropolitan Police, when I was seconded to help them solve a series of gangland murders back in the seventies. I've used the same deductive skills to solve Betty Fish's Murder. It's never been solved you know."

"I know," I nodded.

"Well, this is what happened. She had a secret lover..."

"Hold on," I said, "are you serious? Do you know how old she was?"

"The old ones are the worst, or the best if you know what I mean." He winked.

I shivered at the thought of exactly what he meant.

Walter continued: "I've still got all the old press cuttings from the time of the murder. It was definitely a lover. The mysterious visitor, the money she had stashed away. I think it was a younger man who was only after her for her money but pretended to love her. My old girl, God rest her soul, always said there was more to that murder than a simple burglary. She knew Betty very well you know, used to clean for her, every Thursday morning. She whispered the name of the man who did it from her deathbed."

"Who was it then?" I asked impatiently.

"I can't tell you that, not yet. There's still some loose ends to clear up. All in good time."

The front door opened and Ralph came out lighting a cigarette: "Are you still here Mick?" he shouted as he came up the path towards us.

"Just going," I said, "Walter's been telling me his theories about Betty Fish's death. Reckons he knows who did it."

"Oh," Ralph looked disinterested. Then he got angry, turning on Walter, who was smiling inanely in his own secret world. "I remember your older brother William. He was a fucking romancer as well, didn't know when to shut his stupid gob. You lot never change."

Walter looked stunned.

He mumbled: "Sorry boys, got to go, University Challenge is on, I never miss that."

He scurried off down the road.

I laughed: "Why didn't I think of that, he's such a boring bastard, thanks Ralph."

"Think nothing of it little bruv," he said, something of the old confident Ralph showing in his triumphant smile.

I telephoned the office in California when I got back to the hotel, but there was only so much I could sort out by remote control. I would have to return soon to attend to the growing number of projects that were coming to fruition. Perhaps in a few days time after doing what I could for my mother and seeing Linda and my daughters one more time.

I still didn't know where I stood with Angel or what to do about my relationship with Ramona.

CHAPTER 22

Over breakfast the next morning, we got talking to a couple at the next table. The man, a casually dressed young professional, sounded concerned.

"Our firm is looking for a site for a new production facility," he said, "so we're on a kind of scouting mission, having meetings with the local Development Agency and the council. Now, I'm not so sure."

"Why's that?" I asked, hoping for a quick answer. I'd planned to spend the day with Ramona. Breakfast was just the beginning.

"Have you seen the headlines?"

He handed me a copy of The Elchurch Gazette.

'Drug Death Toll Increases'

Under the headline was a story about the death of a drug addict on the Backfields Estate. I scanned the article. It seemed the police had concerns about drugs related crime on the Backfields and in other areas of the town.

A smaller article warned of impending trouble on the estate: *'Tension Mounts on the Backfields as police raids continue.'*

I handed the newspaper back. "Don't believe it," I said. "Most of the people on that estate are decent and law-abiding, just like you and me. It's sensationalism, that's all."

"I don't know," he sighed. "I'll be the mug running the factory. We've got young children. We don't want to expose them to that sort of thing."

"It's the same everywhere," I argued. "There's good areas and bad, good people and bad."

"That may be," he said, "but why should we take the risk? There's plenty of other places desperate for jobs."

"Only you can decide that," I said. "Could I have another

look."

I scanned the article again. "There, it says, '*According to a police spokesman they are in control of the situation. The small minority of criminals on the estate are being targeted.*'" I gulped. *'The man who died, Walter Swift, a man in his forties ...'*

"Are you all right Mick?" Ramona asked.

I mumbled: "Sorry. It's just something I read." I turned to the young couple: "Perhaps you've got a point. Please excuse me, there's something I have to do."

I left the hotel promising Ramona I'd see her in a couple of hours, and drove to Meadow Road. When I got there the place was deserted. I worried that something had happened to Mam.

A neighbour called out. "They've gone for a spin, her daughter-in-law came in that big car. It's a lovely day for it, isn't it?"

"Thanks," I said. I wasn't in the mood to chat.

I drove to the beach and sat on the stone wall that surrounded the disused docks. The tide was out. I stared into the deep black mud.

Could I really be thinking my brother was the murderer after all? Was he capable of such a thing? I squeezed the image of Betty Fish and her nemesis, struggling behind the window, from under the mud, and concentrated hard.

There had been something familiar about the figure who disappeared around the side of the house that day. Was Walter Swift right? Could Ralph have been Betty Fish's young lover? That I couldn't imagine. That was impossible. Wasn't it?

What about Mr Jackson – Jacko's father, how did his death fit in? Did it fit in at all? In my imagination, I even had Ralph fixing the brakes on the car in which Will and Steve had met their deaths. Ralph became an Angel of Death, looming out of the mud, his averted gaze, his vagueness, even his self-assured cockiness as a young man, became nothing but pawns on the chessboard of his evilness.

I must have sat there staring into that filthy mud for two or three hours because by the time I got back to the hotel it was almost lunchtime. By then I'd convinced myself that when I talked to my brother, he'd laugh. 'You've spent too much time in fairyland, it's addled your brain,' he'd say.

I intended to go to my room, have a shower and then get off somewhere for the afternoon with Ramona, but as I walked into reception Matthew rushed up to me.

"You've got to help me Mick."

He was distressed, his voice faltering and his eyes flaring with panic.

"It's Trev, my father," he said. "I don't know what's happening to him, he's started drinking again. I can't get any sense out of him. I remember when I was young, how he used to lose control for months at a time, it's ruined his life."

Matthew's face still showed the bruising from the beating he'd received a few days before, but worse than that, his manner had changed. The happy, confident young man had become a frightened nervous victim. Seeing Matthew like that helped me put aside my own problems for a while, I welcomed the distraction.

"It'll be all right Matthew, let's see if we can sort this out. I'll get us both a drink."

Matthew sat down nervously on a sofa in reception while I went to the bar and brought back a double brandy for him and a glass of orange juice for me. Matthew swallowed half the brandy. I sipped the juice.

"Dad called at ours early last night, pissed and pathetic. My mother threw him out. I went after him. I spent most of the evening trying to get sense out him and keep him sober. He had to work, so we walked to the Majestic, he did start to sober up, but when we got there Robbo went spare and demanded to know where he'd been. I tried to smooth things over but Robbo told me to piss off. Sorry – I'm talking too much."

"No, go on. So did you piss off?"

"Yes, I was knackered by then, I'm still sore after the other night. But later I went back, it was after midnight. Robbo laughed at me, told me he'd sent Dad home. I went to the

Tophill, but that bloody woman he lives with told me to get lost as well. I wouldn't go until she told me where Trev was, so she said he'd gone off to do some sort of special job for Robbo, and he was on the Backfields, in an empty house, near the school."

Matthew lifted his glass and downed the rest of the brandy. "Is that it?"

"When I got there I banged the door until a light came on. Dad answered, he looked terrible, and the place stank. He wouldn't let me in, said he'd tell me about it in the morning. I couldn't get any more sense out of him so went home and slept as best as I could."

"Do you want another drink?" I asked.

"No, there's no time, and I'm feeling better now."

"So did you go back this morning?"

"I've just come from there. I couldn't get an answer, but I'm sure there was somebody in. I'm worried something bad has happened. Will you help me please Mick? Dad respects you."

"Sure," I said. "Let's get over there now."

When we got to the gate of the house, we paused. It was dilapidated and dirty. The ground floor windows were boarded up, the boards rotten and broken. The front lawn was strewn with bits of old beds, sodden mattresses and rusty bicycle frames. The metal gate lay off its hinges on the overgrown concrete path. We banged on the front door but got no response.

"Let's try around the back," I suggested.

We found an alley, overgrown with privet and bramble. A rotten wooden fence protected the rear of the house. It collapsed easily when we shoved it. The back garden was even more of a mess than the front; completely covered by brambles and weeds, and decorated with rubbish. We pushed our way cautiously through the undergrowth until we reached the back door.

The windows at either side of the door were covered on the inside with dirty torn curtains. On the broken concrete path, a dustbin had fallen. It didn't surprise me to see a used syringe near the doorstep. I didn't want to alarm Matthew so pushed it aside with my foot until it disappeared into the weed covered drain inlet.

I pushed the handle of the door. It opened easily. We crept into a small kitchen, which was more disgusting than the back garden, full of dirty plates and empty packets of convenience food mashed up with take away cartons half full with mould. The place stank of urine and stale tobacco.

There was no one in the downstairs rooms but we heard something moving upstairs. We climbed the uncarpeted stairs carefully. Someone groaned in a bedroom. I pushed at the door but it was locked. We went into another bedroom and saw what looked like a heap of blankets in a corner. Matthew pulled the blankets away to reveal a groggy looking Trev, at his side an empty vodka bottle.

"Dad, Dad," he called out, "are you all right?"

"Fuck off." Trev's voice was weak and tired. "Leave me alone."

"Come on Dad, get up."

Trev struggled into a sitting position and slumped against the wall. He picked the empty bottle up and with a look of disgust threw it across the room. The bottle hit the windowpane, smashed it and flew outside where it landed with a dull thump on the overgrown lawn. I looked out of the window to see that a crowd of neighbours had gathered on the pavement outside the house. One of them, it was the old lady that I'd encountered when I'd been talking to the beat officer, saw me and shouted up.

"I've called the police. We've had enough of your sort around here."

I turned back into the room and shook my head at the state Trev was in: "What have you been up to?" I asked. "How did you get yourself into such a mess so quickly?"

"Fucking Snobby, the bastard, he set me up. Can't you see, I had to do it? I had no choice."

"What are you talking about Dad?" Matthew asked, trying to lift Trev to his feet.

"It's not my fault," he said. "I didn't start anything."

"Who's in the other room?"

"Just some junkie, leave him alone."

"Why is the door locked?"

"Snobby wants me to keep an eye on him for a while. Don't worry about him, it's his own fault. Anyone who sticks that shit up their arm deserves what they get."

"Sounds like he's in pain," I said. "Don't you have a key?"

"It's on the windowsill in the bathroom." Trev squeezed his eyes together and shook his head. "Ouch!" he said.

I retrieved the key and opened the door. Crouched in the far corner of the room was a very freaked out Len White.

"What the fuck!" I exclaimed.

Len looked up at me, his face flat and featureless. "Mick," he slurred. "Nice to see you. Fancy a smoke? I've got loads and loads."

On the floor of the room, I noticed a syringe and the remains of what I took to be heroin fixes. A dried up mess of vomit spread out from Len's position. I gagged and almost puked myself.

"How? Who? Why?"

There was the sound of wood splintering. Seconds later four uniformed police officers came charging up the stairs towards me. I put up my hands instinctively and they were cuffed together.

"But," I protested, "we only just got here, this has nothing to do with us."

"You can explain down the station."

As the four of us were brought out of the house, the neighbours cheered.

The police didn't spend too much time questioning me before they accepted my story. Pogo came to the station at my request and helped get Matthew out of there as well. They decided to keep Trev in for a little longer.

"I'm sorry for any inconvenience Mr Matthews," DC James Conway said, "but we have to be sure, in the circumstances. Actually, we've been keeping an eye on that house for some time."

"I understand," I said. "Will there be any charges?"

"It's not very likely, to be honest there's not much we can

charge anyone with. Though I'm a bit surprised at the behaviour of Mr White, hc has a responsible job. Thomas now, he's a different sort of character. He's well known to us, over the years."

"Trev's all right, he's just been unlucky that's all."

"I suppose you could say that," he said.

"When will he be released?"

"Well there are still some matters we need to discuss with him. You and his son can go now. I imagine we'll let Mr White out later after the doctor's been. I can't understand how someone of that age could do that sort of thing. You'd think he'd have learned by now."

"That's puzzling me too," I said. "I never saw Len as the sort to indulge in hard drugs like that. Perhaps I don't know him as well as I thought."

After all the excitement, I needed that shower more than ever. I dropped Matthew off outside his house, promising to keep him up to date on any information that came through from Pogo about his father.

When I got back to the hotel, Ramona was gone again. She'd left a long note. The gist of it was that she felt she was in the way, and would I give her a call when I got back to the States. I felt relieved, at least I'd be able to sift through the mud without worrying about her, and make some decisions about our future.

Len was released a few hours later and came to my room to talk. It was a dangerous time, coming down off heroin. He'd cleaned himself up, but looked drawn and tired. He dropped into an armchair.

"What happened?" I asked. "How did you get yourself into that mess?"

"I'm so fucking pissed off with myself, Mick, so fucking pissed off. That arsehole Robbo. No, arsehole is too polite a word for that low-life scum-sucking piece of shit."

"How can you blame him? I assume you stuck the needle in your own arm?"

"Like fuck I did. You know that night at the so-called party in the Majestic?"

"Yes."

"Well, he caught me snooping around the kitchen – he's a vicious bastard. He wouldn't believe me when I told him I was just taking a professional interest. He thought I was some sort of filth or something. He locked me in a storeroom and his boys gave me a good seeing to. Then later I was taken to that house, bound and gagged, where his henchmen, forced that evil crap into my body."

"Did you tell the police this?"

"No fucking chance, you can't trust those bastards either. Didn't you see all the big nobs there in the Majestic sucking up to David fucking Robinson. It's best to forget it. I just need to go cold turkey for a couple of days. Thank God you found me when you did. I heard they found some poor fucker from the Backfields dead the other night."

I knew him," I said. "Walter, he was a bit of a pratt, but I never took him to be into heroin or anything like that."

The mud stirred again, Snobby's face laughing cruelly at me through the mists of my past life. I knew, of course, that Snobby couldn't have killed Betty Fish, because he was with me at the time. Every other bad thing in my life though, was his fault.

"And that bloody solicitor friend of yours isn't so sparkling white either. Pongo, or whatever his name is. He's got his fingers in too many pies." Len stood up.

He paced up and down the room. "I'm sorry, I'm just strung out that's all. How did I let myself get into this bloody mess? All my life I've kept away from that evil stuff and now – well, just look at me."

Len shivered and clutched himself, trying to squeeze the poison out of his blood.

"What you said about Pogo then," I asked. "What did you mean?"

"Nothing, it's only bar room chat, you don't want to listen to me."

"No, I'd like to know," I insisted.

"That bastard old friend of yours, Robbo – you know what he's capable of. If he can do this to me." Len paused. "Get me a drink or a joint or something Mick. This is driving me bonkers."

"In a minute," I said. "Tell me about Pogo."

"I reckon that Robbo's got something on him. I heard that he's under investigation by the police or the government or something. There's nothing quite so bad as a bent member of the legal community."

"Nah," I protested. "Pogo Bent? Never. He's always been as straight as a poker. He's too nervous to get mixed up in anything shady."

"Well I hear that him and his cronies down the Lodge, or wherever it is they go, have got this town well and truly stitched up. I'm sorry I came back now, fucking dirty grey shitheap."

I knew then that Len was over the worse, his anger would sustain him.

CHAPTER 23

I needed to find out more about Walter Swift's death so I could get my suspicions about Ralph settled one way or the other. After I left Len, I went to Meadow Road. It had just got dark. The house was unlit and the door was locked. No one responded to my insistent knocking. I was just about to get into my car and drive off when I noticed that there were lights on in Angel's house across the road. She was back.

Angel came to the door in a bathrobe, her wet hair pulled tightly back away from her face. She was eating a sandwich.

"Mick," she said, her mouth full of bread, "I didn't expect you. You'd better come in."

She led me into the front room. There was a smartly dressed man in his fifties sitting on the sofa with a file open on his lap. The man closed the file and looked up. I'd looked into those cold eyes before. It was Angel's cousin Kenny, Betty Fish's son.

He stood up with a smile that did nothing to illuminate the darkness behind his eyes.

"I was just off," he said. "Nice to see you again Mick."

Angel looked at me anxiously after she saw him to the door.

"I didn't realise you were still mixed up with him," I said.

"He is my cousin. Neither of us has any other family left, none to speak of anyway."

"I'm glad you're back."

"I was just going to have some coffee," she said. "Do you want some?"

"Yes please."

I briefed Angel on what had been happening since I'd seen her last. I even told her about Ramona coming back and leaving again. She seemed relaxed about the whole thing, but when I told her my suspicions about my older brother, she showed more interest.

"If you don't mind, I'll make a few phone calls," she said. "I'll try and find out what's been going on around here."

After ten minutes on the phone in the other room Angel came back in.

"I'll go and get changed," she said, "then we're going to have a visitor. It's a gentleman called Charles, better known as Charlie Peace. He's another colleague of mine. He'll be here in about half an hour. Luckily, he's staying locally."

Angel changed into a dark purple tracksuit. We sat down to wait.

"What does Charlie do?" I asked.

"I haven't told you much about my work, have I?" she said. "I don't suppose it matters if I tell you a bit more, especially since Charlie's coming."

I waited.

"I work for a government department that's very close to the outfit at customs. We're not as high-profile as they are. We get the job done in a different way."

"Are you sure you're not a spy?" I asked, only half-jokingly.

"Of course," she hesitated, "but we do work undercover a lot. Most of the work is patient investigation and analysis. When we've got enough information we pass it on to the real boys in blue and they take it from there. I guess I'm a kind of researcher. Because I'm from the area they gave me this job."

"What job?"

"The job I've been doing for the past nine months or so. I'm investigating the local operation of what we suspect, or should I say, know, is an international crime organisation."

"What, like the Mafia?" I asked, open-mouthed.

"Not exactly, the truth is, it's not really organised enough to be called an organisation, but there are some very nasty characters involved. David Robinson is one of them."

"Snobby? I should have guessed."

"That's why I'm concentrating on his local operation. He's too volatile for his own or his pals' good. It's been too easy to gather a portfolio on him and in the process we've picked up information about other members of this loose crime network, from other parts of the world. We're nearly ready to make our move. The incidents around here have sped things up a bit, that's all."

"I always thought he was an evil bastard," I said.

The doorbell rang and Charlie came in. He was a tall good-looking man in his sixties with distinguished grey hair. He greeted Angel warmly.

"Good evening Mr Matthews, Angel's told me all about you, I suppose she's told you about me as well."

"Just a bit," I said.

"Good, then we won't have to start from scratch. I'm the Departmental Liaison Officer, it's my job to co-ordinate the operation we're running here and to ensure the local bobbies are kept up to speed, and co-operate with us of course."

I nodded.

He draped his dark grey overcoat over the arm of the chair.

"I think you can help us," he said, sitting down and leaning towards me conspiratorially. "By some coincidence, you seem to be involved in just about everything we're investigating: the drugs, our friend Mr Robinson, possibly the death of Walter Swift. And of course, you're involved with our dear little Angel here."

They were so cool and professional that I realised I didn't know Angel at all. I wondered what I was doing there, privy to their secret world. Charlie and Angel continued to question me for the next two or three hours. Angel did most of the talking, Charlie was content to sit silently, observing, occasionally nodding, looking intelligent.

I told them about Ralph, and Snobby, about Trev and Pogo. I told them about Betty Fish and about Jacko's father, I told them about Jimmy and my mother. I told them more about my relationship with Ramona. Afterwards I felt as if I'd been through intensive psychotherapy.

They wanted to talk to Trev, Matthew, and Len White. I telephoned to see if Matthew or Len were on duty and fortunately they both were. Angel sat with me on the drive back to the hotel while Charlie followed in his own car. As we left Angel's house, I noticed a light on in my mother's house opposite, and Linda's people carrier parked outside.

There was a lot of activity on the streets of the estate as we drove through. Here and there groups of young people were gathering, hanging about on street corners or outside someone's house. Other groups of older residents were also assembled outside their houses, pointing and chattering. There was a lot of police activity as well, and we passed some officers who were obviously having a hard time trying to settle a nasty argument between two opposing groups. We drove on towards the hotel.

"What do you think all that was about?" I asked Angel.

"We get those sort of nights on the estate sometimes," she said. "Don't worry about it, things will settle down soon."

The hotel was quiet. Matthew greeted us enthusiastically but Len was still strung out and nervous. We went into the deserted bar where Matthew poured drinks for everybody. After a few minutes I slipped away and drove to the Backfields, determined to sort things out with Ralph.

The hubbub on the estate had increased. It seemed like the whole population was on the streets. I passed by Death Row on the way to Meadow Road. A crowd of teenagers were yelling and jostling all over the road. There must have been at least a hundred people in that one group. I drove slowly as they parted reluctantly before the car.

Just as I thought I'd passed them without incident, a boy of about eleven fell across the bonnet. I knew he couldn't have been seriously hurt. But it was enough to cause the rest of the crowd to go berserk and chase after the car, throwing stones and bottles.

I pressed the accelerator and drove quickly past Death Row, taking the next left into the lower end of Meadow Road. I checked my mirror as I sped up the street. Thankfully, no one was following. I parked the car outside Mam's house behind Linda's Espace.

Further up the street, a few neighbours were babbling excitedly and making disapproving noises at a gang of young boys, who were taunting them from the opposite side of the road.

I noticed a familiar red scar, Tim, Matthew's younger brother, was in the gang. I could also see Robbie, the boy who tried to burgle his old friend's house.

The front door was open so I went straight into the living room. My two daughters were on the floor sorting through some CDs.

"Hello girls," I said. "What's going on here then?"

All the eyes in the room turned to me. There was Ralph with downcast eyes, Linda, her usual pragmatic self, clearing empty teacups, Auntie Glenys, stopped in mid-flow by my entrance and Bernard, Linda's husband, fidgeting with his glasses.

"Where's Mam?" I asked.

Ralph shook his head: "She's upstairs in bed, the doctor's on the way. She's not been too good Mick. We went for a drive, she was fine at first, but later, when we stopped for supper on the motorway, she took a turn for the worse."

We heard raised voices from the street outside, Bernard got up and locked the front door.

"Why is everyone so wound up tonight?" I asked.

"Haven't you heard Mick," Auntie Glenys said. "The police have been raiding drug dealers and criminals all day. They've been speeding up in their Black Marias, they've been knocking doors down, they've been chasing people all over the roofs even. But as usual they took it too far. One of the police cars knocked a young girl over. She was only six."

"Everyone's gone mad," Bernard said.

"Perhaps you and the girls should get out of here," I suggested to Linda. "By the look of that mob, there's no telling what will happen."

I heard a smashing sound from outside. I ran to the front door, and flung it open. The neighbours had gone and a growing mob of angry youngsters was assembling around my car. Someone had thrown something through the windscreen.

I took my mobile phone from my pocket and dialled the police. They'd do their best, but they were busy.

Someone in the crowd pointed at me and shouted: "There he is, the pig that knocked Darren over."

I ducked back inside, locked the door, and went into the living room.

"Just hold on," I said. "The police will be here soon."

More glass smashed. Bernard went into the parlour. Moments later he returned.

"The mob is getting bigger, and angrier. Someone's put a brick through the window of the front room. I think we'd better get out of here. Come on Linda, come on Jodie and Suzannah. Let's go – now!"

Ralph became animated for the first time: "You can't go out there. We'll get out the back way and make a run for it down the alleyways."

Everyone started jostling at once, grabbing coats and making for the back door.

"What about Mam?" I said. "I'll go and get her, if she can walk."

I ran upstairs with Ralph, and left Bernard and Linda to lead the girls and Glenys to safety. My mother was sitting up in bed in a confused state.

"What's going on? Is that you Jimmy? Where's the boys? It's dark."

"Come on Mam," I said. "It's us, Mick and Ralph, we've got to get out of here."

"Oh you're good boys. Where are you taking me?"

"Somewhere safe Mam," Ralph said.

We helped her off the bed and found a dressing gown on the back of the door.

"My tin," she said. "Where's my tin?"

Ralph helped her into the dressing gown while I scanned the room. Mam's biscuit tin was on the windowsill. I moved over and grabbed it. I looked out of the window at the scene in the street. The crowd had grown. I was spotted and someone threw a stone at the window. I ducked aside. The stone smashed through the glass and landed on Mam's pillows.

"Fuck, come on Ralph, hurry up."

We managed to stumble our way down the stairs. I stole a glance through the broken front room window and was horrified to see that the mob had become more daring. Several of them were edging down the path towards the front door. One of them was carrying a bottle of petrol, with a rag stuffed in the top. He lit the rag and pulled his arm back. We carried on to the back door and hobbled out to find Auntie Glenys waiting for us at the bottom of the garden.

"Come on boys, come on Lizzie," she urged.

Gladys helped us support Mam and together we scrambled down the dark back alleys. I looked back, flames were already visible through the back windows of the house. The sirens of the emergency services cut through the cool night air, and urged us on.

We caught up with the others by the school gates. They were locked, so we hurried further down School Lane. Everyone else on the estate seemed to be running in the opposite direction, towards Meadow Road where the flames and the smoke from Mam's house were growing in intensity.

We came to the house near the school, where the woman who'd complained to the beat officer lived. She was standing on her doorstep, holding a poker in her hand.

She called out: "Come on, you lot, come in out of the madness, you'll be safe here."

We stayed in the house while the rioting subsided. Mam was very weak so I called for an ambulance. Ralph went with her to the hospital. We were told she would be kept in for observation.

I telephoned the South Beach Hotel. Angel was just leaving to go home after questioning Len, Matthew, and Trev. She came to pick me up.

We got out of the car in Angel's drive, and went across the road to survey the wreckage. By then the fire service had done all they could but the house was a shell, like a gap where a tooth had been ripped out. The houses on either side were hardly damaged. There were several police and fire officers sifting through the debris. One of them was the young detective James Conway.

"Hello again," I said.

He nodded. "Can you tell me exactly what happened here?"

Conway made some notes as we talked and Angel listened intently: "That's enough for now," he said. "You can make a full statement when you've recovered, there's not much you can do here tonight."

CHAPTER 24

When we arrived at the hospital, we met Linda, Bernard, and the girls coming towards us from the ward. Linda looked surprised to see Angel but didn't comment.

"Mam is stable, but critical," Linda said. "There's nothing we can do here, so we're going back to our hotel. Ralph's got all the details."

"Thank you, I'll let you know if anything changes."

Ralph was pacing in the corridor outside the ward. He stopped and looked at me, eyes streaming with tears.

"She's going to die Mick, I know it. That bastard is going to pay for this."

"No Ralph, don't say that, she won't die – not Mam. Let the police deal with it, they'll find out who was responsible and sort it out."

"Since when have the police done the likes of us any favours? The likes of me anyway. And I already know who did it, who's behind all this – and the cops aren't going to give a toss."

"What do you mean?" I asked.

"It's that toe-rag Robinson, he's got his filthy claws into everything, including the police. Who do you think is responsible for all the drug problems in this town? All the crime?"

Angel shuffled uncomfortably at my side.

"I've been talking," he said. "Since I came back, there's still one or two people here with a brain cell – they know what's going on."

"All right Ralph, maybe there's something in what you say, but now is not the time."

"I'm off out for a fag," Ralph said. "Mam is sleeping. They've given her something."

I sat at Mam's bedside with Angel.

"What do you make of all that?" I asked her.

She shrugged. "I don't know Mick, but I'm worried Ralph is going to ruin the investigation. I think perhaps we should all get together for a briefing, before Robinson takes fright and brings the shutters down."

"When? Where?"

"As soon as possible, tomorrow afternoon, at mine. In the meantime it's best that you stay with Ralph, watch he doesn't go off. I'll get Charlie to come and talk to us all – he's a genius at that sort of thing."

After a reassuring chat with a doctor, who convinced us Mam was not going to die that night, Angel dropped me and Ralph off at the hotel.

"Will the bar still be open?" Ralph asked.

"I don't know," I said. "Let's go and look."

Len and Matthew were still awake, drinking and smoking in the bar. When Matthew saw us he slipped off his stool and came towards us.

"Thank God you're all right," he said. "We heard all about it. There's cops everywhere, they've pulled Tim in, and loads of others."

Len got us some drinks and we sat down around a table. I told them about Angel's idea of a debriefing, but didn't say too much about what its context might be. I wasn't certain what her intentions were and didn't want to break any Official Secrets' Acts.

In the morning the police came to interview me briefly and afterwards we got a cab to Meadow Road.

When we arrived I crossed the road to examine the remains of the small council house. Grey metal crowd-control barriers were stretched across the front of the plot, and across the front of the two houses at either side. Beyond the barriers investigators were turning over the still smouldering rubble, assisted by workers in fluorescent jackets and hard hats.

I couldn't bear to look at the scene for very long, it stirred up too much of that black mud that lay at the depths of my psyche. Ralph said nothing but vibrated with anger at my side.

Charlie, Angel, Matthew, and Ralph were reclining in Angel's comfortable furniture, while Len White entertained them with anecdotes about his time on the road.

Angel went to the kitchen and returned with a tray of coffee and biscuits. Len grabbed a cup and filled it to the brim.

His hands trembled as he gulped the coffee. "I'm getting there," he said. "I'll beat this shit."

We spent the next hour or two going over everything we knew about Snobby and his operation. Angel asked the questions while Charlie nodded and observed, making notes in shorthand.

Charlie stood up and stretched lazily. "We'll give you all a break for the time being," he said. "I've got to get back to my hotel and make some calls, do some serious liaising. Don't go away, will you?"

After he left, the rest of us had a chance to catch up with each other. Most of our attention was focused on the riot the night before. At one point we stood on the small lawn in front of Angel's house and looked across at the wreckage, pointing and prodding like tourists. Angel took some photographs.

"You'll appreciate these one day," she said, "when you can look back and laugh."

I glanced across at Ralph, he wasn't laughing.

We went back into the lounge for more coffee. Len and Ralph, tempted by the stillness and beauty of the late summer day went into the garden for a walk amongst the trees of the still standing apple orchard.

"Have you seen your father yet?" I asked Matthew.

"I've never seen him so riled up," he said. "The police released him without charge, yet he's so angry. He's gone off somewhere, I don't know where. He went to the Tophill and collected his dog. According to his girlfriend he didn't say much, just stamped around the house for a few minutes and then he was gone. I hope he'll be all right."

"I'm sure he will be," I said. "He used to go off with his dog when he was a boy too. I didn't realise he still kept a dog. What sort is it?"

"It's a kind of sheepdog, black and white, long-haired. He's always had a dog, this one's called Smokey."

"That's what he called the sheepdog he had years ago," I said. "I always wanted a dog like Smokey myself. I wonder where he's gone?"

"I know he's taken to spending a lot of time at the reservoir lately, he says it gives him a place to think."

"We'd best leave him alone," I said. "Give him some room to sort it out for himself, he's had a rough time of it."

Angel sat in silence next to us. Len and Ralph came in from the garden.

"This is so kind of you Angel," Len said. "It's makes a big difference to be fussed over for once, even if you do have ulterior motives."

Ralph still looked miserable.

"What's up Ralph?" I asked.

"I'm sorry, I'll be all right."

"Did you say Trev's gone to the reservoir Matthew?" Angel asked.

"Possibly, why?"

"It's just that you said he was very angry. Robinson lives near there. Do you think he's out for revenge?"

Matthew looked concerned. "Do you think we should go after him? He may do something silly."

"Perhaps we should wait for Charlie to come back to finish the statements you've made," Angel said. "It's nearly over, and then Robinson will no doubt be pulled in. We don't want to risk any foul-ups at this stage."

"But what if my dad fouls things up for you? The mood he's in at the moment, who knows." Matthew said. "There's something else," he added.

"What?"

"His girlfriend also told me that he'd taken his gun, it's a shotgun. He uses it to shoot rabbits."

"He's still doing that?" I asked.

"Maybe you're right," Angel said. "I'd better phone Charlie

to let him know where we've gone."

We went outside and waited while Angel telephoned Charlie. She joined us soon after.

"He didn't answer, so I've left a message on his mobile phone's answering service," she said, unlocking the doors of her car.

We all squeezed in and Angel drove. "God knows why all you lot are coming along," she said. "You're like a gang of small boys."

Len chuckled. "If Robbo's going to get his, then I want to be there to spit on his grave. The bastard's got it coming."

Angel shook her head and sighed.

"Do you know where Snobby lives?" I asked Angel.

She tapped her head: "It's all up here, I know where he lives. I know his ex-directory telephone number. I even know his shoe size."

"But we can't just knock his door and say: 'Excuse me, but has Trev been here with his dog and a gun,' can we?"

"You've got a point," she said.

"I know a place where Dad likes to go," Matthew said. "It's a clearing in the woods next to the reservoir, not far from one of the car parks. We could try there, I suppose."

"Worth a go," I said.

The reservoir was situated just a few miles from the Backfields Estate, but in terms of financial success the dwellings that we passed as we approached it, might have been a million miles away. Some resembled whitewashed castles hidden discretely behind tall conifers, others shouted at us from behind vast locked gates at the edge of the road. Angel pointed Snobby's house out to us, it stood louder and brasher than any other we'd passed, fronted by magnificent lawns and neatly pruned shrubbery. The car park Matthew had referred to was a few hundred yards further on.

A courting couple in the only other vehicle in the car park didn't even notice us as we tumbled out of Angel's car and set off into the woods following a vague path between the trees.

"I'm sure it's along here," Matthew whispered. "I came here with him once, but that was in winter and it looked so different."

The trees thinned out and gave way to a large clearing. At the centre of the clearing was a wooden picnic table. Trev was standing with his back to us, looming over Snobby and Pogo, who were shivering with fear on the bench.

They called out, pleading for us to stop the lunatic. Trev swung around, bringing the shotgun into view.

I edged forward, the others moving cautiously beside me.

Len shouted out hysterically: "Go Trev, go, get the bastard."

Trev's dog, Smokey barked and leapt about excitedly.

"Stay back," Trev screamed.

We all stopped. The dog went for Snobby, snarling and nipping at his legs. Trev tried to shoo him away with his foot.

Without warning, Ralph took the opportunity of Trev's lapse in concentration, bounded forward, and with a few enormous strides threw himself at Trev, wrapping his arms around his legs. Trev fell backwards. The two chambers of the gun discharged, the contents of their cartridges sent high over the trees with a loud bang. Snobby stood up grinning. Pogo was stuck to the bench, still quaking with fear.

"Thank God for that," I said to the others. "That bastard isn't worth swinging for."

Ralph disentangled himself from a thrashing Trev and propelled himself over the bench, his hands outstretched reaching for Snobby's throat.

"He's mine," he screamed. "Leave him to me, I've waited a long time."

Snobby dodged to the side. Ralph's flying body caught him on the shoulder. The two of them fell to the ground in a tangle of limbs. Snobby quickly regained his feet and with a frightened backward glance crashed into the trees at the other end of the clearing. Ralph got to his feet, and chased after him.

Afraid of what Ralph would do if he caught up with Snobby, I followed, fighting Smokey off as I ran through the clearing. By the time I hit the undergrowth between the trees, I'd lost sight of them.

I pushed through the woods, pausing every few seconds,

hoping to hear the sounds of fighting or of two men running. I heard water. The trees thinned until I arrived at a grassy bank between the woods and the reservoir.

To my right, stretching across the reservoir was a concrete embankment that sloped sharply down towards me. Water flowed across the weir in a thin sheet over the concrete to the shallows below. At the top of the embankment Snobby and Ralph were struggling, and yelling at each other.

I struggled up the damp grass and took a tentative step onto the ledge. The water to my right was calm and deep, and flowed over the concrete to a depth of about two inches.

I made slow progress. Snobby and Ralph continued to struggle and scream at each other. A few yards from where they were, the concrete had given way and left a gap of a few feet. I paused.

"Stop it you two," I shouted. "Leave it."

Ralph distracted by the sound of my voice, loosened his grip on Snobby. Snobby took advantage and yanked free. He turned to face Ralph, panting for breath.

"What's got into you Ralph?" I shouted. "Let the authorities deal with him."

"What do you know Mick?" Ralph glanced at me before fixing on his target. His shoulders tensed, he was ready to attack again.

Snobby cupped his hands to his mouth and shouted: "Call this maniac off. He doesn't know what he's dealing with."

Ralph shouted. "You've screwed my life up for too long. You killed my baby. You told Marie I'd had an affair, we were going to get married, that day, when we argued, it was your fault."

Snobby sneered: "An affair? What did you expect me to do? You were fucking my mother, my fucking mother! I saw you."

"She wanted it as much as I did. Can you blame her with you as a son and that bastard wife-beater of a husband she had? Just like you, an evil little shit."

"And my mother wasn't the only married woman you shagged, you always had a thing about older women, didn't you Ralph? What's the matter, didn't you get enough milk from your own mother's sagging tits?"

"Shut your filthy mouth up. You do nothing but fuck people's lives up."

"Me? Fuck people's lives up. I had you sussed out when I was still in nappies. You liked them even older, old enough to be your granny – fucking pervert."

Ralph lunged, lost his foothold and slipped. The momentum carried him forward and he crashed into Snobby causing them both to fall, arms and legs flailing, to the concrete bottomed shallows below. Snobby banged his head and lay motionless. Ralph rolled around groaning before passing out.

I stayed with Ralph until a helicopter arrived to take him to hospital. He was still unconscious but was breathing regularly, as far as I could tell. There was nothing anyone could do for Snobby.

From that moment the world, or at least my world, seemed a much brighter place. After the helicopter lifted Snobby's body and my unconscious brother away, I made my way back to the grass bank where the others, who had finally caught up, were waiting.

They questioned me eagerly. When I told them about Snobby, Len and Trev clapped. Matthew stared open-mouthed. Angel examined me closely.

"Are you sure you're not hurt?" she said.

"Yes, I'm good. What happened to Pogo?"

"Little prick fucked off," Trev said. "But not until I scared the shit out of him, he couldn't stop talking. I felt sorry for him in the end. Snobby had him by the balls."

"How do you mean?" I asked.

Angel explained: "When Pogo was a newly qualified solicitor, Snobby, who was only a small time gangster then, got him involved in some dubious property deals. Snobby ran a protection racket locally, not big money at first, but when the victims didn't pay, he extorted deeds out of them. Pogo acted as Snobby's legal adviser. Since then Snobby's had him in his pocket."

CHAPTER 25

The police and the fire service had finished with the ruins of the house; the builders would be arriving later to begin the task of removing the rubble. The rain-soaked ashes of my childhood beckoned me in. I dodged the barriers, picked my way cautiously over the debris, and stepped into the black mud.

The charred remains of the materials that make a life lay piled up around me. Here, the contents of the kitchen, a twisted stainless steel sink, the broken door of the gas cooker, saucepans without handles, cupboard hinges without doors. There, the living room, springs from a sofa, a burnt wisp of carpet, fragments of glass from a picture frame. The bedrooms and the bathroom huddled in similar piles, all thoroughly sorted and sifted for evidence.

Near the rear of the gap was a mountain of material that I didn't recognise; it appeared to have suffered less damage than the other heaps. I poked at the mound, stacked up like the earth from an open grave. It was the contents of the attic.

I found a heavy wooden box that I'd stashed up there before I left for London the first time. In the box a collection of photographs, untouched by the flames. I saw myself with Will and Steve on a sunny day in a park. That was the day, I thought, when we were out of our heads on acid, the picture taken with my cheap camera by a passing schoolgirl.

I smiled at a snapshot of Angel as a teenager, smiling herself at the camera, her eyes showing, even then, the strength tinged with sadness she still possessed.

I put the box down and tugged at a small bundle of black, shrivelled by the fire. It came apart in my hands and I recognised the fibres of what had once been my favourite jacket. That's where it went. I recalled my mother's spring-cleaning frenzy when I thought it had been lost forever.

A small bundle fell from the black mass, disintegrating as it tumbled down the pile. As it split apart, a treasure emerged, the letters I'd hidden away in my pocket, the letters I'd stolen from the chaos in Jacko's shed. I grabbed my prize eagerly and scrambled out of the devastation.

What had happened to Jacko? Didn't someone tell me that he died young, strangled by the icy fingers of alcoholism? What about his mother? What route through the maya of life did she take after the death of her husband? Still young and attractive then, I guessed she couldn't have become more miserable.

I shuffled the envelopes carefully, though damp and dirty with soot, they looked salvageable. The faded handwriting on the outside of the envelopes still said the same one word – *Elizabeth*. Why were they hidden in Jacko's shed? Who was Elizabeth? Betty Fish perhaps?

I sat in the bay window with Angel, looked out and down at the memory of my family home, and opened the letters carefully. A lorry deposited an empty skip on the other side of the road. We read the letters chronologically from the stack, bottom to top. The first letter consisted of a single sheet of paper torn from a school exercise book. It had just four words written on it in block capitals with an untidy scrawl: *'I KNOW YOU'R GAME'.*

I put the paper back into its envelope and opened the next one, and then all the others, ten in all. The second letter read:

'BRING TWENTY POUNDS TOO THE SCOOL GETES AT SEVN O CLOK OR I WIL TELL THE TAX ABOUT THE MONEY YOUV GOT HIDEN.'

The rest of the letters continued in the same way with the amount rising a little each time. The tenth and last letter demanded the sum of: *'ONE HYNDRUD POUNDS'.*

"Looks like someone was being blackmailed," I said.

"I don't know," Angel said. "It looks like a childish prank to me."

"Then why were they in Jacko's shed?"

"It's such a long time ago," she said. "We'll never find out."

"Perhaps Trev will know something about Jacko's mother; he's lived on the estate all his life. Let's go and ask him."

"I'm tired, after everything. Can't it wait?"

"Oh come on, strike while the iron's hot. How about we just go to the Carpenter's, he might be there, if not, he might be on the Tophill."

Trev was in the Carpenter's. He seemed relaxed and happy.

"Jacko? I remember, his mother lives in Meadow Road, not far from you Angel, in the private houses on your side of the street, it's not far from here either, come to think of it. It's a big white house, next to where Good Stores used to be. She married an Italian, Florini. I think?"

We left Trev with a fresh pint and walked from the pub to the house. We rang the doorbell but got no answer, so we made our way around the side of the house and into the back garden. An old man and a woman of around sixty were sitting around a plastic patio table sipping coffee. The woman was still beautiful but with a careworn look.

"Excuse me," I said, as we approached them.

They looked at us suspiciously.

"We're not selling anything," I reassured them. "It's Mr and Mrs Florini, isn't it?"

"Don't I know you?" Mrs Florini's brow furrowed.

"It's Mick Matthews, my mother lives ... used to live, just up the road. I was a friend of your son's, a long time ago."

"I remember, you've been away."

The old man stood up, shielding his wife protectively. "What can we do for you Mr Matthews?"

"Stop it Tony," his wife said. "Go and make some fresh coffee, this man has had a very traumatic time. It was his mother's house that burned down."

"Oh, I see, please accept my apologies Mr and Mrs Matthews."

Angel smiled at his mistake.

We sat down in green plastic chairs. "Do you remember, your son, he had a puppy, and it died, choked on a bone?"

She winced and nodded.

"Well, I found something, in the shed afterwards, it's a mystery to us and we thought you could help."

She shrugged.

Angel reached into her handbag and produced the bundle of letters. She dropped them on the table. Mrs Florini picked up one of the envelopes and a pair of reading glasses and peered at them. Her face went white and she dropped them back onto the table as if they'd burnt her fingers.

"How did you find out?" she asked, ashen-faced.

"Take it easy," I said. "Are you all right?"

She composed herself. "I found them in the shed, it was the day before he died. I put them back exactly where I found them, he was very fussy about his things, and I didn't want to risk his temper, he was in a foul mood that day. I realised what they were after he died but by then they were gone. I thought they'd been thrown away, after..."

"Hang on," I said. "What did you think they were?"

"Well, obviously, he was blackmailing that poor woman, the one who got murdered, her name was Elizabeth. He must have killed her and taken the letters back. When he was found dead, I was glad. Justice had been done."

"Got into a fight, didn't he?"

"That's what they said at the time, but I don't know..."

"What do you mean?"

"Sorry, I've said too much. I'm sorry..."

I stood up angrily. "No, come on, this is important."

She gulped. "I think it was Ralph, your brother. We were having an affair, he said he loved me, couldn't bear to see me hurt by..."

I sat down, shocked.

Her husband returned with the coffee.

"I'm sorry," she said. "I've got a headache. I need to lie down. These people won't be wanting coffee after all."

"What's going on?" he said. "What have you said to her?

He stood close to his wife, guarding her.

I retrieved the letters from the table and we left.

We paced around Angel's house, occasionally stopping to

warm ourselves by the open log fire in the hearth of the living room. Neither of us knew what to do next.

"I still don't get it," I said. "Ralph is not a killer, he gets angry yes, but he isn't capable of that."

"You saw him with Snobby," she said.

"That was different, he was trying to catch him, not kill him."

"I'm sorry Mick." Angel put her arms on my shoulders and looked me in the eyes. "I think Mrs Florini is right – there's other evidence, things you don't know, things you can never know."

"Why Angel?"

She let her hands drop and turned away. "It's my job Mick, I can't even tell you."

"That's crap," I said, "and you know it. And what about the letters anyway?"

"It could only have been Mr Jackson, he used to do a bit of gardening for her, and general handyman stuff sometimes. I think he found out she had a stash of money hidden away. There must have been a struggle."

"So, that's it then?"

I felt powerless. I needed to keep strong for Mam and for Ralph. I didn't have any energy left to fight.

Angel picked the letters up from the coffee table. She walked over to the fire and threw them in.

"It's for the best," she said.

I sighed and walked into the back room, the room where Betty Fish had met her death in the bright, sunny days of my childhood. Angel joined me and we stood side by side looking out of the window, over the lawn and at the orchard, where the apples were just ripening on the trees.

I noticed some movement. I leant closer to the window and tapped it with my knuckles. A gang of four young teenage boys broke cover from the trees and legged it towards the wall at the bottom of the garden.

I brooded the rest of the day away and went to bed early.

I woke later than usual to the smell of freshly-brewed coffee.

Angel was sitting at the kitchen table reading a newspaper. She stood up and kissed me on the cheek.

"Sit down," she said. "I'll get you a cup. Do you want any toast?"

"No thanks. I have to get going soon."

We sipped the coffee. Angel stared at me absently.

"What's up?" I asked. "Why are you looking at me like that?"

She shook her head. "Oh, I don't know, just thinking you know, about how things could have been."

"You mean us?"

"I guess so, but there you are, you can't go back."

"You're right," I said, "but maybe we can go forward. What do you think?"

Angel sighed. "It's all so complicated Mick – you've got your life over there, and we're not so young, and..."

"And what?"

"Nothing."

"There's always a way," I said.

"Perhaps," she said. "But now is not the time. I hope it goes well in the hospital. I'll pop in later this morning."

I stood up and kissed her on the cheek. It was soft and sensuous. I wanted to wrap my arms around her and get lost in her warmth.

"See you later," I said.

Ralph was still improving. He was sitting up sipping a cup of insipid-looking tea when I arrived. He didn't look happy. I sat in the chair next to his bed.

"Have you seen Mam today?" he asked, his voice barely audible.

"Not yet," I said, looking at him closely to see if I could detect anything of the murderer in him.

Ralph nodded and sipped.

"Are you all right?" I asked.

He shrugged. "Got to get on with it," he croaked.

"Have they told you anything new?"

"Not really. They don't tell you much. There's some internal damage, they think it will heal on its own."

"Yeah, it was quite a fall you had. You're doing well considering. Snobby wasn't so lucky."

"Good riddance, piece of scum he was."

"I know, but I still don't get what he did to you."

"It doesn't matter."

"I suppose not, now that he's gone."

"One down," Ralph said quietly.

"What do you mean?"

Ralph shook himself. "Ah, you know, one less turd of evil shit in the world – that's all."

"I'd better go and see Mam," I said.

Ralph nodded and laid his head on the pillow. I took the cup from his hand and put it on the bedside cabinet.

Mam was lying down with more tubes and wires poking in and out of her than Ralph had. She turned her head towards me and smiled when I went in.

"You came," she said weakly.

I kissed her forehead and sat on the edge of the bed, taking her free hand in mine.

"I'm so glad you're here Mick, it's been lovely having you around – despite all this."

"Yes Mam," I said, holding back the tears.

"How's the house, all gone I expect?"

"No need to worry about that now. Just concentrate on getting better.

"Where's Ralph?" she asked.

"He's fine, don't worry, he's just laid up for a day or two."

Her eyes opened in alarm. "Laid up, is he all right?"

"Yes, he is, he had a bit of a fall, that's all, hurt his back."

Mam's eyelids closed. "He's a good boy." Her eyes snapped open again. "He needs looking after. Promise me you'll look after him for me. I know he's older, but he's fragile. You're strong. You've always looked after yourself.

"Of course I will, don't worry."

She fell asleep.

I sat with Mam for a while, thinking about Ralph. I'd

always thought of him as strong and capable, not as a mixed up murderer. He'd always had a different bond with Mam than I had. If I'd been the sort of child who cared about such things I would have been traumatised by such favouritism. Maybe I had been?

Mam shifted and moaned a little in her sleep. It was obvious that she was drifting towards her end. What did all the rest of it matter?

I went outside for a smoke, delaying the moment when I'd have to tell Ralph just how ill Mam was. Angel was walking towards the hospital entrance from the direction of the car park. Walking a pace behind her, his face stuck to a mobile phone, was her cousin Kenny.

Angel waved as she approached me. Kenny stopped on the pavement and continued his conversation.

"Hi Mick," she said.

"What's he doing here?" I asked. "I don't want him in there."

"No, no," she said, "he's just giving me a lift. Car problems."

"He gives me the creeps," I said." I don't know why you bother with him."

"He is my cousin."

I grunted. It was none of my business, but if I was going to get involved with Angel again, the presence of that creature was a factor I had to consider.

"How are they?" Angel asked.

Kenny finished his phone call and approached us.

"Mick," he nodded.

I nodded back.

"Sorry Angel," he said. "I've got to go and sort something out. It shouldn't take long. Let me know when you're ready."

We went into the hospital.

"Ralph is good," I said, "if a bit down in the dumps, but I don't know how to deal with him, after what you told me."

"Best not to say anything," she said. "It's ancient history, sometimes it's better to let things lie. I expect he'll be going back to Canada when all this is over."

"I'll have to think about it."

Mam was still asleep, she looked peaceful enough.

Ralph was lying down, staring at the wall.

"How's Mam?" he asked, when he saw us.

"She's resting," I said. "She's fine, asking about you. I didn't tell her much, just that you'd had a fall, but were OK."

"Good."

Despite our efforts to make conversation, Ralph was morose and uncommunicative.

"Um," I said, "Sorry, I've got some calls to make – see how things are going back in the States. I'll come back later."

Ralph grunted. He looked defeated.

"I'll drop you off home Angel, no need to bother your cousin."

Angel shook her head. "It's all right. I think I'll stay with Ralph for a bit, maybe see Mam when she wakes up."

Fair enough. Perhaps she could get some life out of him.

There was a large black car with tinted windows parked opposite mine. It reminded me of the car Charles Peace had driven up in. I drove past it on my way out of the car park. The window was lowered. Kenny was sitting in the driver's seat, mobile phone clamped against his face again. I felt an involuntary shiver as I drove on to the hotel.

Matthew and Len were sitting in reception, smoking and drinking beer.

"Bit early for that," I said.

"Mick." Matthew stood up. "How's your mother? And your brother?"

"All right," I said. "Considering."

"My dad's been arrested, because of the gun. I hope he doesn't get charged."

"Me too," I said. The truth was, I didn't really care. If some idiot ran around brandishing a shotgun they deserved everything they got – even if it was Trev.

I sat down.

"Looks like Pogo is going to wriggle out of it," Len said.

"Typical," Matthew said. "It's who you know."

"And what you know about them," Len added. "What was it all about?" he asked. "All those cops and men in suits. It's like one of your Hollywood movies."

"I don't think we'll ever know the whole story."

I needed to rest and think.

Everything was good back in LA, better than good, it was getting boring. I chuckled to myself, boring in LA?

The phone rang.

"It's me."

"Hi Angel."

"I'm still in the hospital. It's Ralph. Sorry Mick, you'd better get back here."

"What's happened?"

"I'm not sure. I was with Mam, she was still sleeping. When I got back to Ralph's ward, they were rushing him to the operating theatre."

"On my way."

I parked in the same car park I'd left less than an hour earlier. At least creepy Kenny was gone. I hurried through the corridors to the ward. Ralph's bed was empty. I went back into the corridor. Angel was coming towards me.

"He's still in theatre," she said.

"Do you know why?"

"Something about his spleen, it may have ruptured or something, they weren't expecting it."

Ralph died. That sad, defeated look on his face as he slumped on the bed was all I could remember of him, the rest was a painful blur. I sat with Angel on a bench outside the hospital for an hour. Numbness began to replace the pain, but the blur remained. What would I say to Mam?

Kenny came to pick Angel up. It didn't seem important.

Angel hugged me as she stood up to leave. "Are you sure? I can stay if you like."

"No, it's better you go now, we can catch up later."

Back at her bedside, it seemed to me that Mam was fading quickly. Every breath released a little more of her spirit. Her eyes opened slowly and scanned the ceiling before resting on mine.

"Mick?"

I squeezed her hand.

"I want everything to be right, before I go," she said, each word draining too much of the little energy she had left. "I want ... you ... make sure ... Ralph ... looked after. Papers ... where are my papers. My tin."

She raised her head an inch before it dropped back onto the pillows.

"It's all right Mam, it's safe, and the papers are safe."

She sighed. Her eyes closed. She was dying. I stopped myself thinking about what would come next. I didn't want to wish her life away.

Mam woke up mumbling. I had to appear cheerful for her. I had to offer her comfort until her dying breath. I had to bear the unbearable sadness that filled me to the skin.

"The tin," she said.

"It's all right Mam," I said. "It's all safe.

Mam's eyes closed, she was smiling and mumbling, not surprising considering the amount of opiates in her blood.

"Ah Jimmy," she sighed. "He was a beautiful baby."

Her eyes opened, she stared dreamily into the distance.

"Ssh," I said, "it's all right, everything is all right."

"If only you'd stayed Jimmy, we could ..."

She fell asleep.

A doctor came in and took me aside.

"You're going to have to prepare yourself," she said. "Is there anyone else, any other close relatives?"

I thought of Ralph and shook my head.

"No one?"

"Well, yes, of course," I said, thinking about Linda and the girls. I didn't want them to see their grandmother dying, but it wasn't my call.

The doctor nodded. "I'll leave it to you."

I phoned Linda, who drove straight to the hospital with Jodie and Suzannah. Mam opened her eyes once more, giving her granddaughters a chance to say goodbye, if only with their presence.

Afterwards the twins sat silently in the back of Linda's car. I stood with Linda in the car park, not knowing what to do next.

"You should come with us Mick," Linda said. "You shouldn't be on your own now."

"I don't know."

"I'm glad you called us Mick, it was the right thing to do."

I nodded. "Yes," I said.

"How was she, before..."

"Yes, she was, you know, ready for it."

"Did she say anything?"

"Not really, though she was rambling about Jimmy and Ralph."

"Ah," Linda said.

"What?"

"I don't suppose it matters now."

"What?"

"It was obvious to me. At first I thought you knew. Ralph was Jimmy's son."

I shook my head. "That doesn't make sense. Jimmy was gay."

"Of course," she said, "but when they first met during the war, he didn't know what he was, it was the times, it was like that then. She met your father soon after, when he was demobbed."

"How do you know all this?" I asked.

"Mam had to talk to someone. Jimmy left for London before the end of the war. He didn't know she was pregnant, not until he came back all those years later and he saw Ralph."

I shook my head. "Why didn't she tell us?"

"She told Ralph. Well he found out, he heard them talking. It did something to him. He changed after that, didn't want anyone else to know. I suppose it was some sort of identity crisis, but it switched something off – or on, in his mind. And that horrible man didn't help."

"What man?"

"Snobby, whatever he was called. He found out, years ago,

got it out of Ralph when he was drunk, used what he knew to try to control him, crippled his confidence, ruined his relationships."

"Mam told you all this?"

"Most of it. Ralph needed someone to talk to sometimes."

"Poor Ralph."

I looked at Linda then, with a new admiration, I was beginning to understand her at last. I wondered how things would have turned out if I hadn't run away to America twenty years earlier. Linda was one of the good guys, I did love her, in a way, but the feelings I had for Angel were in a different class.

"Thank you," I said, kissing Linda on the cheek, "for being there for them."

I let Angel deal with all the funeral arrangements. It wasn't too bad. On the day, it was just something to be endured. The weeks passed. Everything ticked away as usual in California. Angel took some time off work and we just hung around the house waiting for the formalities to finish.

As Len had said, Pogo carried on with his business just as before. Trev was released with a caution, but I couldn't face seeing him, or anyone else. I just wanted to get out of the Backfields for the last time.

The house phone rang. Angel picked the handset up.

"Hello."

"Yes."

"OK."

"All right."

"Will do."

"I suppose that's that then."

"Good luck."

"That was Kenny," she said, as she put the phone down. "He's got a job in Eastern Europe somewhere, he's already on his way there."

"Good," I said.

"I need a change too, I've been thinking about resigning."

"Oh."

"What about you Mick? This can't go on, all this moping."

"You're right," I sighed.

"And what about us?" she asked. "We've never really talked about it."

I looked across at her. She was sitting on the edge of the armchair fiddling with her hands. She was all I had, all I wanted. Perhaps this could be our chance.

"Come to LA with me," I said "Sell up, we can start again. Someone with your talents and experience can go a long way over there – if that's what you want. You wouldn't have to do anything if you didn't want to. Yes, the more I think about it, the better it sounds. What do you think?"

Angel shook her head, but she was smiling.

"I love you Angel. We could even get married, if you want."

She laughed. "Steady on Mick, we've only just met."

We stood up and embraced. I was sobbing.

"It will be all right Mick. I will come with you, but I won't sell up. Maybe I'll rent the house out. You never know, I'm trained to have an escape route."

I laughed through the sobs.

A month later a beautiful sunset welcomed us to our new life in Los Angeles.

2013

I'd become so engrossed with that past version of me that it took a moment to remember I was a sixty-three year old man hiding in a hotel in a town I'd escaped from decades earlier.

There was nothing left for me there, but there wasn't much in LA either. Oh, why was I so miserable? I was lucky, wasn't I? I was just a boy from the Backfields who'd spent most of his life living the dream in Hollywood, everyone else's dream anyway, but my nightmare. The place was a shallow artificial lagoon, surrounded by sharks. It wasn't a paradise – it was purgatory.

Who was I? Where did I belong? Could the allegations in the emails be true? Were Ralph and Mam murdered? How was Angel involved? Why had she really left me so suddenly five years earlier?

I was exhausted, both physically and emotionally. Reading those manuscripts had exhumed nothing but grief and confusion, and it was all swirling around in my mind, overwhelming me.

It was around 5am. I was knackered. I lay face down on the bed, my head buried in the pillows, hoping I could ignore the demons long enough to fall asleep.

BOOK 3
2013

CHAPTER 26

I woke at eight disorientated and still knackered, the room littered with loose sheets of paper, each one imprinted with a snippet from my life. I took a cool shower and went down for breakfast.

I managed half a slice of toast and jam. A young man came to my table with a jug of fresh coffee. He reminded me of Matthew. What had become of him, I wondered? The waiter produced a clean cup and saucer from somewhere and poured the coffee into it.

"Give me a wave if you want any more," he said.

"Thanks."

"And if there's anything else I can help with let me know."

"Actually," I said, "there is something. Matthew Thomas, does he still work here?"

"Yes of course, he's the hotel manager."

That was good news, Matthew was a decent young man, not so young by then of course, he'd be approaching solid middle age, twenty years is a long time in a life,.

I wandered into reception. Matthew was behind the desk, dressed in a grey suit, looking very much the manager of a large modern hotel. He looked up from the computer screen as I approached.

"Good morning sir," he said, with a polite smile.

"Hi Matthew."

His smile widened. He came around to the front of the desk

and hugged me.

"It's so good to see you."

I was taken aback by his warm welcome. "You too," I said.

"I don't suppose you fancy a coffee and a chat?" he asked.

"I've had coffee," I hesitated, seeing his disappointment, "but I am hungry, maybe we can talk over breakfast?"

"Yes, that would be great."

I took a step towards the dining room.

"No, not here, I know somewhere far better," he whispered.

I laughed. "Aren't you supposed to be working?"

"No, I've got the morning off, I was just sorting something out, it's all done now."

"That's dedication to the job."

"Not really, it's just something that had to be done, it will make my life easier later."

"Fair enough."

"Do you mind walking?" he asked.

"It's good to walk. Where are we going?"

"There's a café in the visitor centre further along the South Beach. They do a good breakfast, all the usuals."

"Do they do beans on toast?" I asked. "That's what I fancy right now, maybe some hash browns."

"Ha – classic, of course they do."

We walked along the cycle path that ran between the road and the beach. It was already occupied by a stream of cyclists and dog walkers.

"It's not far," Matthew said, "no more than a 20 minute stroll."

"It's nice," I said. "Not like when me and your dad were knocking about down here, all rust and sewage then. How is old Trev by the way?"

"Ah well, that's what I wanted to talk to you about, he's not been himself, always going on about the old days, talks about you a lot."

"Sorry to hear that, what do you think it is?"

"I'm not sure, it's like he's thinking too much, and remembering, regretting."

"What's he been saying about me?"

"It's nothing I'm sure, just his age I expect, he's not thinking straight."

"What do you mean?"

"Well, he cries a lot. I often catch him when he thinks I'm not looking. When I saw you, I thought…"

He wiped his eyes with his sleeve.

I patted his shoulder awkwardly.

Matthew continued. "You know, because he talks about you a lot, it might do him good if you were to talk to him."

"Of course," I said. "Where is he now?"

"He's got a little flat on the Backfields, he's on his own there, it's not brilliant but he wants to stay independent."

"Will he be in now?"

"Yes, he doesn't get out much, a bit of shopping, and the surgery, and the Carpenters once a week or so."

"Bugger the beans on toast, let's go and see Trev now."

Matthew smiled. "Thank you Mick. I'll get my car. You can wait here if you like, save the walk."

"I don't mind the walk, but I think I will wait."

"All right," he said. "I won't be long."

"No, take your time. I'll go and sit on the rocks over there and watch the sea. It's a long time since I've done that here."

Alone on the rocks I stared out at the brown water of the estuary, thinking of the secrets beneath its gently lapping surface. When was it? Fifty years earlier, a couple of teenagers had dug in that wet sand for worms. I winced as I remembered how we used to thread their squishy bodies onto barbed hooks, how we used to toss them at the end of our traces through the surface of the watery veil that hid those murky worlds.

Trev was the king at that sort of thing; he always knew the best place to dig worms, and the luckiest place to cast them into the water, wriggling for their doomed lives.

I clambered over the slippery rocks and stood on the thin strip of muddy sand between the water and the embankment. I imagined myself at thirteen, tripping along those shores, bunking off school, smoking cheap cigarettes, looking for something for nothing.

I came to realise of course that nothing's for nothing, but it was too late for all that. I was just an old man revisiting his childhood haunts; my life was done, defined and packaged, a story of naivety until the end. I'd been a stupid bastard all my life, nothing was going to change that.

I kicked at a lump of seaweed, it was like a discarded mermaid wig, splayed on the sand. A small crab, no bigger than a dime scurried from underneath towards the water. With one step I could crush that creature, extinguish what scrap of life it had.

I sighed. Was that all I was, a tiny helpless speck of consciousness, living only at the whim of some unseen, uncaring entity?

I began to regret my decision to return once again to The Backfields. I should have left things as they were. I was doing all right, finally. I was as busy as I'd ever been and had a new girlfriend. I regretted opening those emails, I could just as easily have dumped them in my spam folder, and then things would have carried on very nicely.

The internet was full of trolls and tossers, why had I let that particular creep infect me with its stench? Why should I care about the death of an old woman fifty years in the past? Christ, how many billions of other human beings had come into and gone out of existence since then? And not many of them with an ending as easy and as quick as old Betty Fish.

I'd had enough. I'd see Trev, be polite, respectful, no doubt we'd reminisce a bit, then I'd slink back to my lovely house in LA and carry on where I left off with the beautiful Helene, maybe pay a visit to Linda and the girls in London before I flew back.

What was the matter with me? I was thinking too much, forgetting about Angel's treachery, and about Mam and Ralph. I owed it to them, or at least I owed it to that part of me that was created by them. Ah fuck! I was confused.

I heard the honk of a car horn and clambered back over the rocks to the roadside. Matthew was sitting at the wheel of a smart family car. He swept aside the detritus from the front seat as I opened the door.

"Excuse the mess," he said, "kids."

"Oh, how many?"

"A boy and a girl," he said. "Emily is twelve and Arthur is fourteen. Great kids, both of them."

"Must be nice to see them grow up," I said. "I didn't have that chance with my two girls."

"Sorry," he said. "Yes it is nice."

"It's my fault. Chasing rainbows to the Land of Oz."

"Are you still in Hollywood?" he asked.

"Yes, for my sins."

He laughed. "Still, it's going well. Isn't it?"

"Yeah yeah," I said. "It's all good."

"Are you back in Elchurch to see family?"

"There's no one left for me here now. No, it's not that."

"OK," he said.

Ten minutes later we arrived on The Backfields Estate. Matthew stopped the car outside the same building I'd hidden in the night before.

"It doesn't look much," he said, "but Dad's flat is cosy enough. You'd better wait here. I'll go and warn him, he might be in his underwear or something."

I laughed. "Probably a good idea then."

Matthew opened the door of the block and went in. I stared out of the car window over the field, still characterless, just a patch of damp green and brown with no life on its surface.

The door of the building opened and Matthew came out with a young girl, it looked like the same girl I'd seen the night before. She went back inside and Matthew came back to the car.

"He's not there," he said, as he got in. "Medina, that's the girl I was talking to, who also happens to be Arthur's girlfriend, don't ask. Anyway, Medina said he went out earlier mumbling about blackberries."

"Blackberries?"

"Oh, he's always mumbling about something, he's probably just popped to the shop. We can wait here, but he takes his time sometimes, goes for walks around the estate. Best if I drive round a bit, the shops first, if you don't mind."

"Of course not."

Trev was not in any of the shops on the main road so we drove back into the estate, turning left into Meadow Road before the Carpenters.

"He might be in there," I said.

"No, he doesn't do that anymore, it would kill him, just a couple of halves, once a week, he's happy with that."

We were passing Mam's old house and Angel's opposite.

"Must be strange for you," Matthew said, "after all this time – ah look, there's that woman, Angela is it? Do you want to say hello?"

I panicked. "No, drive on, don't stop."

"All right," he said.

I shrank in my seat and peered out as we passed. Angel was walking down the street towards her house loaded with shopping bags, every inch the suburban housewife.

We found Trev, sitting on a bench at the top of Meadow Road, slumped forwards, staring at his feet. Matthew stopped the car a few yards along the road.

"It might be better if I leave you to it," Matthew said.

"Good idea," I said. "I'll sneak up on him, give him a surprise."

Matthew laughed. "Good luck with that."

As I got out of the car he handed me a business card. "All my details are on there, when you're ready."

"Thanks. And, do me a favour, don't tell anyone you've seen me, please."

"Sure," he said.

Matthew drove away. Trev was still staring at his feet. I sat next to him on the bench.

"Never imagined we'd be doing this," I said. "A pair of old gits sitting on the old codgers' bench."

Trev sat up straight and looked at me. "Mick – fuck me!"

"I'd rather not."

We both laughed and hugged awkwardly, neither of us knowing whether to stand up or keep sitting.

"You're looking good Mick. What are you doing here?"

"Matthew dropped me off. I'm staying at his hotel."

"Oh!" he didn't seem satisfied.

"You mean, what am I doing in Elchurch?"

"Aye," Trev sighed. He had become an old man in the last twenty years, a proper old man. He looked tired and worn out. There wasn't much of that fair-haired hero left.

"It's complicated," I said, "might take a while. We could go for a pint," I remembered what Matthew had said about Trev and drinking, "or a coffee, or something?"

"We could go to the community hall," he said. "It's only round the corner, it'll be quiet now, all the old biddies are at home making lunch. We can get a cuppa there."

The community centre was a small red-brick building, the size of a detached bungalow, blue gloss painted frames around the large windows.

"It's closed," I said.

"I've got a key. I'm on the committee."

"They gave you a key?"

"Aye," he said. "I thought it was funny too."

Neither of us spoke. As Trev brewed a pot of tea. I looked around the room, there was a display on one of the walls: **History of The Backfields Estate,** in thick black letters. I walked over to get a better look.

A large map of the estate was fixed to the wall. Pins and coloured string linked locations on the map to cards stuck all around it.

An orange thread led from a point on Meadow Road to a card headed 'Good Stores'. On the card it said that the shop had opened in 1953 and closed in 1978. I wasn't surprised to see a pin stuck in the location of Angel's house. The card connected to that pin was headed *'Unsolved Murder.'* I started to read. *'In 1963, a widow, Mrs Betty ...''*

"Tea's ready," Trev called out.

I joined him at a table near the kitchen.

"What's all that about?" I asked, pointing at the map.

"It's a little project we've got on the go. We're hoping to put it on a computer, if we can get the funding. I've told them I can do it myself but they won't listen."

"So, how's things then Trev?"

He shrugged and avoided eye contact.

"Bit of a whizz on the computer then are you?"

"Aye, done a bit, over the years like," he mumbled.

"What is it Trev, what's the matter?"

"I'm sorry Mick. I don't know what's the matter with me. It's all so pointless."

"No Trev no. We all feel like that now and again. It will pass, it always does."

"No Mick, it's gone too far, it's destroyed me. There's no way back for me now. I'm sorry Mick, I shouldn't have dragged you into it, should have let things be."

"What do you mean?"

"It was me who sent the emails," he said. "It was me, my obsession, and now..."

"What the fuck Trev? You? Why?"

"I was stupid Mick, I got things into my head. It was after Angel came back on her own. I kept expecting to see you, but you never came. Then I found out what she'd done, what she was involved in. I liked your mother, and your brother, they didn't deserve it. I was so sure."

"And now?"

"I don't know, Mick. I think I'm going mad."

"Hold on Trev. Take it easy. Whatever it is, I'm glad I came back. I've got a lot of unanswered questions myself. You did me a favour sending those emails."

Someone was fiddling with the front door.

"It's the old biddies coming back," he said. "We'd better go, there's some kind of social this afternoon."

"Oh Christ," I said," I don't want to get dragged into that – come on, I'll phone for a cab, we'll go back to the hotel. We can get some lunch there too. Are you up for that?"

"Oh, I don't know, look at me."

"Don't be daft, you look fine. Anyway, what does it matter?"

Back at the hotel we had lunch in my suite. I put the television on for background – to help get Trev relaxed.

He looked around at the expensive furnishings. "You've done well for yourself, fair play, but you always were the clever one, the one who knew where he was going."

"That's not true, I just got lucky. You were the one who everyone looked up to, you knew everything, you were never afraid, you..."

"Oh stop it Mick, that's bollocks."

"It's not Trev, you were a true leader, an inspiration."

"I was a nobody, Mick."

"All right," I said. "Anyway, it doesn't matter about that now, let's get down to business, we've got things to do, mysteries to solve. Let's go over everything we've got."

CHAPTER 27

"This is weird, don't you think?" Trev said, waving his arm around the room.

"I'm getting used to weirdness," I said. "It's been a weird few weeks, since I started getting those emails."

"Sorry about that."

"Are you ready to talk now? I'm on your side in all this, you know. Let's compare notes."

We talked for a couple of hours. I showed Trev the manuscripts I'd found, reading bits out, dramatising some of the highlights.

"We didn't really break into that poor woman's house, did we?" he said. "Nah, it's not true is it? It's just a book."

I laughed.

I logged into my account on my tablet and re-read the emails Trev had sent. Trev expanded on the semi-cryptic messages they contained, but what it boiled down to was that he believed Angel murdered Ralph and probably Mam too.

"I'm still not sure where you got these ideas from," I said.

"I saw the files Mick. I didn't mean to look, but she left me there on my own, and I just sort of noticed them."

"Left you where?"

"In her house. I went there to fix her computer. She had a shock when I turned up, but tried to hide it. I used to do all that, help people around the estate with their computers, got a bit of beer money out of it, when I was still a drinker."

"What files, on the computer?"

"There was a cupboard, I opened it looking for a paperclip, the CD drawer on her PC was jammed, there's a trick you can do with a paperclip. There were shelves full of box files, all labelled and dated."

"I remember them," I said. "I thought she got rid of them,

before we went to LA."

"There was a file labelled 'David Robinson', I opened it."

"What was in it?"

"Lots of papers, some photographs, one or two newspaper cuttings, lists of dates. times, places. There were pictures of you and me in there Mick, from years ago, when we were kids, it was creepy."

"Doesn't make sense," I said. "How is that possible?"

"I don't know. I didn't have time to see much before Angel came back. I was spooked. I shoved the file back in the cupboard and pretended to fiddle with the computer."

"Was that it?"

"There was a list of names, some were crossed out, I didn't have time to read them all, but Snobby's was there, and somebody called James something, then I noticed Ralph's name."

"Crossed out?"

"Yes."

"What happened next?"

"I sorted the computer out, she was chuffed, gave me an extra tenner. I haven't seen much of her since."

"So how did you get from that to thinking she'd killed Ralph?"

I had to put a new password on her email account. It didn't occur to me then, but much later, after I saw her arguing with Pogo ..."

"Pogo, is he still around then?"

"Oh yes, smug little bastard, and he was smug with her that night. It was at a do in The Majestic. Strange thing was, she took it on the chin. She let a twat like Pogo get the better of her."

"That's not the Angel I know," I said. "She'd have sliced him to pieces."

"That's what I mean," Trev said. "So it got me thinking, you know, Pogo and her, and that led me to thinking about you, and all of that, and we never really did find out what happened, did we."

"No."

"Thing is, she never changed the password on the email account I'd set up, like I told her to, hardly anyone does. I logged on. I saw the emails between her and the other one."

"What other one?"

"He calls himself Smileyone, he must be one of her lot, you know, a spy, a spook, whatever they are."

"What was in the emails?"

"I'll show you," he said.

Trev used the laptop provided by the hotel. "There, it's mostly spam. Ah, that's new. Look, she hasn't even read it herself."

A couple of clicks later I read the email aloud.

'The Fox is loose but the hounds are hungry'

What do you think it means?" I asked.

"It's always the same, that's how they talk to each other, after a while you see patterns, you start to get the gist."

"So who is the Fox?"

"I know it sounds far-fetched, but I think Angel and Smileyone are involved in something big. The Fox is probably someone who's onto them. I think they're still involved in crime, but on the other side, and crimes against the whole world."

"Something that big? Here in Elchurch? That's not likely, is it? I mean it's just a little run-down dump at the back end of beyond."

Trev raised his eyebrows.

"Sorry, I didn't mean to slag off the town like that. I know how you've spent all your life here, and even though I've been away for most of mine, I've never left it in spirit. But you've got to admit, it's an unlikely place for anything that big to happen."

"Perhaps they're scared of this Fox. They know someone's on to them. Maybe it's me?"

"Or me," I said."

"Listen Mick, this world isn't what it seems, you know. The people you think run things are only puppets. It's all just a big front for the New World Order."

Oh Christ, I thought. Trev was one of those conspiracy

crazies. I'd come thousands of miles, lost weeks of sleep, left a promising relationship, to travel back in time at the whim of someone who thought the Duke of Edinburgh was a lizard. Perhaps he was so deluded that he'd set it all up himself, planted those emails, he was Smileyone.

"Aw Trev," I said. "You don't believe in all that do you?

"What do you mean?"

He looked bewildered, childlike. I couldn't do it, couldn't slap him down like that.

"Oh I don't know," I said. "Who knows what goes on, nobody does really."

"Exactly," he said, "nobody knows."

"I haven't had much sleep lately," I said. "How about we take a break, come back to it later. I might have a lie down. You're welcome to stay, there's plenty of room."

"It's a lot to take in I know. I've got to get back anyway, my granddaughter always pops in after school on a Tuesday."

"Right, do you want a lift?"

"No, I'll walk, it's not far."

"OK. See you later."

"I'll do a bit more digging by then." Trev said.

I gave Trev my business card. "My cell number's on there if you need it. Take it easy."

After Trev left I went online to check the news sites out, to reconnect with the reality I was used to, to put some distance between realising I'd been dragged into the fantasies of a nut-job and having to figure out what to do next.

There was still a chance he was right, not right about it being a global plot, but right about Angel's involvement in Mam's and Ralph's deaths. After all, it wasn't just the emails. There was all that other stuff with Pogo, and Angel was still active in some way, I'd heard her admitting as much on the phone when I was hiding in her attic. Maybe I'd do just a little more digging, before giving up on it all and heading back to LA to patch things up with Helene.

It was time to look Pogo up, not that I believed Trev's version of Angel's encounter with him, but it was worth checking out. I searched online for his office and rang to make an appointment. I felt it was best to disguise my voice, for all I knew Pogo could be working hand-in-hand with Angel, it was best to keep my options open. I shook my head; best to stop thinking like that, or I'd be wearing a tin-foil hat.

I put on my best rich American's accent and told the receptionist I was a visiting businessman about to invest in the area, and was looking for a local legal representative. After some whispering in the background I was told that luckily, Mr Summers had a cancellation that afternoon and could I come to the office at 3.30.

It was time for a bit of lunch, but I didn't fancy staying in the hotel, so decided to go for a drive

The car I'd hired was an immaculately kept grey family sized hatchback. The tinted windows were a nice touch. I wanted to keep a low profile, especially under the circumstances. The exit road from the hotel car park curved to the left, towards the West, along the coast road. I'd drive in that direction for a few miles and try and find a pub or somewhere to eat. I was looking forward to the meditative state that driving brought me when I needed to think.

It was pointless, the roads were too unfamiliar, and there was no space for me to think about anything other than negotiating them. I needed to resolve the Angel dilemma and didn't have time to go on some daft drive, so headed for the Backfields. The answer had to be there, that's where everything had happened.

I couldn't resist parking in the street opposite Angel's house, aware that if someone spotted me they'd assume I was a spy from the dole office or a plain-clothes policeman on a stake-out. The tinted windows helped.

I sat there for half an hour or so, the car radio tuned to a local station to keep me company and to familiarise myself with the local vibe again. I wasn't actively listening to the radio, just using its drone to smooth the irrelevancies in my mind, so that I could focus on figuring out what to do next.

Should I continue to pursue the idea that had been sparked

by Trev's gibberish? That old saying, 'if in doubt – don't' kept asserting itself and eventually I convinced myself that even if Angel was a black-hearted ghoul, then it didn't matter anyway. Dusk was falling on my life and the only sensible thing to do was to get back into my cave and wrap up warm.

My hand moved towards the ignition key. It was time to go back to LA and say goodbye to the Backfields for the last time, there was nothing left for me there, except a few vaguely known cousins and spoiled memories.

I also had my girls to think about, my lovely daughters, both already in their forties, and my grandchildren, Ben, the eldest, thirteen years old, the same age I was when I witnessed the event that had overshadowed my life ever since. Fifty years is a long time.

But if I gave up the shadow would still be there. I needed the light of understanding to dissolve that darkness. My hand hesitated as it touched the key. I sighed and sat back. It was too soon to surrender, and I had that meeting with Pogo later, perhaps after that I'd realise how stupid and paranoid I was being. I decided to wait in the car for a few minutes more and then get down to town to see Pogo. I would decide after that meeting.

I relaxed, and the meaningless drone of the radio resolved into something that could be parsed into intelligible sentences. It was a phone-in programme; the topics seemed to be homelessness, crime and drugs.

"It's a fact I tell you, it's everywhere, all over the estate, and the police, they do nothing."

"Yes caller, I understand you don't want to give your name, but do you actually live on The Backfields?"

"All my life, man and boy, and I'm telling you, it's never been this bad, society is falling apart – and the authorities are doing nothing."

"Why do you think that is sir?"

"Ah well, that's the way they want it isn't it, you know, it's the New World Order."

Christ! It was Trev's voice.

"Ah – okay, now, what about the criminals – the gangs?"

241

Derec Jones

"Never mind the criminals, it's the police you've got to watch, and then there's the spooks – the people who are above the law, protected, I could name a few names, even here, in Elchurch."

"Very interesting, thank you. Now, I've got other callers on the lines."

I let the drone fade into the background. Poor bugger Trev, I couldn't leave him to disintegrate. I was convinced that's what would happen if all this wasn't resolved. Perhaps I could take him to the States with me? It would make my trip to Elchurch worthwhile after all.

Yes, good, that was it. It all made sense. I doubted he'd ever left the country before, it would give him a new perspective. He was an unlucky sod, and I had the power to change that.

A car stopped outside Angel's house, a tall old man got out and walked up the path to towards the front door. Angel opened the door before he got there, she looked calm and relaxed, and just as beautiful as she was when she left LA five years earlier.

Angel and the man gave each other a friendly hug and went inside. Did I know him? I couldn't be sure but from that distance I was sure he was Kenny, Angel's cousin. That seemed odd to me, in the fifteen years she lived with me in America, she never mentioned him, and as far as I knew, had no contact with him, but then, a lot could have happened in the five years since.

I might have waited and followed him when he left but I had to get to Pogo's. After that I would see Trev again and convince him to come on that visit to the States.

The receptionist made a big show of pimping up Pogo in the five minutes she kept me waiting to see him. He was very busy, she said, he was still in demand even though he should have retired, important clients, she said, but the office was shabby.

The phone on her desk rang.

"Yes Mr Summers."

She put the phone down and looked at me. "Would you like to go through," she said, pointing at a brown door.

"Thank you."

I pushed the door open and walked into a large sparsely furnished office. An older, greyer Pogo was sitting behind a leather-topped desk, a diary lay open on its surface.

He stood up as the door swung shut behind me.

"Good afternoon Mr ... Bloody hell, it's you, Mick, isn't it? I thought it was going to be..."

"Sorry about that," I said, "it's just that I don't want too many people knowing I'm in town."

Pogo stood up and extended his hand. "Nice to see you again," he said, smiling, but his hand was clammy and he was shaking, obviously making an effort to control his nerves.

"Sit down," he said.

I sat down opposite Pogo and nodded, waiting for him to talk. I wanted to test those fragile nerves of his, hoping he'd let something slip that would help me.

"Um, so what can I do for you Mick?" he asked, anxiously rubbing his sweaty hands together.

Even though I was almost a hundred percent certain Trev's ramblings were only fantasies, I decided to pretend I was on to something.

"There is evidence," I said, putting on as serious a tone as I could muster, "that my mother and Ralph, you remember Ralph don't you?"

Pogo nodded jerkily. "Yes, yes, your brother."

"Yes, well, it looks like they were murdered. The investigations into their deaths are being reopened."

Pogo fiddled with his diary, he wouldn't look me in the eye.

"Pogo!" I said sharply. "What's going on? Do you know something?"

"Not now Mick, not here."

I was taken aback, that reaction was not what I expected or what I wanted. "So when then, and where?"

"I don't know. How about we meet somewhere later, after seven? I've got appointments until late this evening."

I didn't believe him about the appointments but needed some time to think things through myself.

"OK," I said. "I'll come back here at seven. Don't tell anyone about this."

"All right, but make sure you come on your own, or I won't have anything to say to you."

I left an obviously shocked Pogo in his office and walked quickly to my car. I didn't want to lose the momentum.

When I got back to the car I noticed a missed call from a number I didn't recognise. I called the number.

A young female voice answered. "Yo! You will speak now."

"Oh sorry," I said. "Someone called me from this number."

"Oh yeah," she said, "hang on."

A moment later Trev's voice came on the line. "Hi Mick, where are you?"

"I'm in town, just about to go back to the hotel. What is it?"

"I've found something else out, it proves I'm right, there's no doubt."

"Are you at your flat?" I asked. "I can pick you up. We can go back to the hotel."

Trev was waiting on the pavement outside the flats. He was clutching a crumpled orange carrier-bag to his chest as if it was a sick baby. He sat in the passenger seat, cradling the carrier-bag on his lap.

"It's all in here," he said, as we drove away.

It made me feel sad to see my childhood hero reduced to a rambling old maniac. That tall confident master of the Backfields, diminished to a scared and deluded old man obsessed by conspiracy theories, his world a dark nasty place where ordinary people were exploited and manipulated by an alien elite.

The reality was that he was that he was right in a way. In a fair world Trev would have become a respected senior citizen, treasured for his abilities and experience, instead he was a feeble pleb, forced to watch mutely from the sidelines as the dignitaries paraded their privilege and power.

"What is it you've got in there then Trev?" I asked.

"Best leave it until we get to the hotel," he said. "You don't know who's watching or listening." He put a finger to his lips.

"Ssh," he whispered.

"Fair enough," I said.

I decided to introduce the idea of inviting him back to LA with me. It was probably best to be direct, considering the state of his mind.

"So Trev," I said, "how do you fancy a holiday in America?"

"What?"

"You know, come back to the States with me for a while, a break, I can show you the sights."

Trev laughed. "Don't be daft Mick."

"Seriously," I said. All expenses paid, you'll love it over there."

"No Mick no."

I could see he was getting agitated.

"If you're worrying about the money, then don't. I've got more than enough of that, enough to buy half of Elchurch, millions. And I could do with someone friendly around, to keep an eye on things. I could even give you a job."

"A job?"

"Yes, and it wouldn't matter if you did very much or not, my accountants would probably make a profit out of you anyway."

Trev whistled and clutched onto the orange bag like a comfort blanket. I thought I'd better let it go for the time being, give the idea some time to percolate, perhaps he'd come round.

I ordered a plate of sandwiches at reception on the way to the suite.

"Is Matthew on duty?" Trev asked the receptionist.

"Not yet," the young man said. "There's a big function tonight, he's coming in later. Is there any message?"

Trev shook his head.

"Matthew's a good bloke," I said to Trev in the lift. "You should be proud of him."

"I am," he said. "I love all my children, and my grandchildren, but Matthew is the one who's achieved the most, considering his mother."

"You've got a proper clutch."

"Aye, Twelve," he said proudly, "and eight grandchildren."

"Yes, you've been busy."

Trev smiled. Perhaps I was being too patronising, I mean, anyone who's fathered twelve children must deserve some respect. In his own way Trev was more successful than I was.

Trev wouldn't talk about the contents of his plastic bag until the sandwiches were delivered, so I told him about seeing Angel and Kenny, and about my encounter with Pogo.

"Very dodgy," he said. "I'll come with you when you go and see him later."

"No, I'll be all right. I promised Pogo I'd go on my own."

"Well be careful Mick, you know he's a slippery sod."

The sandwiches came but neither of us could be bothered to eat them.

"I'll put them in the fridge," I said. "Perhaps you'll fancy them later. Now, what's in the bag?"

"Where's your phone?" Trev asked.

"Here," I said, pulling it from my pocket.

"Give it here."

I shrugged and handed Trev the phone. He stood up, walked across the room and into the bathroom.

"Those things," he said, as he came back phoneless, "they can listen through them, they can even take videos without you knowing."

"OK," I said.

Trev tipped the contents of the orange bag onto the bed – it was a jumble of electronics, bits of motherboard and wires. He picked up a metal rectangle the size of a cigarette packet.

"It's a hard drive, it's all on here," he said. "All we've got to do is hook it up to a computer. I tried to do it in the library, my computer is too old, but they didn't like me fiddling with the equipment."

"Where did you get it?" I asked.

"I used to have a shed full of this sort of stuff, bits that I'd collected from all those computer repairs over the years. The flat is too small for that, but I've still got a few bits."

"What's so special about that one?"

"It's Angel's old hard drive. I replaced it for her that time, it was wrecked, but the files are still accessible with the right equipment. Pass me that laptop."

I hesitated. "It's the hotel's."

"Don't worry, I know what I'm doing. I've got all the bits I need."

Trev poked at the laptop, turning it over and examining it closely.

"I'm going to have to disassemble it," he said. "It's going to take a while."

"All right. I've got to go anyway, to see Pogo. I'll leave you to it. If there's anything you want, just put it on my tab. I'll let them know downstairs, all right?"

"Yes yes," Trev said, too engrossed in his task to look up.

I drove back into town and parked the car across the road from Pogo's office. The front door was locked. I pressed what looked like a bell push but nothing happened. I banged my fist on the panels. Pogo opened the door and stood still in the doorway, he looked shocked, his eyes wide and staring.

"Let me in then," I said.

"Oh, sorry." He jerked out of his trance and stood aside.

He led me down the corridor to a room at the back of the building.

"I'll just be a moment," he said, the door slamming and shutting me in.

I was in total darkness. "What?" I said. "Pogo, for Christ's sake, what's this all about?"

There was no response from Pogo. I fumbled at the wall near the door and found a light switch. The room lit up dimly with a single low wattage bulb hanging from the centre of the ceiling. The shelves were lined with dusty box files and there was a small table and a stool in the middle of the room.

I pulled and pushed at the door but it was firmly locked. I grabbed the stool and swung it at the door, but it didn't make a dent since the door was solid old wood. If I kept hitting it, it would give way eventually, I was sure. I hit the door again and again until it showed signs of cracking. Then the stool disintegrated into a dozen pieces and I was left holding a leg.

I was knackered so leant back against the table to rest. I'd try again when I was able. I'd rip the legs off the table if I had to. That little twat wasn't going to get the better of me.

Someone knocked the door politely. I stood up. "Get me fucking out of here you little shit," I screamed.

"Stand back, Mick," Pogo shouted through the door. "Take it easy, sorry."

I leant back against the table, maybe it was just a silly mistake and there I was behaving like a caged gorilla.

The door swung open. It wasn't Pogo framed in the doorway, but Angel, and she was pointing a gun at me.

CHAPTER 28

I stared speechlessly.

There were tears in Angel's eyes.

"You shouldn't have done this, shouldn't have started digging."

Kenny appeared next to her, Pogo was hovering in the background, rubbing his hands together anxiously.

"Stand back," he commanded.

I didn't move. I couldn't move.

"Do as he says, Mick," Angel said, her hand shaking. "It's for the best."

Kenny moved quickly towards me. Before I could react he had me in an arm-lock.

That brought me to life, but it was too late. He was strong considering his age. I didn't resist when he tied my hands together or when he pushed me to the floor and bound my legs with thick canvas strips.

I looked up at Angel, she lowered the gun.

Kenny extracted a softer cotton strip from his pocket and tied it carefully around my face as a gag.

"It won't hurt, as long as you don't struggle too much."

He took my mobile from my pocket and handed it to Angel.

"What are you going to do with him?" Pogo asked. "You can't leave him here forever."

"Nothing is forever," Kenny said, looking coldly at Pogo.

Pogo shivered.

Pogo and Kenny went out of sight along the corridor. Angel paused in the doorway.

"Sorry," she whispered, as she closed the door and locked me in.

So, Trev was right about Angel. Did that mean he was right about everything else as well? Was there really a global conspiracy? I had to stop thinking like that, it would drive me mad, and couldn't be true. If it was, then my whole life, everything, would have been a sham.

I'd met some weird people in Hollywood, people you wouldn't expect to be lunatics, people who believed in everything from Scientology to crop circles, chemtrails to lizards, but I'd never come so close to adopting such crazy beliefs myself. No, no, no. I had to think logically, find a way out of this.

I struggled with my bonds until I was exhausted, I could hardly breathe, but the guy who'd tied them was too good, I was helpless.

I got my breath under control and tried to focus on staying positive. This is what was going to happen: Angel was going to come back, she would explain everything, she was caught up in something, and that meant she had to pretend to go along with it in order to protect herself and to protect me.

She would set me free and we would fall into each others' arms, declaring our undying love. Afterwards, with the help of a top team of detectives and spooks, we would round up the villains, save the world, and live happily ever after on Meadow Road, or in LA, whichever Angel preferred.

Angel did come back. She stood in the doorway looking distraught. I tried to speak through the gag but all that came out were unintelligible grunts.

"I'm sorry," she said. "Sorry about this, sorry about leaving you in California, sorry about ever having met you, and sorry for ruining your life. I will set you free, I will take that gag off, but first I want to explain. You need to know the full story before judging me."

I would listen to what she had to say, it's not as if I had any choice anyway. Afterwards, if she kept her word, I would ... I would what?

"First you've got to know, I did not kill your mother and your brother. You must believe me Mick. I loved Mam, you know that, and Ralph, he was complicated, but he was a good man."

Kenny returned, Pogo at his heels like a lapdog. Without

warning, he pushed Angel hard into the room. She fell forward awkwardly and landed on top of me.

Kenny laughed. "I guess you two have a lot of catching up to do. I'll leave you to it while I decide what to do with you. He slammed the door and locked it.

Angel struggled to her feet and staggered to the other side of the room. She sat against the wall opposite me getting her breath back. She eased herself off the floor, obviously bruised by her fall. She fiddled with the knots that held my bonds in place. The gag fell away.

Angel stepped away from me. "The others are too tight, I'm going to need a knife."

"Why Angel?" I asked, bewildered by what was happening.

"He's dangerous Mick, he's a killer."

"But why? All those years..."

"I couldn't live with it Mick, seeing you every day, and knowing what I knew, it was driving me mad, Mick. I had to leave."

"What are you talking about?"

"It was me. I started it, back then, in the summer of 1963."

"Started what?"

"Everything, I started everything. She was a disgusting old harridan, manipulative, controlling, it wasn't my fault."

"Are you talking about Betty Fish?"

"It was an accident, she pushed and she pushed, and I lashed out, she fell..."

"But what about Jacko's father, the letters?"

"That was him, he wrote the letters, as a backup, he said."

"Kenny?"

"Yes, he was always there for me, that's what I thought. But he was using me, Mick. I was only thirteen, he was like an older brother. Betty hated him, almost as much as she hated my father. Kenny came to live with us, when he was a teenager. Then he went away to college, didn't come back, not until his mother died. He found out what I'd done, said he'd protect me. He called himself a soldier, said he'd protect me, but he didn't, he used me, Mick."

She paused and looked at me for a reaction.

"Go on," I said.

"He followed me everywhere, kept notes, took photos, recorded things. He'd been recruited by then, and he was good, but he was mad, Mick, obsessive."

"What about later? Snobby, the international crime thing?"

"That was true, mostly" she said. "By then Kenny was a seasoned operator. He was pulling the strings, Snobby was the fall guy."

"What about that other bloke you were working with, the older guy, Charlie Peace?"

"Another stooge. Kenny likes to keep himself out of the line of fire, to keep himself clean. He uses people Mick, like everyone else uses tissues or something, they're just a resource. It was all Kenny."

"So, let me get this right. Ralph didn't kill Jacko's father after all?"

Angel shook her head. "It was Kenny, to protect me, he said. He was framing him. He planted the letters, killed Jackson, tipped the police off, but when they got there the letters were gone. I had quite a shock when you found them in the ashes."

"But you let me believe my brother was a murderer."

"I know," she sobbed.

"And the fire?"

"That was just a fluke, for Kenny. He took advantage of the riots, put his own man in to instigate the attack on Mam's house. I didn't know until afterwards Mick, he bragged about it all."

"But why?"

"He didn't like you poking around, it was you he was after."

"Shit. You're right, I should have let things be."

"You only did what you thought was right, you weren't to know you were dealing with a violent sociopath."

"And Ralph? did he kill Ralph?"

"I don't know, Mick. I really don't know. I believe he did, I'm sorry. He was hanging around in the hospital, he's capable of anything. He didn't like Ralph, I know that. Something to do with a woman, years before. Kenny doesn't forget or forgive. He's very patient."

"Why didn't you let me go after all that then? Why did you come to LA with me?"

"It was over by then Mick. He'd lost interest, got assigned to something big in the Balkans. And I loved you Mick, I've always loved you, from that first day, outside my house on the Backfields. I thought it would be a new start, and it worked, until Kenny got bored and tracked me down. Sent me emails, hinting he'd let the truth out, he had all the evidence he needed to prove I killed his mother. I couldn't look at you without feeling sick with guilt."

My mind was engaged in a frenzied search through my memory, revisiting, analysing, putting things together. How could I have been such an idiot? How could fifty years of a life be based on lies?

I hung my head. My joints were aching with the pressure of the bonds and their contact with the unyielding floor. I shuffled uncomfortably.

"I'll get you out of this. You don't deserve this," she said.

I looked up at her tearful face. She was a 63 year old woman, an experienced, skilful, intelligent woman, still beautiful, but she was also a scared and confused little girl, just as I was a terrified little boy. We were still the same babes in the wood we were when we first met half a century earlier. She was still that 13 year old girl desperately grasping on to the platform of that tree-house.

"Where's your phone?" I asked, suddenly regaining some mental capacity. "Or mine?"

"In my bag."

She wasn't carrying a bag.

"You need something to pick at the knots," I said. "Something metal, there must be a spoon or something."

Angel became animated, looking around the room, moving along the shelves, moving files aside to search behind them.

"The files," I said. "They must have metal fasteners."

Angel grabbed the nearest file. "Brilliant," she said.

Angel worried away at the knots around my hands with the metal clip. It took a few minutes and perversely, I wouldn't have minded if it had taken longer, I was enjoying the feel of her hands against mine as she struggled to cut the knots.

I took over when my hands were free and hacked at the canvas around my ankles.

I stood up unsteadily, pushing through the pain and the stiffness. We faced each other across the room. We were equal again. There were still so many questions but they were jumbled in my head. The answers would be irrelevant anyway, unless we could escape and avoid becoming the latest victims of Angel's psychopathic cousin.

"What next?" I asked.

"He's bound to come back," she said. "Perhaps we can do something then. You could pretend to be tied up."

"He's got a gun."

"Yes, and he's a trained killer, but he's getting on a bit, not as quick as he used to be. We can overpower him. You're in good shape Mick, must be that Californian lifestyle, and, I've learned a few tricks over the years."

"And he's got a rubbish henchman. Pogo couldn't walk a dog without tripping over its lead."

Angel laughed. "Sorry," she said. "I've missed you."

"I've missed you too," I said. "But this isn't something I can put in a box in the attic. This is my whole life, a life of lies. I haven't got a clue what to think, or what to feel. Besides, he's a murderer, and you're..."

"I know," she said. "But it doesn't matter about me, you're the victim here."

I looked at her. She was distressed and anxious, resigned to spending whatever life she had left in a state of penitence, and probably imprisonment. I couldn't imagine what she'd felt like as a teenager, the horror of what she'd done like a worm eating her from the inside.

"No," I said. "I am not a victim. We are not victims."

A light flickered in her eyes. I looked away. No. It was too soon for truth and reconciliation. First we had to survive.

There was movement outside the door, we both stepped back to the wall and waited. I considered sitting down and pretending to be tied up, as Angel had suggested, but it was too late, the door was opening.

Pogo and Kenny stood in the doorway. Kenny was pointing a gun at us. He was swaying on his feet, laughing. Was he drunk? Pogo stood next to him, fidgeting like he was bursting to take a piss.

"Ha! Young love eh, Summers. What do you think of that?" Kenny spat into the room. "Disgusting creatures, aren't they, Summers?"

Pogo's jaw quivered but he couldn't speak.

"We know what happens to disgusting creatures don't we?"

A huge crash of glass came from the front of the building. Pogo screamed and grabbed Kenny's arm for protection.

"You stupid moron," Kenny said, flicking Pogo aside like an irritating puppy.

Pogo fell heavily against the door frame and crumpled to the floor. Someone was shouting from the front of the building. Kenny turned his head to look down the corridor. Angel launched herself forwards and grabbed Kenny's neck. They both fell struggling to the floor.

There was a gunshot!

Kenny staggered to his feet, the gun hanging loosely in his hand. Angel was lying motionless on the floor. A disembodied scream came from deep inside me, passing through my awareness and out into the room. My consciousness became a detached observer as instinct drove my body towards the man with the gun.

In slow motion he found his bearings and levelled his weapon at me, I watched myself as I floated towards certain death. The seconds stretched into eternity. His finger tightened on the trigger. It was good. In that moment, I made peace with myself and with the world. In the end it's just a story, a series of scenes, and one of them has to be the last.

His head jerked back, he lurched forward like a loose puppet. The gun fired, but by then his hand was splayed out from his body and the bullet thudded harmlessly into the wall.

The slow motion sequence ended and real time resumed. A pile of bodies rolled into the room. It was Trev and Matthew.

They pinned Kenny to the floor. Trev looked up at me triumphantly.

"We got the bastards," he said.

I clambered over them to where Angel was lying. There was blood oozing from her side, but she was conscious. She smiled at me with tear-filled eyes. She looked defeated.

"I do love you, Mick." She lifted her arm towards me.

I knelt down and clasped her hand in mine. She was that spirited, troubled, young girl, reaching out to me, trusting me to save her falling from the tree, that light in her eyes giving meaning to my existence. I felt a surge of raw life again, the real, the only meaning there was. Without her there was no life. Whatever she'd done could never be as important as who she was. I knew she'd survive, knew we'd be together again.

Her eyes closed.

"I love you, Angel."

She smiled weakly.

Sirens and flashing blue lights announced the arrival of the police and the medics. The building was overrun with people in uniforms. Kenny and Pogo were handcuffed and led away. Angel was tied into a stretcher.

At the hospital, two uniformed police officers sat in the corridor outside the room. Inside, Angel's eyes opened and looked at me silently.

"You're going to be all right," I said, squeezing her hand.

"There are no more secrets," she said.

I leant forward and kissed her on the cheek.

"I know."

- The End -